'Full of strangeness and striking sentences that made me stop and savour Lucy's world.'

ALISON MOORE, Booker Prize shortlisted author of ***The Lighthouse***

'DEAR LUCY is about keeping promises against huge odds. This gorgeous novel does exactly that: the opening pages promise transcendent writing, remarkable characters, and a slowly unfolding mystery. But what happened and why is only part of what keeps you reading . . .'

CHARLOTTE ROGAN, *New York Times* bestselling author of ***The Lifeboat***

'A novel which explores a variety of themes such as motherhood, life force, choice, faith and personal morals. DEAR LUCY is a rewarding and compulsive novel, written in a beautiful, at times poetic style.'

JESS RICHARDS, author of ***Snake Ropes,*** shortlisted for the **COSTA FIRST NOVEL AWARD**

'A rare and precious novel – moving, captivating and expertly written in a voice unlike any other. DEAR LUCY is full of characters who are heartbreakingly human; full of hope, desperation, love and joy.'

HAYLEY TANNER, author of ***Vaclav and Lena***

'This is gothic noir that is full of heart and pathos. Lucy's lyric voice comes barrelling off the page, and you will be utterly transfixed by the twists and turns of her journey.'

GABE HUDSON, author of ***Dear Mr. President***

'DEAR LUCY is one of those rare delights that you cannot put down, and once you do, you can't forget.'

ANN HOOD, *New York Times* bestselling author of ***The Red Thread***

A native of Orange County, California, JULIE SARKISSIAN attended Princeton University, where she won the Francis Leon Paige Award for creative writing. She holds an MFA in Fiction from the New School in New York, her short fiction has appeared in *Tin House Magazine* and *Quick Fictions*, and she has written for the *New York Times*, *New York Observer* and the *Huffington Post*.

Julie currently lives in Brooklyn Heights, New York, with her husband. **Dear Lucy** is her first novel.

Visit Julie's website at
www.**juliesarkissian**.com

Follow Julie on Twitter **@SarkissianJulie**

Like **Dear Lucy** on Facebook at
www.**facebook.com/pages/Dear-Lucy**

DEAR LUCY

HODDER

First
published in Great
Britain in 2013 by Hodder &
Stoughton An Hachette UK company.
This paperback edition published in 2014 .1.
Copyright © Julie Sarkissian 2013. The right of
Julie Sarkissian to be identified as the Author of the
Work has been asserted by her in accordance with the
Copyright, Designs and Patents Act 1988. All rights reserved.
No part of this publication may be reproduced, stored in a
retrieval system, or transmitted, in any form or by any means
without the prior written permission of the publisher, nor be otherwise circulated in any form of binding or cover other than that in
which it is published and without a similar condition being imposed
on the subsequent purchaser. All characters in this publication are
fictitious and any resemblance to real persons, living or dead is purely
coincidental. A CIP catalogue record for this title is available from
the British Library. ISBN 978 1 444 76760 5. Printed and bound by
CPI Group (UK) Ltd, Croydon, CR0 4YY. Hodder & Stoughton
policy is to use papers that are natural, renewable and recyclable
products and made from wood grown in sustainable forests.
The logging and manufacturing processes are expected
to conform to the environmental regulations of the
country of origin. Hodder & Stoughton Ltd,
338 Euston Road, London NW1 3BH
www.hodder.co.uk

To Mom and Dad

PART I

Since the Beginning of You

LUCY

Everyone is asleep but me.

I look quick in every room to see that nobody is missing and nobody is. That is good because if someone is missing I have to leave to go find them and then who would get the eggs? Because they have never known a girl who was as gentle with the eggs.

I go down the stairs quiet like I am something without any weight. I open the door in the dark and the cold sucks my skin towards it. It is the morning but there is no sun yet, just white light around the edges.

It is the time to get the eggs. Time for my best thing.

The foxes I can hear them still digging. They come in the chicken house at night. We try to keep them out with wire. Sometimes they dig under the wire. If you think a fox is a smart animal then you are right. What do the foxes do after they dig under the wire? Well, they eat the chickens and break the eggs is one thing.

But they are scared of the day and of me, so they are gone.

The eggs they shine with their white and I do not need the light to find them. The foxes need no light either. I am a little like the fox, he is a little like me.

I get the eggs for our breakfast. They are alive. When you eat something that is alive you take the life for yourself. You can't think of it as taking life from another thing, you think of it as giving life to yourself. That is what Samantha told me when I asked about eggs for breakfast.

Samantha knows. There is something growing inside of her too.

Every person gets three eggs but Samantha, she gets four eggs. I count the eggs, one two three for me, one two three for you, one two three four for her. Missus makes her have extra so the baby will be big enough when it comes out, but Samantha, she saves the extra for me. I say, what about the baby? and she says, the baby's fine, you take it.

Mister thought I would not be as gentle with the eggs but I am as gentle with the eggs. My favorite is to put them in my apron pockets because then I feel them against my body underneath. Then I know something but I can't say it. It's not a secret but I don't have the words yet. I am still looking for them. But even without the words, I know how to be so gentle.

My pockets they are heavy but they rub against my legs and it feels nice like someone who would hug your legs. It isn't really a place to hug but that is why you would want it. Because you thought nobody would remember that place.

I touch one of the eggs with my cheek. The egg, I feel him trying to kiss me through the shell. He is trying so hard for the kiss. I know about trying so hard. It is when there isn't even one piece of you that isn't trying so hard. I kiss him back, and it is probably his last kiss because what happens next is that he is opened up and put on the skillet. That is part of what breakfast is.

I tell the egg to find the baby in Samantha's stomach and give all his life to her. Then he is not scared about being opened up. He knows it is time for him to give his life to the baby and knowing that makes him brave, which is doing something even if you think you are too scared. Then I hear the bell. Mister is gonging the bell, which means time to get up. No, not for me. For the others who are still sleeping. I wonder if Mum mum hears that it is time to get up. She is in the city, which is with Monte.

But I am still inside where the chickens live, which is called the chicken coop. Now I know I am late bringing in the eggs. I rush to bring them home. *Rush*, that word means do something fast and try not to drop anything.

I come back to the house holding my apron with the eggs like kittens. They sleep all wrapped together so when one wakes up the other says, it's okay, go back to sleep. The light in the kitchen it looks like how warm feels. I see Samantha on the inside because her hair glows. That means light is made inside it. It is a big braid like a rope you could climb up to be near her face, which is the prettiest place in the kitchen. Her eyes are green and if there was something on the other side of them you could see through to it. Do you know how to remember green? Well, it is the same as grass while it is growing.

I take one hand to open the door and keep one around my apron. An egg jumps out.

"Lucy, use a basket. When you don't use a basket, then the eggs break." Mister is standing next to the skillet. When the skillet is hot with oil he puts his beard inside his shirt. "Then we don't have food for breakfast. And everyone is hungry."

"I am gentle with the eggs, Mister," I say. "Missus said, 'Have you ever known a girl who was as gentle with the eggs?'"

Missus doesn't say anything. Today Missus forgot to tell her face to wake up. She is stirring a bowl and watching the grits turn around and around by the spoon. Mister he makes the eggs and Missus she makes the grits and that is what breakfast is. *Missus, Missus, say how good I always am with the eggs.* That is my wish but she doesn't look up. A lot of the times wishing doesn't make things happen any better than they would without your wishing. But it is something hard to learn, not to use your time to wish things.

"Missus, Missus." I have to say it louder because her ears are still asleep. So I say it louder and louder, "Missus, did you ever know a girl who was as good with the eggs?"

Because my first job, it was getting the eggs. And when I

brought them my fingers were so gentle and soft with them and they weren't scared of me so they didn't break. And Missus said that she had never known a girl who was as good with the eggs and her face looked like when Mum mum found an earring that fell off. It made me feel good inside myself like I found it for her. Even though I didn't.

"Lucy, give it a rest," says Samantha. "Come sit by me and leave Missus alone."

But Missus is the only one who knows about me being the best girl with the eggs. Samantha, she only does the weeding because of the baby making her heavy. So she doesn't know about being gentle with the eggs. Only Missus knows and I need to find the words to make Missus say to everyone how good I am with the eggs and they will let me stay on the farm so Mum mum will know where to find me. But sometimes when I don't have the words to say something one side of my body goes one way to find them and the other side goes the other. Then none of me is left to remember the words with.

"Missus." I am using all my air to carry the words to her.

"Lucy, be good and bring Mister the eggs," Missus says.

But if Mister says how many times do I have to tell you to use a basket and everyone is hungry, then Missus has to tell Mister that I am the best girl with the eggs. So he will know too. So everyone will know I am doing a good job at being Lucy on the farm.

"Lucy, you are usually gentle with the eggs, but look what's happening now," Missus says. "The eggs are breaking. You have to pay attention to be good with eggs."

And she starts stirring.

The skillet is hot and dancing with oil. Mister makes sure the skillet is hot when I come inside so he can crack the eggs and not use any time waiting. He wants to get to the time where he tells us all what to do that day and then we do it and then he sells some of the things we do and some of the things that grow. That is what a farm is.

"Damn it, Lucy," he says, which is not a thing you are allowed to say. "Get over here."

He takes the eggs out of my apron. He is fighting to get them all out but they aren't ready. They are flipping like fish if you get them out of water. An egg jumps out again. It is a noise I hate to hear.

"Get that one off the floor," says Mister. "We can't waste any food. I have to keep you all fed."

I get that one with a spoon and bring it to Mister. Mister flops the rest on the skillet and it sizzles, which is a word I know. It means the noise of the eggs when the pan is hot enough to cook them and the sound when you almost step on a snake.

Then Mister says, "That corner there, that's for you. The rest of us aren't going to eat off the floor because you carry the eggs in your apron."

I look at the corner. *That corner* means that Mister does not think I am as gentle with the eggs. I want Missus to say it to him but she is not saying it to him so I will do it.

"I am gentle with the eggs, Mister, have you ever known a girl who was as gentle with the eggs?"

"That's enough!" Mister says very loud, which is yelling, and he bangs the skillet, which is hot with oil. It is noise you hear during the rain and makes you want to stay under the blanket. It is a noise that means he does not think I am as gentle with the eggs.

Missus has to tell him I am gentle with the eggs. But she is stirring and watching the grits go around and she is not saying anything. I think it is the stirring that makes it so Missus cannot remember how I am good with the eggs. I need to make her stop.

I take Missus's stirring elbow with my strength because the stirring is making her forget because of how many times the spoon goes around and around. She stops stirring. Now is when she will say it! She closes her eyes longer than blinking. Then she opens them. Now she needs to open her mouth too, so the words will come.

"Now say it! Now say it!"

But she still doesn't say it. Her mouth stays closed and small.

Mister grabs my arms, harder than I could grab the stirring elbow.

"Lucy, come sit by me!" yells Samantha.

But Missus still doesn't say it.

And now I know. I know the grits being stirred is what is making it so Missus cannot remember I am the most gentle. I use my strength to push over the pot full of all the forgetting. Now it is on the floor. Now Missus will remember how I was the most gentle.

"Say it!" I say. "Say it!"

But she still doesn't say it. And now I know the grits on the floor are making her forget I was the most gentle girl with the eggs. The forgetting grits are too hot to hold and they slip through my fingers but I still hold on. I open the kitchen door and throw them away, far enough away so Missus won't be able to forget anymore and I say, "Say it! Say it! Say that I am the most gentle with the eggs!"

Then Mister takes my arm again and I am getting thrown away. Thrown away on the porch with the forgetting grits in between my toes, making my toes forget how gentle I was. Mister bangs shut the door. I use my forgetting grits hands on the door but the door forgets how to open. So I bang on the door loud enough to make them remember, make them remember, it was me. I was the girl who was gentlest with the eggs. Make them remember so they will let me stay on the farm where Mum mum can find me.

MISSUS

Life constantly reminds us of all the things that could have been different if betrayal weren't in human nature. I have heard people in church ask, if the Lord had wanted us to be perfect and not make any mistakes, then why did he make us capable of sin?

Those people don't understand. He gave us free will because He loved us. He trusted us. And we betrayed it. We didn't deserve it. We did wrong by Him. Not the other way around, and we continue to pay and pay and pay for it. Nobody is spared. We all pay.

Stella betrayed us, that is true. I would never deny that. Though when I feel she did so out of spite, I have to remind myself that it was because of her condition, our condition, the human condition, born from our original betrayal of Him. I have to remind myself that nobody is spared, that we are all indebted to pay for that first mistake.

LUCY

When we are weeding I take my arms out of my dress. I know that you mustn't ever, not ever, take your clothes off in front of other people. Because when Mum mum came out and saw me she said, "How could you lift your clothes up in public like that? You're going to get yourself into big trouble. What would have happened if I hadn't come out when I did? What did you expect was going to happen to you?"

Well, I didn't lift them up because of what did I expect. I did it because of the sun on my legs and the game with no words.

That was when she said to me, "You mustn't ever, not ever, lift up your clothes in front of other people."

But now nobody is here except Samantha and she isn't other people. I take my arms out of my dress and tie the sleeves around my waist and lift up the skirt and the sun does its dance all over. The sun's feet tickle and press and I make music with my breathing because music is what you need when you want to do a dance.

"Lucy, how do you plan on weeding with your dress balled up like that? You're going to have to do most of it. I can barely lean over my belly to get ahold of anything. Come on, Mister wants this done quick."

The weeds take the life out of the plants, that's why you kill them. The way you kill them is pull them out of the ground. They might tell you they want to stay in the ground and they might look pretty but you have to pull them out anyway. The farm is about taking the life from something and putting it somewhere else.

But we are so far from the house it doesn't matter about having my dress balled up like that or how I am going to have to do most of it. Here we can open our mouths to swallow the sun and Samantha can braid my hair like water pouring over me with no wetness. Here there is no Mister to yell when it's not done quick or an egg falls out during breakfast.

"Mister, he did not believe about how I was the gentlest with the eggs," I tell Samantha.

"Oh, he thinks you're fine with them."

"But then he was yelling."

"Yeah, but you were provoking him." Her hands in my hair, it is a feeling I never want to end. "He's nice enough if you don't provoke him. Which you've got to stop doing."

"Which is provoking?"

"Doing things you know he'll yell at you for."

"I don't do anything so he'll yell at me."

"I know that's not why you do it, but when you see it's happening, you gotta quit it, get it?"

"Yes."

"I can't always be there to help you, but you know I would if I could, right?

"Right." Right is a thing you say when the other person says right.

I open up the back of her dress. She lets me. She is afraid of the burning but she wants to feel the sun more than she is afraid. She lets her arms go loose so I can take them out of the dress. That is how she tells me that she wants to be outside of her dress. Not every time is a time when you need words to tell things. Then I tie the sleeves behind her back, so she can feel the sun and so the sun, it can feel her too.

"I can take care of myself," Samantha says. "I just worry about you."

"Don't be scared, Samantha," I say.

"Take care of yourself, then, and I won't be."

"Okay," I say, and she smiles. So I know what I said was a right thing to say. Then I touch the best part of her, which is her hair. I practice my braiding so I can show the baby how to braid his hair.

"Samantha, will the baby have orange hair?"

"No way to know," she says.

"Even though he's made out of you?"

"Well, he's not all me. He's part me and part someone else."

"Who is the someone else?"

"A boy. It takes a boy and a girl to make a baby. Don't you know that?"

"Which boy? Wilson's boys?"

"No." Samantha pulls on a weed but it doesn't come up. She tugs and tugs but its roots are grabbing fists of the underdirt. "A boy from a long time ago. From when I lived at home. Plus, Wilson's boys are too young to make babies."

"Why did you make a baby with the boy? So you and the boy could love it together?"

"Something like that."

"And be there from its very beginning? Since its very first day?"

"Sure."

"What else is there about the boy?"

"Not much."

"But what?" I go into the dirt where Samantha was tugging. I am careful not to dig into the tomato root. I am good at helping the plants grow ever since I've been Lucy on the farm. I know how you have to be loving in your touching the dirt like it is the thick fur on a wild animal. You don't want it to get scared and hurt you, or run away. I use my fingers to be gentle and strong at the same time and get the weed that wouldn't let go.

"Stuff, I guess."

"What stuff?"

"Let me think of a way to say it, so you'll understand it."

"Okay."

"Okay." Samantha says it in a funny voice that sounds like a smile and messes up the braid she made in my hair.

Samantha wants to say something so I can understand it. Not just shake her head like flies are trying to land on her and say, I just don't know about you, Lucy. That is all some other people do when I say things. They just shake and shake their heads and maybe laugh and say, I just don't know about you, Lucy. I just don't know.

Well, what don't you know? Whatever you want to know, I will tell you.

That's what I will say when someone asks me that again.

Then Samantha says, "Isn't it funny how the world is always turning?"

"How does it turn?"

"Turning, like this." Samantha gets up and spins in a circle.

"Why does it turn?"

"It turns because of the moon. Or the sun. Or something. I learned why in school."

"I don't feel any turning."

She sits down. She puts her hands on the ground. She puts her ear near the dirt so it almost touches like listening for a secret that is about to come. "I know. It's weird. But it's true."

Now there has been some time since Samantha said she had to think of a way. I put my head down near to the ground to be next to her and the secrets.

"Did you think of a way yet?" I ask.

"A way to what?"

"To tell me about the boy."

She laughs, but not because of a joke. "That was like a minute ago. So, no."

"But how did you choose him to be the other half?"

"Sometimes you get to choose the other half, and sometimes you don't."

"But—"

"No, Lucy. No more questions."

MISSUS

The situation was not good, we learned from the doctors at the hospital. In fact, it was very bad. I was missing half a cervix. It was only half the size necessary to hold a fetus full term. If an egg did implant, there was no hope for life.

Back at the farm, we couldn't look each other in the eye. But neither could we avoid it. There had been no shyness between us all these months of happy marriage, and now a space was between us, the size of the missing half. I was to blame, but Mister acted like the guilty one. I should have said, stop, it's my fault, I'm to blame, it's my missing half, not yours. But I couldn't say it. I was ashamed I couldn't say it, and the sounds of the animals made our silence louder.

Sometime later Mister said, "What do they know?"

I was outside sewing. We had a rocking chair on the front porch. After dinner, I sewed and rocked. I always got my best sewing done on the rocker. I grew up with store-bought clothes, but my mother had taught me to sew to make sure that she never forgot, and then I never forgot either.

"I have an idea," Mister said.

He got down on his knees. He took my sewing out of my hand. It felt romantic, like a grand gesture, like we were going to try something new, he was going to carry me to the bedroom or have me right there on the porch. It felt like my husband was capable of anything.

But instead, he clasped our hands together, he bowed his head, and he said a prayer.

He told the Lord that if He were to bless us with a child, we would love it like no other child had been loved because it would be a reflection of our love for Him and our love for each other. Take pity on us, Lord, let us be with child. We know God helps those who help themselves. We will do anything.

He looked up at me. His eyes were glistening. I wanted to tell him I loved him, but I couldn't. I felt the nothing stir, inside the missing half.

LUCY

Samantha sits on her bed and writes in her book. It lives under her pillow. When you love something you sleep with it close to your face. Because then it will be the first thing you see when you wake up. She pats the bed next to her, which means that is a place for me to sit. We look in her book together. What she is writing is words.

"Which word is this?" I say.

"These words say, *get out*."

"Which word is this?"

"These words say, *of here*."

Then she laughs so I do too. That shows how I know that she is funny.

"Which word is that?"

"That word says, *Lucy!*"

"This is the Lucy word?"

"That's the one! Practice copying it. Then when you're famous you can give people your autograph."

She takes out a paper from her very own book and gives me her pencil to make the word and I use the pencil to touch the paper. I practice looking just at the Lucy word, just at the Lucy word. But the Lucy word feels me looking at it. It doesn't like how heavy it is to have me look at it. It starts running over the page, sneaking behind other words. When Samantha sees my eyes chasing it she points to where it is hiding.

"It's here. Don't let your eye wander off it."

"Which word is your baby's autograph?"

"I don't know yet."

"Why not?"

"Because I don't know him yet."

"Then why do you know he's a boy?"

"I don't actually know. That's just something Missus thinks."

"Why does Missus think that?"

"Who knows?" Samantha braids a piece of my hair with a piece of her hair. It makes me laugh because you don't think a braid is made with two different people's hair, but then it is and it is even prettier.

"But I've heard," says Samantha, "that sometimes a baby will whisper their own name to the mother, just to make sure she gets it right?"

"What does he think the name will be?"

"Who?"

"The boy that made half the baby."

"I'm not sure."

"Why don't you ask him?"

"Because I don't know where he is."

"Even though he is half the baby?"

"Yeah."

"Why?"

"Well, because people don't want us to be together."

"But you are the family."

"Yeah, but they think it's an evil thing that we were doing and that when we get together again we'll do more evil things."

"Did you do an evil thing?" Sometimes I do not have a lot of good behavior and people tell me what I am doing is a bad, evil thing.

"Of course not. It can't be an evil thing because it's what

makes babies. God wouldn't give people babies for doing something evil, would he?"

"No." God only gives you things if you are very grateful and have good behavior, which is maybe why God has not given me a lot of things so far.

"It wasn't an evil thing, people are just stupid and like to have things their way all the time. You know."

"Is this his word?" I point to a word in her book.

"Whose word?"

"The boy that's half your baby?"

"No."

"Which is the one?"

"How come you wanna see it?"

"Because he's the other half."

"Well, it's not on this page."

"What is his name?"

"You can call him the father."

"His name is The Father?"

"No, but you can say, when you want to say his name, the father of the baby."

"Why not his name?"

"Because." Samantha closes her book.

"Because why?"

"Because people like to talk too much."

"What do people like to say?"

"All kinds of stupid things." Samantha puts the book under her pillow. "I wouldn't want you to get confused about what's what."

"I never had one."

"Had what?"

"The father of me."

"Everyone has a father of them."

Then the door opens and it is Mister that opened it because now he is in the room.

"This came for you today," Mister says.

He gives Samantha a paper that has a letter inside it. On the front of the paper it says these letters SAMANTHA and then these letters ALLEN and some numbers. I am looking at the letters and some numbers but Samantha is not looking at them. She is looking at Mister.

"Gee, thanks," she says. But thanks is not how her voice sounds.

She does not look at it. She is looking at Mister and Mister is looking at her because maybe he wants to know about the insides of what he gave her. That is what I want to know about. But I also know that whenever Mister gives Samantha the things that come for her she never looks at the insides and I just wonder and wonder and never know.

"All right," Mister says, and shuts the door again.

Samantha does not open up the paper, even though that is what I would do if someone gave me that kind of thing. Mum mum, she would give me those same ones if I had enough words to know what was inside. Because when you are away from someone and you love them, then you write down all the things you would say to them if they were there. Like what Mum mum does for Monte. Then you hope that they read all the things you wrote down. Samantha puts the paper behind her bed and I hear the noise it makes when it hits the floor. And now all the things the person is trying to say, they are underneath the bed.

"Why don't you read the insides?"

"Because I already know what it says."

"How do you know already what it says?"

"I've heard it all before."

"Which things is it that you've heard all before?"

"Same old things." She shakes her head and our braid swings like the low branches in the wind and then comes apart.

"Because you are very smart, you know about things even when you've never read them."

"No, not that. Just this person is not so hard to figure out. Anyway, I promise it's boring inside that letter." Samantha puts her hands in her hair and it waves like sheets on the clothesline.

"Let's talk about something more interesting. So, what about your father?" Samantha says. "What do you know about him? Other than your mom never let you meet him."

"I know that I never had one."

"Lucy, everyone has a father. Remember what I told you about how you need a boy and a girl to make a baby? There aren't any exceptions."

"Mum mum told me I didn't have a father."

"She probably told you lots of things that aren't true. That's part of the fun of having kids, right? You get all the control."

"No, Mum mum told me only true things. Like how to be good. Mum mum knew how to have good behavior and she was always trying to make me learn it too."

"She just said you were bad so she didn't have to deal with you." Samantha lies on the bed and looks at the top of the room. I do too so I can see the same things as Samantha does. Which is nothing except one crack. I look at the crack. "How do you think you ended up here?" she says. "How do you think I ended up here?"

"Because this is a place where I can get taken care of. Other places I might go people wouldn't know how to."

"Your mother should have taken care of you."

"I didn't have any good behavior so it was too hard."

"What about school?"

"School couldn't know how to take care of me."

"Nobody here takes care of you either. Here you just have to work all the time."

"You take care of me."

"You and me, we could live some other place and I could still take care of you. There's nothing here that helps you any. It's not about you, it's about her not wanting to deal. That's how your mother sees it."

"That is not how Mum mum sees it."

"Yes, it is. She's just looking out for herself."

"No. She thinks that I will wait here and never leave the farm and then she will come to get me."

"Don't play dumb, Lucy."

"I'm not playing."

"Then don't be dumb, Lucy. You don't need to be here. After I get this baby out, then we'll figure something out together."

"I'm supposed to be here so I can wait here and Mum mum will know where to find me. She knows what the best place is because she is my family. She has been there since the beginning of me."

"But where is she now?" Samantha's words are angry and scared. She is angry and scared because she thinks Mum mum will never be coming, but I know that Mum mum will be coming. "Who cares if someone is there from the beginning if they just end up leaving you?"

"Don't worry, she will be coming."

Then I put my arms around Samantha to quiet the thing inside her. She sucks in some of her crying through her nose. She hits the bed with her hand one time and another and another and puts the blanket in her mouth and bites on it and the noises she makes in her throat can't come out her mouth.

Then she puts her hands on the sides of my face near my ears and looks at me and looks hard. Her eyes they are big and green and glass and beautiful and I try to look to see what is on the other side of them but there are just her eyes and her eyes. She whispers. That means secret. That means listen and don't tell anyone else.

"Lucy, we can't count on them. They think they know what's best for us, but they don't. We gotta figure it out on our own. You hear me? We can't count on anyone but each other."

SAMANTHA

Mom slipped this into my bag before I left.

A *safe place to keep your thoughts*. She wrote that on the first page. *Love, Mom*.

I think what Mom means is, here's somewhere to bury my thoughts, so nobody will ever have to hear them and find out what kind of daughter she has.

So here it goes. Here's what I'm hiding underneath all the dirt.

Allen came around after school. He wasn't really my friend, but I guess he wasn't really *not* my friend. I didn't have many friends so there wasn't much to compare him to. I never invited him. He'd just show up. Sometimes he'd bring Rusty and we'd play fetch or we'd just sit on the back steps and he'd draw and I'd dream up exciting things that seemed highly unlikely to ever happen to me.

He'd stay for dinner and after we ate he'd beg to be alone with me.

"Let's go to your room, just for a minute. I won't try anything, promise."

Sure he wouldn't. I'm sure he just wanted to look at my posters.

I'd say, "Oh, no, my mom would never allow it."

His mouth twisted up, but he tried to hide it and said he understood and that sometimes it was hard to do the right thing. I figured that was just something he was saying. Back then I didn't know he actually meant it.

Then one night I met a real man, and everything changed. I was sitting on the bench outside the depot reading a magazine someone left. There's not much to do in this town.

He got off the bus and lit a cigarette. He was wearing a uniform and was the most handsome man I had ever seen, even counting any guy from any movie.

"Can I bum one?" I said.

"For you, the world," he said.

Then he asked what people did for fun around here.

"Oh, lots," I said.

We walked along the river. We talked about everything. I never knew I had so much to say. He put his jacket down under the bridge. That jacket had been to so many amazing places, I buried my face in it and smelled them all. Afterward he scratched our initials on a tree with a pocketknife.

"Now this tree will never forget what he saw tonight," he said.

"Me neither," I said. "I mean, what happened."

We stayed up past midnight at the Diner Car sitting on the same side of the booth, drinking coffee. I felt like I'd been sleeping for a year and finally woken up, not because of the coffee.

Until the police came. I begged them to let me stay. I dug my nails into his arm. Gotta come with us. No way around it. Your folks are looking for you, they said.

"You gotta go, little darling," my uniform said. "Can't worry your folks."

"Who cares about them? Let them worry."

"A gentleman wouldn't let a girl's folks worry about her."

"Then don't be a gentleman!"

"Go on. We'll see each other again."

"How?" But I didn't want there to be an again. I just wanted to never not be seeing him. I was being dragged away.

"Just know it." He was smiling, I was dragging.

My mom cried and my dad paced around.

"Who were you with?"

"I was with Allen," I told them. "Swear."

"You're lying, we know, we spoke with him."

"He was lying so we wouldn't get in trouble."

"We spoke to the police, Samantha."

"They don't know what Allen looks like."

"How can you lie to us like this?"

"Truth. Cross my heart, hope to die."

I waited by the tree. I waited in our booth. I waited in all the places we'd been together. I never saw him again.

LUCY

The moon is winking, winking at me.
  I hear you, I hear you, I tell him.
  Don't ignore me, Lucy, get up.
  But I was dreaming.
  We all dream, and we all have to get up.
  I know.
  It's time, it's time.

I open my door one little littleness at a time so there aren't any creaks. I climb the stairs to Mister and Missus. I push open the door gentle as whispers. Mister, his smell is there. Which is the last dying parts of a fire and bark stripped off trees and the sour that floats around his words. Missus sleeps like when a person dies and you put them in a box to stay hidden in the ground, with hands on her heart on top of the covers. She has scarves for the day and for the night so her hair will stay warm.

Missus has lipstick too, but, no, not for the everyday. The letters on the bottom are these: *CAJOLING CAROL.* I will buy Mum mum the same kind when I get to live in the city with her after everything is ready for me to come home and she will call me Dear Lucy. I know how pretty it would look on Mum mum. Monte, he likes her to wear makeup because of how pretty she looks. I wear Missus's lipstick sometimes, but I take it off very fast after I look in the mirror and kiss my hand.

I float down the stairs. Samantha's door is my favorite. *Favorite*, that means it is the one you love the best and think about the most. You can smell her if you are next to it because her smell is between the threads of the wood. It is fruit that is almost too heavy for the tree, but still there for a little bit longer. I am at her door, I hold myself against it like I am so tired and falling into bed. I breathe it open and there is Samantha, but she is not doing what the others are doing. She is sitting up and writing in her book.

"Come here, Lucy. Practice your name some more."

And I come here and I practice my name and she writes in her book until I know that the gonging is almost going to happen, so I go to do my most gentle thing, which is get the eggs.

Samantha comes with me while I feed the pigs. They eat slop. That sounds like a noise but really is a word that means it is made of everything. And Mister says pigs eat anything, so they like to eat a food that is made of everything.

"That smell is so gross," Samantha says. "I don't know how you can be around it."

She sits on the fence and I am inside with the pigs.

"In fact, it makes me want to be a vegetarian."

"What is that?"

"It means someone that doesn't eat any meat, or eggs or butter or anything."

"What about breakfast?"

"I'd have to find something else to eat."

"But the eggs don't smell like slop."

"Yeah, but there's something about eating eggs that makes me a hypocrite, you know? I have a baby growing inside me and I'm eating what might as well be a baby chicken."

"Why is an egg a might-as-well-be-a-baby-chicken?"

"Because that's where the baby chickens come from. They come from the eggs."

I poured the pigs all their slop and now they are eating it fast, each pig faster than the pig next to them.

"The eggs become baby chickens?"

"Yeah, didn't you know that?"

"No."

"Guess you missed that day in health class. Yeah, we just eat them before they're ready to hatch. If we didn't eat them, they'd hatch into baby chickens. Come on, I'll show you. Help me down, will you? I'm getting so fat."

Then we go and Samantha shows me that the eggs are might-as-well-be-the-baby-chickens. They start in their shells. They do secret growing inside their shells and then the shells break and they do the rest of their growing out in the world so everyone can watch. And I know Samantha is right about things that grow inside because there is something growing inside of her too.

After the chickens we walk away from the farm to the place by the river because Samantha says her feet are killing her. When she says that she means she wants to put her feet in the water and have the water run over them.

"This is pretty much my favorite place," she says.

"In the whole world?"

"Yeah, I love it down here. It's pretty much the only place that doesn't make me wish I was somewhere else. What about you, Lucy?"

"Yes," I say. "Pretty much."

And I make a pile of all the hottest stones and press them against my face one and then another and then another until all their hotness runs inside me now, like the lives of the going-to-be-baby-chickens, inside the eggs.

At night I dream the eggs are saying to me, Lucy, Lucy, you've just got to keep us until we're ready to hatch. Lucy, listen to us, if you leave us here in the chicken coop, we're just surely going to die on the skillet or get sold in the market. Lucy, we want to be born.

They say, Rescue us and you can be our mother. In the dream I am smiling with them and they are smiling with me.

Rescue us, Lucy, rescue us and you can be our mother.

I run down the stairs. I fall on the last step but it doesn't hurt the way falling usually feels. Because all the hurt is in my insides so I can't feel any of the hurt on my outside.

The sky is getting more white around the edges. I am late with the eggs. Some of my jobs on the farm is to get the eggs. The foxes, we keep them out with wire, but at night they dig under and what they do when they're inside is they break the eggs and eat the chickens.

I go with my feet with my no shoes and the dirt is smooth as stones and now I am in the coop and there are the eggs all broken and the fox is chewing with his fangs and I am saying, get out! Get out! But he just smiles at me, happy as he can be, there is no sound in my voice, all the sounds are stuck inside my head.

Get the eggs, get the eggs, get the eggs, save them all!

They are broken all on top of me. I am trying to lick them up, save them in my mouth.

Then I wake up. Dreams aren't real, except the things they tell you. And I know this morning I need to beat the fox, he is almost at the coop, I can feel it. I need to get the eggs for the baby. He can't get them for himself. I am the only one gentle enough. I need to rush more than I did before, down the steps faster, out the door faster, through the cold faster, save the eggs faster. Grab this one faster and that one faster. And some are breaking but I need to keep taking them for the baby. Taking a living thing, giving its life to another.

MISSUS

Stella. He is saying her name in his sleep. It keeps me up and finally I nudge him awake, so I can get some rest.

We had always loved Stella. Even after her betrayal, we never stopped loving Stella. We had loved her since the first time she was mentioned to us by Rodger Marvin. He told us not to get our hopes up, but we already knew she was ours. We knew because of all that we had been praying and because we knew the Lord keeps his promises and he had promised both of us. We couldn't have both got it wrong.

We never doubted it, we just wondered to Him and to each other, when will it come? Will it be soon? Every day until the day she came, we wondered, will it be today?

"I'm sorry I had to wake you. You were talking in your sleep."

"What was I saying?"

"I couldn't make it out."

I don't want to weigh him down with her memory, first thing like this, to stay with him throughout the day. It's better to start the morning with the people who are still with you, not the people who have left you.

Better to start the morning with hello.

Not with good-bye.

Good-bye, Mother, good-bye, Daddy.

LUCY

We sit on the outdoor steps in the time before the bell gongs for us to get into bed.

Samantha says, "You're shivering. Go put on a sweater."

But I do not have a sweater so I do not go put one on.

"Go put on a sweater. Don't you have a sweater?"

But I do not have a sweater so I do not say.

Then Samantha is gone, and then she is back and I put on a sweater.

"Didn't your mom pack you any warm clothes? God, my mom packed me enough for ten pregnancies."

But I do not have any warm clothes so I do not say.

"It's okay, you can keep mine."

Then Samantha asks, "Are you upset about what happened with the eggs this morning, Lucy?"

But I don't say. All my words are inside. They can't come out. Inside, inside they are fighting each other, all the yeses and the noes and the shoulds and shouldn'ts. They have mended me shut from the inside out.

"You can still visit them. The only difference is now you don't have to do any work when you're there. It'll be more fun that way."

"But Mister said I can't even go near the coop."

"You can hang out with the other animals."

"But those other animals knock me down and ruin my dress."

"So you'll stay at a safe distance. The other animals are more interesting anyway."

"But I was trying to get the eggs for baby, so he'll get big and strong. Baby still needs the eggs."

"He'll still have them, don't worry. And you know what? You can think about the eggs, even though you can't be with them. That's something Mister can't take away from you."

"It that like you and the father of the baby?"

"Is what like that?"

"Is that the same way that you are sad that you are not with the father of the baby?"

"Uh-huh."

"You can think about him, even though you are not with him?"

"That's right."

"And what do you think?"

"What do I think?"

"When you think about him, what do you think about?"

"Well, let's see. When he looked at me, he made me feel like we were the only two people in the whole world." Samantha smiles at her hands. She is moving them like rolling a ball of dough. "Like we had the whole world, just to ourselves."

"How does he make that feeling?"

"Because even though we had just met, he knew me better than anyone else ever had, or ever could."

"That's the same as a mother and her baby."

"No." Samantha puts our hands together like sewing. "It's not the same at all."

"What else about the father?"

"He likes his coffee black. And he's a gentleman."

Samantha drops our hands apart. Her smile drops away too. I want to put us back together but her hands are hiding in her pockets now.

"Tell more, Samantha."

"Later."

"Okay." *Later* means a promise that something will happen, but just not yet. "And now I can think of the eggs."

"Yeah, you can think about them now, even if you can't be with them now."

But something more is inside me. It started down deep inside me but now it rises up up and through my mind and out of my mouth.

"Samantha?"

"Yes?"

"But what is his name?"

"Why do you want to know?"

"If I ever meet him or see him or hear his name I will know that he is the one. That loves you so much to make a baby. To be there on its very first day."

Samantha sighs. I know her face. It is the one I have when I am trying to have good behavior but it is hard to make it come out. "If you must know," she says, "it's Allen. But don't go gabbing that all around town."

"Allen." That is a word that will never go missing.

Then Missus rushes out and says, "Girls! Come look, come look!"

"What is it?" Samantha says.

"Girls!" Missus says. "Come look!"

We follow Missus to the front steps and under the front steps is the cat on the farm. She is lying on the grass under the steps and also what is lying on the grass under the steps are tiny baby cats sucking on their mother. The cat on the farm blinks her eyes at me and tells me it is okay to stay and watch as long as I am very gentle.

"Gross," Samantha says. "They look like skinned mice." She goes inside.

And Missus and me, we sit on steps and watch the babies suck and suck and grow. Even though we can only see the sucking part we are watching the growing part too.

"The miracle of birth," says Missus.

SAMANTHA

It didn't take much more than a month for me to realize I was in a situation. I didn't try to tell myself anything different. I'm not stupid.

I needed a place where I could hear myself think, and that wasn't school, or my backyard with Allen breathing over my shoulder. I started spending the day at the bus depot. The people waiting there weren't from around here, and I knew the guys who worked there wouldn't tell my parents. They saw plenty of people coming in from trouble and going back to trouble. They didn't mind one more. People left their brochures and magazines lying around and I read those.

When I got bored, I walked along the river and picked up rocks I liked the looks of. I made paths and little walls with the rocks, going nowhere, keeping nothing at bay. I put my feet in the water until they turned red from being cold and couldn't feel anything. I dropped rocks onto my toes and felt nothing. It was a great feeling, though I couldn't feel it. I sat under the bridge, traced our initials in the tree, gave myself splinters, sucked them out, and listed all the things I remembered about him, each one like a little candy I was saving for later, but would never get to eat. Then when the time was right, I went back home and pretended I had been in school.

"How was school, dear?" asked my mother.

"Great!"

I had to think of something. It'd been weeks and so far I'd come up with nothing. Allen had to climb a fence to get from his house to my house. He'd shown me a couple of places with holes in the boards so he could climb up and over without any help, but I'd never done it. Until now.

I stuck my finger in the hole and hoisted myself up. I almost broke off my finger, but I managed to get one leg about half over. I clawed the rest of me all the way up and balanced at the top, trying to picture how to fall so I wouldn't get too hurt, so I wouldn't break anything, wouldn't have to explain anything, so my normal life, that didn't feel normal at all anymore, could continue.

Just belly flop, I guessed.

I took a deep breath. I scooted my butt off the top of the fence and tried to position myself parallel to the ground. But before a thought could go through my head I was in the dirt on my shoulder, both hands on the ground, one in front of me, one to the side.

I couldn't breathe for a minute. I sat up and vomited a little. That seemed like a good sign.

My right cheek and shoulder were scraped up. I took a bath and put on a long-sleeved dress and kept my hair over my face during dinner. I said a little prayer that night when I went to sleep. The next day I hurt so bad I could hardly make it out the door in the morning to pretend to go to school. I sat at the depot and held my shoulder and cried. I went to the river to nurse my wrists in the freezing water.

And then, I was fine.

I waited and waited.

No blood. No nothing. My face scabbed over, my shoulder healed.

I was fine.

It was too.

I was going to have to think of something else.

The next time Allen came over I told him he could kiss me. We were on the back steps.

"Just like that?" His face was open and bright, but he was looking at his hands.

"Well, do you want to or not?"

"Yes, of course, but I figured you wanted to make it special."

"This is special enough for me. This isn't special enough for you?"

"It's always special with you."

If it was always special with me, why couldn't he ever look straight at my face?

"Then what are you waiting for?"

LUCY

I was wearing a pretty dress when I came here. It was my favorite dress because of the flowers on the collar. But now it is dirty and breaking into pieces which is what happens when something is too old to be what it was in its beginning and covered in slop which is a food that is made of everything and the smell is in every stitch.

"This dress has seen its day," Missus says. "Come with me."

Then Missus says I can wear an old dress of hers until my stitching is good enough to make my own because that is the rule about getting a new dress if you are living on the farm. The one she picks for me is brown and heavy. I feel like I am walking through water and every step weighs more in the dress than when I don't wear the dress. Me and Missus are leaving her room to go down the stairs to the room where we practice the stitching.

But before we leave I see there is a dress hanging around with the other dresses except this one is red with a round skirt like twirling. I know that is really my real dress because it is like the dresses that Mum mum wanted me to wear when she wanted me to be pretty and with good behavior.

"I want this to be my dress, Missus." I reach out to touch. What it feels like is the outside of a peach which is soft but still protects the inside.

"That's the dress I wore on my first date with Mister."

"What is a first date?"

"We went to a home-improvement exposition at the fair-grounds. He seemed to know more about what the people were showing off than the people themselves."

"It is like a dress Mum mum wears."

Missus smiles. She likes thinking of Mum mum in her beautiful dresses. I smile too.

"Mum mum bought me dresses in every color and having all those is what it feels like to be a rainbow."

"It sounds very nice. But what happened to all those dresses?"

"They got too small and she didn't want to buy me any new ones because I didn't go to parties after that. Then sometimes I would wear pants even though Mum mum said that real ladies didn't wear pants."

"Would you like to try some pants now? You can do your chores more easily in them."

"I would like to wear the red dress."

"That is not an everyday dress, Lucy. That is a dress you wear to go somewhere special." Missus's breathing is loud but her words are quiet, like whispers, which is the way to tell a secret. "A special party, with dancing. And boys."

"But I never go to a special dance."

Missus does not say anything.

"Can I put on the party dress? I will see if I can look pretty in it."

"You don't need to look pretty. You're not going anywhere special today, dear. This is the kind of dress you wear to go somewhere special, where special things might happen to you."

Her eyes are seeing something far away. She takes the dress and holds it over her and smoothes it like she is trying to make it stick to her but it doesn't work. You need to get inside of it to make it stick to you.

Then she undoes the zipper in the back of my dress and says, "But you know? It has been a long time since this dress has gotten any attention. A pretty dress deserves some attention every now and again. We wouldn't want it to think it's been forgotten, don't you think?"

"Yes." *Yes* is what you say when someone says *Don't you think?*

I look like I have climbed into an apple and it became part of my body. It shows my knees and my ankles and arms. When I see them in this dress I know those are all parts that I love the best.

Missus says I look very pretty. That is because I have done the right thing climbing inside the dress.

"Could I have some lipstick with my dress?"

"When you go to the dance, you can wear lipstick."

But I know the lipstick is the right thing with the dress. They belong close together like the pieces of your hair in a braid. I want to show Mum mum I have good behavior and I know what things need to go together.

"Mum mum, she put me in a white dress with a big pink bow and we went to the party. She said to play very nicely with the other children but I couldn't because they wouldn't play with me. I kept calling but they didn't look at me because I wasn't pretty enough with no lipstick on." Now Missus will know about how I need the lipstick.

I was saying, Here I am, let's play very nicely together, but they were pretending they didn't have any ears for me. So I called louder and louder and louder and they laughed and I grabbed one of the girl's hair and I said, Why can't you hear me?

"Then the next time Mum mum went to a party she put me in her bedroom and made it so I couldn't get out. But I put on lipstick when she was gone. I put on all the lipstick so there was none left and put some even not on my mouth and Mum mum came home with a man and they saw me. Mum mum said the man left because I scared him away."

"You didn't know any better. You were just a child, you didn't understand what the lipstick was for."

"But after that I got to go to another party because Mum mum couldn't leave me."

"Well, now you know lipstick is just for special occasions."

"It's for right now. The lipstick belongs to the dress."

"No, no. Now let's get you out of this dress and into something more practical." Missus touches my back where the dress opens.

"Just a little lipstick to see how I can be pretty."

"Dress-up time is over for now, Lucy."

"Just a little lipstick so I can see what I will look like at the party."

"Let's get going. We've spent enough time enjoying this pretty dress. There's work to do and it isn't fair not to do your part."

Missus tries to undo the back of the dress but I spin away from her.

"Just a little lipstick and I will look like a very pretty girl."

I run over to where the lipstick is. I know because sometimes I wear it as a secret. Missus walks hard and fast over to me and tries to take it out of my hand. But I already have it all the way up and I very fast put some on my mouth and then a little more and a little more.

"Lucy! You mustn't use that lipstick now! It's only for special occasions!" Missus yells to me, but I feel myself getting torn in two and so I can't move any direction I want to. I see Mum mum smiling into my smile as she put on the lipstick and I saw in her face that she was looking at a very pretty girl. I know I am Lucy on the farm right now. But inside I am Lucy going to the party. I want to see what Mum mum saw. I want to see Lucy ready for the party.

"Put it down!" Missus yells. "We have to save it for the dance!"

She is trying to get the lipstick away from my mouth but that is where I want the lipstick to be. I am stronger than Missus, I know, but I don't want to hurt her.

Now Missus is on the floor. She sucks in her air fast, like slipping on a rock walking along the river. You don't know if the slipping will make you fall down, or if you can keep walking. That means scared, but Missus shouldn't be scared because now I look so pretty. I know how pretty because I see it in the mirror.

"Do I look pretty now?" I ask.

Missus gets up slowly and touches my shoulders very, very gentle like sunshine landing on a flower petal. There is so much sunshine but it doesn't move the flower, not at all. That is gentle.

"Now do you see how pretty I am?" I ask.

We look at me in the mirror. Missus smiles. She isn't a little scared anymore. She is happy now, which is the feeling of my legs when the eggs rub against them in my skirt.

"Yes, Stella, you look lovely."

MISSUS

The day finally came. I was cooking a late dinner when there was a knock on the door.

"Here she is, the little beauty," Rodger Marvin said. He handed me the bundle. It was our Stella. "The young mother is so grateful."

"Well, Rodger, she's not the mother."

Rodger laughed. "Yes, well, the young lady. She left town tonight, heading to the city. She's set up in a very nice boarding home. The church is paying for her to take nursing classes. And really, she thanks the Lord for the two of you."

I didn't care about the girl and her plans for the future. I didn't say that to Rodger Marvin. I didn't want to be rude. We owed him so much. But I didn't care. The sooner we could all forget about the young lady, the better.

We invited him in for dinner. Mister finished the cooking, set all the plates, served the food, and took away the plates. The kitchen had always been my territory but I wouldn't take her out of my arms. Mister knew that, without me having to say. There is a lot that passes between us, without needing to be said aloud. He has always trusted me.

During the meal she fell asleep in my arms. I went upstairs without excusing myself. I set her in her crib that Mister had built. He used a tree from the woods I had admired. Of course we could afford something store-bought, the farm was prosperous by then. But the way I was raised, things made at home were always better.

Then I tiptoed to our bed and climbed under the covers. As soon as I closed my eyes, Stella started to fuss. I rocked her back to sleep and again tiptoed to bed. As soon as I put my head on the pillow, she began crying. I picked her up and walked around the room singing to her. She fell asleep. I waited next to her crib for a good while, until I was sure she was deep into sleep, but again, as I climbed into bed she awoke. So I lay on the floor by the crib, and with my hand through the slats, holding hers, we both slept through that first night.

For countless nights after that, we slept in that same funny way. But babies grow up, and eventually, Stella didn't need me next to her while she slept. Babies grow up, but a mother's instinct remains as strong as it ever was. So it became a habit; every night, before retiring to my own bedroom, I would lie outside Stella's bedroom door, listening to her breathe.

LUCY

Before I was Lucy on the farm, I was in a yellow dress. The colors of my ribbons in my hair were pink, blue, green, and purple. Mum mum said, Which ribbon would you like in your hair? And I said, All the ribbons, all the colors in my hair like a rainbow. Mum mum said, It's a party, we might as well make merry, and she took all the colored ribbons to the hairdresser, which is where we sat and the woman touched my head and Mum mum drank out of her tall glass and held my hand and said, Dear Lucy, you look so pretty. It was warm because it was the summer and Mum mum took a kerchief to her forehead because her makeup was melting. Then she put more on and it melted off too. She did that again and again and I laughed.

There was a room for the children at the party and Mum mum put me in it. She told me to play nicely with the other children. There was a toy with beads and you could move them all around from one side to the other. That was the toy at the doctor's for children to play with. I knew how to play nicely with that toy. And I went to the toy and played with the toy and a boy said to me, "How old are you anyway?"

"I am twelve."

"That's a toy for a baby, what's a twelve-year-old doing playing with a toy for a baby?" He was laughing and he grabbed the other kid and said, "Look, look, this is the retarded kid my mom was telling us about. She's playing with that baby toy. My mom said not to make her mad because she could do something crazy."

"She doesn't look retarded," another boy said. "I thought she was going to look more retarded, with a mashed-up face or something."

"I don't think she's retarded," a girl said. "I think she's just stupid."

She sat down next to me. She moved some of the beads. The beads she moved were orange beads.

"Are you retarded?" I was looking at the beads and she was looking at me. "It's okay if you are. If you are or if you aren't, you should say so to shut up these boys. They can be real stupid."

"Oh, we're the stupid ones," the boy said.

"Mum mum said she doesn't know about me," I told the girl.

"Your doctor would know about you. Or your teacher. They know about different kinds of people and what to do with them."

"I don't have a teacher."

"Everyone has a teacher."

"Not me. I don't have a daddy or a teacher. Just my Mum mum."

"I know some people that don't have a daddy because he died or ran away on them, but everybody has to have a teacher because it's the law. That way if a kid doesn't want to go to school and begs their mom not to go to school, the mom still has to make them go. Because it's the law. The mom could get arrested if she didn't make them go to school."

"I don't go to school."

"Well, everyone needs to go to school. Especially you. I'll tell my mom to tell your mom and then your mom will have to listen because it's the law and she could get arrested."

I moved some of the beads. They felt like flying in my hand.

"Don't you like to talk?" the girl said.

"I don't have very many words."

"That's okay," the boy called to me. "Let's play a game with no words."

"Mum mum said for me to play nicely with the children."

The boy laughed. "That was a lot of words. *Children* is a big word. Maybe you're not as dumb as you think. Maybe you're a genius and you don't even know it. What's a million times a million?"

The other boy laughed. The girl had purple ribbons at the bottom of her braids. Her dress was purple. My dress was better. That meant that Mum mum loved me more than her Mum mum loved her. Mum mum loved me because she put me in a pretty dress. And she wanted everyone to love me too.

When I made Mum mum cry and she said, "I don't know anymore, I don't know about you," I would forget she loved me. Until the next time she put me in a pretty dress and made her face look a certain way at me.

"Here's a game with no words," the boy said. "Show us what's under your dress and then you win."

"Oh, you are horrible!" the girl said. "You little, greasy, disgusting perverts. My mom must be right about your daddy. How else could you get such a disgusting idea in your head?"

"What exactly did your mom say about my dad?"

"I won't repeat it!"

"Whatever she said there must be a reason she knows so much about it. A firsthand reason!"

"How dare you say something like that about my mother! She's nothing like your sleazy dad! She'd never have anything to do with him!"

"Then how come she's always talking about him?"

"You better take that back!" the girl yelled. The boy laughed again and then the girl ran away.

"So, about the game with no words," the boy said. "This is how you play it."

LUCY

The music wasn't in the children's room. It was in the grown-ups' party. But we could hear it anyway and it was very pretty and very fast and it made you feel like moving. The boy said, about the game with no words, This is how you play it. He took my hand and we went behind the couch. There were other children but we couldn't see them because we were hiding. The couch was green and soft and I liked touching it because it felt like it had fur which meant inside, it was alive.

"Stop touching the couch," the boy said. "That isn't part of the game."

I wanted to tell him it felt like fur but I didn't because that wasn't part of the game. When you don't have enough words you had better to listen to the people that do.

We were sitting behind the couch where the music was pretty and fast. The boy opened his pants and brought them down a little. He sat up on his knees. I saw underneath. He had on white shorts with purple stripes. He took my dress and moved it above my knees. He looked over the couch and came back down. He brought his pants to his knees and put my hands on his knees. There was some hair on his knees and I rubbed it a little. It felt like fur. I liked the feeling like fur.

Then he lifted my dress up around my middle. My legs looked funny with no dress around them but with my fancy shoes and ruffle socks. He put his hands on my knees. His hands were cold and a little wet in between the cracks of his skin but I liked them because they made my skin feel like there were feathers touching me or I was a feather touching him. I laughed because of the feeling of the feathers and my legs looking funny with fancy black buckle shoes and he laughed too and then he moved his hands above my knees and I did too. I felt that his underwears felt like tissue and he didn't have any more fur on the legs above his knees.

Then he put his whole head on my shoulder and rubbed his head around. It was a kitten rounding itself on my ankle. I touched his hair. It was hot and thick and warm and living. I put both my hands in it and grabbed around in it but not hard. Not to hurt, just to feel. He licked my neck. It was a kitten with a big, soft tongue and I licked his neck and it was the first other person I had ever tasted and it tasted like soap and salty rocks.

"I don't care that you're retarded," he said to my ear with heat on the words. "And you don't really act that retarded anyway. Maybe you're smart and you just don't know it."

"I don't know if I am that." My nose was breathing in his hair and my mouth was touching it and my tongue was touching it when I talked. "I don't have the right words for what I am."

He moved his hands and I moved my hands too.

"Not everything needs words," he said.

"This is the game with no words."

He laughed and I laughed too. Laughing at the same time was singing words to the same song. The music was pretty and fast. He licked my neck and it was a frog's belly.

Well, that was my favorite game, the game with no words.

Then the girl came back. She called, "Jeremy, Jeremy." "Shhh," the boy said. I knew that meant no words, not even any sounds. We put our heads together low behind the couch and hid but still moved our hands up higher on each other.

The girl came around to us and said, "Oh, you! You're in for it now."

The boy laughed. "Don't worry about her, she doesn't mean anything she says, she's just a nosy brat with no friends."

We laughed together about the girl. His hair was in his eyes. I wondered how it looked to see me through his hair.

He sat in my lap and pulled up my dress more and put his hand on the inside of my leg and it was a big hand, it made my leg look small even though no part of me ever looked small before then. We were looking at each other and his eyes were brown puddles that didn't spill and I kept watching to see if they would spill and they never did. His heart was beating in a way that means happy but he looked sad. I wanted to ask, Are you sad? But it was a game with no words. He put his head on my shoulder so his mouth was on my neck. I never knew how much my neck wanted to be touched until then. It was a part of me I didn't know anything about until then. I put my hand on his head so he couldn't ever move his head away. I wanted it always to be just right exactly there because I had learned that was the exact right spot.

Mum mum came in fast almost running but falling forward over herself. And she grabbed me up by the elbow and the boy fell over. I laughed because he had no pants. Noises were coming out of his mouth but they weren't words. He sounded like "I-I-I."

"Quiet," Mum mum said, mean and in a whisper. "You keep quiet on our way out of here, I swear, you've humiliated me enough already, I'm serious, Lucy, not a sound."

"I-I-I"—that was the noise the boy was making. My dress fell back down around my legs like it was before the game with no words. The boy jumped up and he jumped his pants up with him.

"I-I-I," the boy said.

"I-I-I," I said back to him.

Mum mum was dragging me out. The boy was standing behind

the couch. "I-I-I," I said to him. Then we had the same noise and that noise was "I-I-I." A man rushed into the room and went to the boy. He was shaking the boy. The man took the boy to the corner and smacked his face. I was making my feet heavy so I could stay and watch the boy. I didn't want to leave the boy with the man because it's wrong to hit someone no matter what they've done.

"Lucy!" Mum mum pulled hard on me but I was making my feet heavy.

"What's the matter with you? Taking advantage of a retarded girl. While a guest at someone else's house. What's wrong with you? What's the matter with you?"

That was what the man said.

What's the matter with you?

I know that question.

What's the matter with you?

When someone asks you that question, there is no answer.

We were gone from the party and Mum mum didn't laugh.

She said, "And this dress, and these shoes."

She cried and her face looked muddy. "I tried because I wanted people to see how pretty you can be."

Mum mum cried. "But you, you don't act pretty. You act nasty. You act disgusting."

Then she cried some more. "You can be a good girl, but when I take you out in the world with me, you ruin it. Why do you always have to ruin it?"

Sadness was squeezing Mum mum's insides so the crying kept coming out.

"I feel so stupid for trying."

"But, Mum mum, I played so nicely with the other children. I played with the other children and they played so nicely with me."

I didn't want to touch her. Her face was wet and red with lots of bumps like bites from spiders you never can catch when they are doing the biting. I thought my finger would stick in her face and I could never get it out and it would be the only thing I would ever feel again.

"I have made a fool of myself so many times."

"I played nicely with the other children."

"It's because of how much I try with you."

"You said play nicely with the other children."

"The harder I try, the more foolish I get."

"But, Mum mum, say that I played nicely with the other children. You said, play nicely with the other children, and I played nicely with the other children."

Mum mum held my head inside her hands. Her face was red and fat and shining because of being covered with tears, which was her disappointment in my bad behavior.

"How much longer do I try? Forever? Is that how long?"

"You said I looked so pretty so that everyone would like me and to play nicely."

"It's never right, however I do it."

"But I played nicely!" I yelled a straight line into her ears.

"However I decide to try, it's always wrong."

"But I played nicely. Say I played nicely."

Then there was quiet. During the quiet Mum mum closed her eyes. Then she opened them.

She said, "I know you did. It's me that can't do anything right."

Then it was later. Mum mum was in her dress but not me. That meant she was going but not me. I said to Mum mum, "I want a fancy dress like you. I want to look pretty and go to the party with you."

Mum mum said, "How about a party with just me and you? You can have a new dress and we'll do whatever we feel like and really just let loose. We'll go shopping for the most fabulous dress. I'll drink a whole bottle of champagne. I'll take off the next day just to recover. How about it? How about it?"

She made me laugh, how fast and how happy she was saying those things.

It made me happy that she said them because then I didn't know they didn't ever happen.

LUCY

No. It is not one of my jobs to get the eggs anymore, but they still call to me in my dream. They roll up to the front door and whisper loud enough for only me to hear, We miss you, Lucy, where have you been? Nobody is saying hello to us or tickling our noses underneath our shells.

I'm sorry but I'm not allowed.

Why not?

Because I wasn't the right person anymore. I was doing it wrong. I broke too many.

Oh, Lucy, we are so lonely. Come rescue us and see how much nicer we are when we're born.

Even nicer than being eggs?

Oh, yes, much nicer.

But I tell them no.

Later I wake up and the moon is winking at me.

No, I say, it's not my job to get them.

It's time, it's time.

Shush, I say. I can't sleep with you winking at me.

I beg for sleep because I know I can't listen to what the eggs want because it isn't what Mister and Missus want and they are the ones I must always obey or Mum mum won't come back to the farm and she is the only one that has been there since the beginning of me.

But the moon is winking and winking and I try to keep my legs heavy but they float up like fog above the river and carry me across the floor and out down the stairs and into the coop. In the coop the eggs aren't saying things anymore but their shells are making them glow in the night like they are each a tooth of a beautiful smile. I pick them up and rub their noses inside their shells and feel their warmth from inside.

I'm sorry but I can't take you all with me. Only a little of you.

Then I get very quiet and listen to which ones need me the most. Then I take them. One, two, three, four, five, six, and carry them into the house. I take my softest sweater that Samantha gave me when I was cold on the back steps and I wrap them all up in it to keep them warm while they grow in their shells and let them have a new house in my drawer.

Then in bed I sleep with no dreams. Until the bell is gonging that it is time to get up and now that means me too.

And the day is Sunday.

On Sunday is the day to go to church. That is where the Lord lives and Sunday is the day he wants all his people to come to his home and tell him how much they love him. People sing songs about him and explain how to make the Lord the most happy and we promise to do it and then afterwards we drink coffee and juice and stand outside in the sun and say hello to everyone else who loves the Lord.

I ask Missus if I can wear the party dress to church.

"Church is not a place to wear a party dress." Missus is putting a hat with flowers on top of her gray head because the flowers have more color than a gray head and the Lord likes colors. That is why he made the flowers have colors. "But you can wear a church dress."

The church dress Missus lets me pick is yellow with little purple flowers so it looks like I am wearing the ground during the days when the flowers are born, which is called the spring. She lets me pick it even though I didn't do any stitching to make a new one. She brushes my hair and puts it behind my ears.

"There, now we can see your pretty face," Missus says, looking at me in the mirror. I know her face. It is a smiling face one second after the smile goes away, but the rest of the face stays the same as it was during the smile. It is the same face she had when I wore lipstick and she called me Stella. I want the Stella face to be the face Missus makes at me. And then Mum mum will come back and Missus will say she never made bad faces at me, only good faces, because I only had good behavior.

"Missus, when I wore the lipstick you said Stella and you knew I was being a good girl and very pretty."

"Oh, did I call you Stella?"

"You said Stella."

"I guess having you young girls in the house is bringing back memories."

"What does having young girls bring back?"

"Memories of Stella, it would seem." Missus holds her stomach like when I ate a piece of slop to know why the pigs liked it, and I didn't taste the badness in my mouth but I felt the badness in my insides.

"Who is Stella? She is very pretty?"

"She was our daughter."

"She is your daughter? That is like me! Like me and Mum mum."

"She used to be our daughter," says Missus. "Now, you know we can't keep breakfast waiting, let's go downstairs."

But I know something. Something that Missus said is wrong. People tell me when I am wrong and I will tell Missus that she is wrong, so she will know a special thing and never forget it.

"Missus!"

"Come along, Lucy." Missus holds open the door and wants me to go through to the can't-keep-it-waiting breakfast.

"But, Missus, a daughter is never used to be. A daughter is always."

"Well, dear, not in this case. Not anymore."

But there was never a time a daughter was not a daughter anymore because a family is the only one that is there since the beginning of you and you can never change the beginning, and I am going to ask Missus, but now she is not holding the door anymore, the door is shutting, and she is going down the stairs because you can't keep breakfast waiting, even if you have questions.

We go downstairs to eat breakfast like a family, which is what we are not. I want Mister to look at how nice I look and make the Stella face at me, which means I am doing a good job of being Lucy on the farm. But he only looks at other things.

"Mister," I say, "this is my new church dress."

"I'm letting her wear it," says Missus. "What's the harm?"

"No harm," he says.

"See, Mister?" I say.

"I see." Mister's face has lots of lines, but none of them are moving, like mud that dried and cracked in the sun. He is not making the Stella face.

Samantha, Missus, Mister, and me all go and sit in the front of the church to get closer to the Lord than anyone else. We all hold hands and feel how much each other loves the Lord. When we don't hold hands Samantha chews her fingers. Missus and Mister close their eyes and rock side to side and sometimes they cry but not because they are sad. It sounds the same as sad crying but it is different. It is the sound of being so happy about the Lord that the happiness overflows and spills out of your eyes.

That is during church and then after church Mister and Missus need to say something to some other church people. "Wait by the refreshments, girls," they tell me and Samantha. And people say hello to other people except for us and the sun melts the top of my head into honey that burns instead of tastes sweet.

A round man comes to stand near us with his special church book in his arms. Everyone that goes to church has a special church book except for me because when you don't have any words you don't need any books, even a special book that the Lord wrote.

"Well, well, well," he says, and sweeps his hat towards the ground. "Samantha."

"Hey," she says.

"You're doing well on the farm? Working out for you the way we hoped? Treating you well?"

"It's a dream come true." Samantha grabs my hand. I grab back. So my hand is for her and her hand is for me. We each have an extra.

He waits for more from her but she is looking at the ground. She is listening for the ground's secrets and not to what the man says.

Then he turns to me. "And we haven't had the pleasure." When he says we he says it extra-long. It is a special way to say a word, just for me. "Though of course I have heard lots about you."

"Lucy," Samantha says.

"Lucy, good afternoon. My name is Rodger Marvin and I am in the business of eternal life. No, I'm not selling maps to the fountain of youth. I only spread the news of salvation through the word of our savior, Jesus Christ."

"Good afternoon," I say.

"I'm sure I needn't even ask if you ladies read the Lord's good word every day?"

Samantha, she wants him to go away. I know because her

mouth is getting heavy and pulling her face towards the ground. But I don't want him to go because his belly is round and looks soft like your hands would get lost in it, like in the dirt when you look for a weed. On the top of his head he has no hair but drops that are shining. I want to rub them together and feel them grow into one big drop. His mouth is big and moves fast and tries to catch your ear with the nice way he sounds.

"I don't read any word any day," I say.

"Blind, busy, or broke, no excuse is good enough not to read the word every day."

"We have other things to worry about. Like being farmhands, remember?" says Samantha. There is dust on Samantha's green-glass eyes because they are not shining anymore. I want to rub it off but it would hurt her to have my finger in her eye. "Come on, Lucy."

She pulls my arm, but I want to stay. Maybe Rodger Marvin has more words he will make just for me.

"Ladies, ladies, ladies, what I'm selling doesn't cost a penny and will make you richer than all the money in the world. I'm extending an invitation to come together with fellow daughters of the Lord to read and study the word together."

"I can't," I say. "Because I'm missing too many words and I don't know where to find them."

My talking opens a curtain because now light is shining on Rodger Marvin's face. He blinks because of the lots of light.

"My dear girl." His voice is louder now. Each word is whole and round and heavy like a stone sinking to the bottom of the river. "God loves all His children equally. Even the different ones like you. Even the ones who hadn't had the opportunity for an education. It doesn't make any difference in His love for you."

"It's hard to have me as your child, Mum mum says, because I don't have any good behavior."

"Not so with the Lord. It's not hard for the Lord to have you as

His child." The curtain between us goes up and up and away and Rodger Marvin's words shine light back on me.

"Mum mum says she doesn't know about me."

Samantha pulls on my arm. "Lucy, Rodger Marvin doesn't care."

"Samantha!" says Rodger Marvin. "Don't be silly!"

Then Mister and Missus find us. Mister and Rodger Marvin shake their hands together. But Missus folds her hands, like closing a book when you do not have enough words to read the insides.

"Afternoon, Rodger," says Mister. "I've come to collect these two. Time to head back to the homestead."

"Good afternoon, Mister, Missus. I just had the pleasure of talking to these fine young ladies, extending an invitation for one of those famous—or infamous, depending where you get your news, from the sinner or the saved—Bible studies of ours, bringing the young folks of our community together to read the Good Word. After all, they are the future." Rodger Marvin smiles using a lot of his teeth to show the most happiness.

"Oh, Rodger, you shouldn't feel you need to take too much of your time talking to these girls," Missus says. She is smiling. But only with her mouth. Her eyes and voice are turned downwards, the wrong direction of smiling.

"It's my job, Missus, and I take my job very seriously. When it's soul-saving you do for a living, you'd better take it seriously. Because you know who else takes their job seriously?"

It is a question but nobody answers.

"The *devil*! Satan himself."

"Of course, Rodger," says Mister.

Missus says, "Well, we are certainly blessed to have a church this invested in its members' personal spiritual journeys. But it just doesn't seem realistic given the girls' respective situations."

"Rodger," Mister says, "you know we are a family that loves the

Word. Your offer is very generous. But Samantha can't make late-night trips to town. And Lucy doesn't read."

"That's what she tells me. But this is a mighty ripe time for her to learn, being as it is with the sad state of her world. The comfort and guidance of His Word would be the single greatest gift a girl like her could ever be given."

Yes. I do want to learn to write down some special letters so I could know them for later, the letters on the lipstick and some of Samantha's special letters that say the names of me and her and whatever the baby will be, the words to say the shapes of things inside of me.

"This might be a ripe time to learn," I say, "because the sad state of her world."

"Yes, it is a certainly a generous offer." Missus is talking loud like we are across the fields from each other. But really we are all right here. "Using your precious time to help enrich their lives. We know how busy you are."

"Wednesday nights in the basement. I reckon you should send them, Mister. You know, the world can be a dangerous place for young girls. The devil can be a charming bugger and our girls need the guidance of His higher power. We all want them safe, don't we now?"

"Of course, Rodger," says Mister.

Rodger Marvin sweeps his hat down to the ground. "I'll be making a special request that He encourage you to send both the girls. I think you'll realize it's in everyone's best interest."

Rodger Marvin takes some backwards steps and waves good-bye.

We are all in the truck. Missus says, "Rodger certainly takes an active interest in the girls."

Mister nods his head, which means yes, he thinks so too.

"But there's no reason for Lucy to come into town to learn to read," Samantha says. "I've been showing her what certain words mean, and I've seen her tracing letters into her book. It might come as a surprise, but I can read, you know."

Mister says his words slow, like they are fireflies inside him and he has to stop and catch each one before he says it. "It would be wise to listen to Rodger Marvin."

Missus opens her mouth but does not say anything. Then she closes it, and opens it again, like she is trying to tell a bad taste to get out but it won't listen.

"It isn't right for Lucy to go into town alone. Someone could take advantage of her." Samantha talks to Mister but what she looks at is all the things that are outside the truck and none of the things that are inside of it.

"Rodger wouldn't let that happen," Mister says.

"If Lucy goes, I'm going with her," Samantha says. "You can't send her off alone!"

"Dear, don't be silly," Missus says. "This was your last trip into town before the baby comes."

"I'm not even close to needing to stay off my feet! You had me weeding just the other day!"

"Quiet," Mister says. "You don't know. You've never had a baby. We're keeping you safe. You and the baby."

"But you promised you wouldn't make me stay inside all the time! We had an agreement!" Samantha's eyes flash like sun hitting the wet rocks.

"Now, dear," Missus says, "it's about keeping you safe. You and the baby. I'd remind you that young girls aren't known to have the best judgment about these things."

"But it's still mine, it's still inside me. And you promised."

"That's enough," Mister says. "You're not going."

Everything else that Samantha says we pretend we don't have ears for it and so she stops saying it. I put my hand on her belly to quiet the thing inside of her. I want to say things to Samantha. I want to say to Samantha, I will always have ears for you. I want to say, Do not be afraid of me learning my words. I want to say, Samantha, why are you afraid of Rodger Marvin? I want to say, There is nothing to be afraid of.

But Mister said that is enough. That means no more talking or else punishment, and what if my punishment is no Rodger Marvin and no finding new words? What if my punishment is a place where Mum mum can't find me?

MISSUS

We were so happy. The three of us. Complete.

There was nothing more we needed. Or wanted.

He reached for me still. But our Stella was already here.

"You don't have to."

"I know I don't have to. But I still desire you."

"We're complete, dear."

"Our family is complete. But I am still a man and you're still my wife."

"There isn't need anymore."

"You're still my wife. Why would my love for you have changed at all? If anything, I love you more now that Stella is in our lives."

"Things are different now, dear. I'm still your wife, of course. But now I'm a mother too. I hear her crying."

"I don't hear anything."

"She is, darling." I peeled off the covers.

He grabbed my hand. "Don't go. She's fine."

"A mother knows."

He didn't say anything more. He understood. He has always trusted me.

He let go of my hand.

LUCY

Even though in the truck she said she wanted to do everything the same, Samantha doesn't fight with Mister when he makes her sleep downstairs. So the baby won't have to bounce up and down the stairs. We sit together in her new bed.

Samantha tells me, "You don't need Rodger Marvin to learn how to read. I've known him my whole life. He worked at the funeral home before he was a preacher. He's not so special. He's just full of himself. He doesn't care about you. Not like I do."

"But he cares about teaching me the word."

"He just likes the sound of his own voice."

"But he likes the sound of God's voice too."

"Oh, please, he probably thinks they're the same thing. And there's no reason why I couldn't go with you."

"Because of the baby getting heavy."

"I could teach you to read. I went to school through eighth grade. I've known how to read for like over ten years or something. I'm an old pro."

She opens her book for me. "I bet you even know some of these words already. Can you find the word *Lucy*? It's on this page here."

I look at the words. The only thing I have seen before is the way that Samantha's words are round and full like lace not small and hard like the words in the Bible. But I want her to think she can make me learn so I pick a word.

"This one says *Lucy*."

"No, that says *uniform*." Her face sinks a little towards the floor.

I turn the page, looking for another Lucy. But I am forgetting what Lucy looks like.

"Is this it? This is *Lucy*? This one says *Lucy*?"

"No, no, none of those."

I keep turning pages hoping that one of them will speak to me like the eggs do, whisper its secret of what word it is. But the words are silent and cold like winter stones at night. They are keeping their secrets all to themselves.

But then as I am turning, turning, I come across something that does speak to me. It is a page that falls out of the book like a leaf after it is too tired to hold on to the tree anymore. I pick it up.

"I know him, he is the fox that steals into the chicken coop."

"That? Allen drew that."

"The fox can see what he is looking for in the dark. The father of the baby, he can come and find you in the dark?"

"No."

"Why?"

"Because he doesn't knew where I am."

"Then we will go to the place that he is."

"I heard he got sent somewhere." Samantha's words come fast like she wants to get rid of them quick. It is hard for me to catch them all.

"Why?"

"To keep us apart."

"We will find him together, so he can be there on the first day. Because that is what family is."

"We can't do that. It would be dangerous to leave so close to my due date."

"After the baby comes? That is when we will find the father? Because he loves you, the father of the baby? That is why he wanted to make a family with you and be there from the beginning?"

"Yeah," says Samantha, very quiet. Maybe that is because it is a secret.

"There was never any boy that ever loved me. Just Mum mum."

"Well, she probably sheltered you too much so you couldn't meet anyone who would appreciate you."

"What is *appreciate*?"

"Like love, kind of."

"You love him? The father of the baby."

"It's been so long since I've seen him," Samantha says. "But I know if I saw him again I'd feel the same."

"What does it feel like?"

"What?"

"Loving him?"

"You know what love feels like."

"But what does it feel like to love the father of the baby?"

"It was like all of a sudden there's a new part of you, that never existed before, but now you can't live without it." Now Samantha's words are small and soft.

"Like the baby? A new part of you and you can't live without it?"

"In some weird way, I suppose." Samantha laughs. "One day you'll see what I mean."

"When?"

"Whenever you fall in love." She puts her head in my lap. "I feel so fat."

"How much longer until the baby?"

"Not long."

"But when?"

"I'm not exactly sure. Hopefully soon."

"Ask him when."

"You ask him."

"How much longer, Baby?" I ask.

Then we are quiet while the baby thinks about how much longer.

Then Samantha says, "He's almost ready."

"Why only almost?"

"He's a little scared, I think."

"Of what?"

"Maybe he's afraid it's going to be cold out here."

"Tell him he can wear the sweater you gave me. I will give it back."

"No, you keep it. I gave it to you. And anyway, compared to living inside someone's stomach, it *is* cold out here."

Then I give her back her book and a piece of paper that has a letter inside falls out. The letters on the front say SAMANTHA and I touch each one and feel the way they come one after another like the inside of a pea.

"What does this say?"

"*Samantha*. Me."

Now I know the *Samantha* word, and know it has always been my favorite.

"Is this for you?" I say.

Samantha doesn't say anything.

"Are you supposed to open it?"

"No," Samantha says.

"What is this called?"

"A letter."

"But what is the outside called?" I use my finger to show the part of it that has the letters SAMANTHA and ALLEN on it. "This part."

"An envelope?"

"Yes." It was a word I was trying to get in my mind so I could see how it felt inside there. "I knew it was a word I liked."

"See, that's what I was trying to tell Mister and Missus. You're a quick study." Samantha takes the envelope and puts it behind the bed.

"But I want to know what the insides sound like."

"Why do you care so much?"

"Because if I had enough words, Mum mum would write me one."

Dear Lucy,

I've been thinking about you. What a funny baby you
were. You didn't gaze up adoringly at your mother like other
people's babies did. It was always so hard for me to get your
attention. Whenever you smiled, I could never tell what at.
It was never anything I could see. I would get down on my
hands and knees, to get to your eye level, and I still couldn't
ever understand what it was you were looking at.

One day you saw the neighbor's kitten in the hallway.
You pointed and laughed. It was the first thing you ever
showed me. My heart smarted like it had been slapped.
I saw how pretty your face would have looked, if you had
been different.

From then on you constantly crawled down the hallway
looking for the kitten. You shrieked with joy when you saw it.
Another mother would have tried to quiet their child; it was
a crowded apartment building. But I didn't. I had to hear your
shrieking constantly. It was nice to know somebody else had
to hear it too.

You put your face right up against its white belly, and even
though it squirmed and scratched, you always managed to
hold it so close. When people stared at the scratches on your
face, I told them I forgot to cut your fingernails. But you didn't
mind the scratches, did you?

Plenty of times I fantasized about hurting that sweet,
innocent creature in front of you, so you could see that I was
in charge of you. So if you started to cry, at least I would know
what I had done to cause it. Other times I needed you to see
the kitten so badly. I convinced myself you would go blind
if you didn't see it, that cataracts were forming on your eyes,
and I would go crazy calling, "Kitty kitty kitty," up and down
the hallway. And sometimes I suspected maybe you and the
kitten were ghosts, and I was stuck somewhere in between

this world and the next. That was why the kitten was the only thing you could really see.

Do you remember the kitten? It was your favorite thing, though that doesn't mean you'll remember. There are so many things you forget. Not like me. I remember the things that made you smile. I remember all your birthday parties, just the two of us, and all the presents I bought you that you found ways to destroy. I remember to write you letters you'll never be able to read, so I also remember not to send them.

Love,

Mum mum

LUCY

Samantha doesn't have to do chores anymore. All she has to do is grow the baby. But she comes with me to do the weeding.

"This is boring, let's go to the river," Samantha says.

"No, I must always obey Mister and Missus. Mister said weed the tomatoes."

The weeds I pull out, Samantha shakes off the dirt and braids them together, so even though they had to leave the underground they aren't alone.

"He'll never know the difference."

"But Mum mum said obey Mister and Missus."

"She'll definitely never know the difference."

"Mister will tell Mum mum not to come back for me. And I won't be the daughter anymore, like Stella."

I find the weed's root and then go deeper, because that is what a root is. Deeper than you ever think. Then I pull, strong and gentle. *Come out, root, Samantha will braid you if you come out and you will be a piece of something so pretty.*

The root comes out. That is brave because it did something even though it was scared.

"Who's Stella?" says Samantha.

"She used to be the daughter, like me."

"Whose daughter?"

"Mister and Missus."

"Can't be," says Samantha. "They weren't able to have kids. Rodger Marvin told me the whole story."

"Missus said. She said Stella was her daughter. And she was very pretty and then Missus touched my shoulder and said Stella."

"Lucy, I wouldn't be here if Mister and Missus had any children. That's why they need me."

"Why is that why they need you?"

"Never mind that part. But whatever Missus said about Stella, she was probably just messing with you. Or else you didn't understand right. But either way, there's no way Mister and Missus ever had any children."

"I did! I did understand right!" I knew when I saw Missus make the Stella face, I knew inside that Stella was the daughter. Because Missus would never make that face if she didn't have the love that you get from being there since the beginning of someone.

I stand up to show Samantha that I did understand. If I stand up, my words will grow taller too and Samantha will see that I did understand. Because Samantha, she has the baby growing inside of her, and she has to know too, about the love of the first day. "I did, Samantha, I did!"

"Shhh, don't get upset." Samantha stands up and puts her arms around me. She smoothes my hair against my head, it tells the words inside they don't have to yell so loud, Samantha can hear me even when I am quiet.

"But I did understand right, Samantha," I say more quiet. "I saw Missus's face when she said Stella."

"Okay, okay. Maybe there's some explanation." Samantha pulls me towards the river. But I cannot go. Even though it is Samantha's favorite place, the only place that doesn't make her wish she was somewhere else.

"No," I say. "I have to do the weeding. Because Stella isn't the daughter anymore, and I will always be the daughter. Missus said Stella got lost and Mum mum can't ever lose me."

MISSUS

Our daughter grew to be a beauty. Not like me. I'm not ashamed to admit it. Everyone at church fawned over her. We feigned modesty and beamed with pride. She participated in the church plays, the school glee club. All eyes on Stella. And none of the attention was lost on her. Even from a young age, she spent so much time in front of the mirror, admiring herself.

"Look, dear, isn't she lovely?" From her doorway Mister and I watched Stella fuss with her hair.

"She certainly is."

"Not like me."

"Don't be silly. You are beautiful."

"But not like that. She is a true beauty."

Stella turned around to see us smiling at her. "Guys, stop! Daddy, make Mom stop."

We all laughed. But in that moment I realized, everyone must know. Everyone who sees us together must know she isn't mine.

"Oh, darling," I told her, "it's just that you take our breath away."

"You're embarrassing me!" She rolled her wide, dark eyes at us, trying to close the door on us, but she was laughing the whole time.

That night he reached for me. I held his face in my hands.

"Oh, darling, isn't she so terribly, terribly lovely? So striking. Doesn't look a thing like us."

"We're lucky to have her as our daughter."

"She's ours, Mister, but is she really our ours?"

"Of course. Who else's would she be?"

"She had a mother once."

"Nonsense. Only you. You are the only mother she has ever had."

"Well, we both know that isn't so. She had to get those looks from somewhere!"

We laughed. I let him have me, one last time. Afterwards I lay awake.

"I just can't stop thinking, everyone must realize she doesn't look anything like either of us," I whispered to Mister. "Do you think everyone knows she isn't mine?"

LUCY

Missus says, "Lucy, you can wear one of my dresses to your Bible lesson. I want you to make a good impression on Rodger Marvin. Show how well behaved you can be. He's very respected around here."

"What's *respected around here*?"

"It means we listen to him and do as he says," she says, and holds my hands, "which is how I'm sure you'll act around him."

"Because of how he is smart and how many words he has."

"He knows a lot about a lot of things. People respect that. And you're going to learn some of what he knows a lot about, proper language, and understanding the Bible and the path the Lord chooses for us.

"How do you like this one?" Missus asks me. Her face is bright. The dress is purple with green lines crossing each other on it and it goes in tight at the waist. "I made this dress for myself. I always preferred home-sewn dresses. There is something special about things made by hand, don't you think?"

"Yes." There is something special about them, and when I am inside, there will be something special about me too.

"Try it on, let's see you in it."

Missus does up the back for me and the waist is tight, very tight like tiny arms are squeezing me around there because they never want to see me go.

"Look, it gives you a shape!" Missus laughs. "Who knew Lucy had shape underneath?"

I laugh too. "I have shape underneath!" It was hiding, like my own secret that even I didn't know.

"An underneath shape," Missus says. Then she takes her scarf off her own hair and ties it around my head. It is the same colors as the dress and they shine against each other like smiling in each other's face. My head is happy to have pretty colors to keep it company again, the way Mum mum used to tie ribbons to it, until I wasn't good enough.

"We have the same type of figure," Missus says. "Big-boned but with a shape underneath."

I laugh again. It makes me feel like sparkling inside, the way the stars say hello to each other from all the different places in the sky.

Missus smiles. She said that we are the same. Me and Mum mum, we were never the same because of how small she was. Sometimes I hurt when I was only trying to feel her. But Missus thinks being big but with shape underneath, that is an all right way to be.

"Here, Lucy, here is a treat for you. Now hold still." Missus has her lipstick, Cajoling Carol, and she brushes it on my lips. It feels like flower petals blowing against each other. We look at me in the mirror and Missus says, "My, what a pretty girl. You look almost as pretty as Stella, the night of her first dance."

"Where was the dance?"

"It was at the school."

"Stella was your daughter and she looked pretty at the first school dance." This shows Missus all the words I have found about Stella. Missus will see I can keep words when I find them, and she will tell me more. "Samantha is the baby's mother and you are Stella's mother."

"Well, I used to be her mother."

"But why not now? I thought mother was forever."

"Stella said good-bye to us, Lucy. Left her mother and her

daddy, can you imagine?" Her eyes are getting bigger, but she is not seeing me anymore. She is not making the nice face at me.

"I would never leave my Mum mum. That is why I am waiting here on the farm for her."

"Yes, you are a good girl. But Stella wasn't good like you."

"Where did Stella go, Missus?"

"She abandoned us. We weren't enough for her."

"Stella didn't stay on the farm with her family?"

"No." Missus shakes her head. She looks one way for Stella, but Stella is not there. She looks the other way for Stella, but Stella is not there either.

"I will help you look for her," I say. Because if you are the mother you must always know where the baby is. That is why I stay on the farm.

"No, Lucy, there isn't any use in that. But what you can do is be very good for Rodger Marvin. Just think how smart he is. If you do everything he says, some of his intelligence will rub off on you."

"There are words that I am looking for and when I find those words I will know that they were the words I was looking for, to tell people about the shapes of things inside me."

"Lucy, Rodger Marvin can help you with those words, just please do as he asks. Will you promise me that?"

"Yes, Missus."

"Lucy, do you know what a promise is?"

"Yes. It is something you can never forget to do."

I am walking to meet Mister outside so he can take me to Rodger Marvin, and the door of Samantha's room opens and the inside whispers, "Lucy, come here."

I go in her room. She says, "What were you and Missus laughing about?"

"We were laughing because of me being big with a shape."

"She was making fun of you?"

"No. She said again that I was pretty like her Stella."

"Stella again? Why are you suddenly obsessed with Stella?"

"Stella used to be her daughter, until she said good-bye."

"What's that supposed to mean?"

"She left them, because she wasn't as good as me. And now they don't know how to find her."

"You didn't understand what she was talking about, Lucy. There was something wrong with Missus's body that made it so they could never have children. If she did say she had a daughter, then she was messing with you for some reason. And what's more, she's probably sending you to Rodger Marvin so he can mess with you too."

"No, that is not why. She's sending me because of his smartness that will rub off on me."

"Don't listen to him, Lucy. He's only going to confuse you."

"But I am looking for some words and I have to try and find them or else I'll never know what they were."

"Please don't give anyone any reason to tease you, okay? Don't talk about living here or why you're here or anything about it here or how we're friends. They'll give you a hard time if they know you live here."

"Is it better to have a soft time?"

"Hard like difficult, like bad, like make you feel bad about yourself."

"Don't be scared, Samantha. Once I find my words I'll tell you lots of things you never knew either."

"I'm not scared. I'm just worried about you. You'll believe anything. They won't see the ways you're special. They'll just see the stupid side of you."

Missus comes and says, "Samantha, I thought you were sleeping. How are you and the baby feeling, dear?"

Samantha closes the door and she does not say how she and the baby are feeling, dear.

SAMANTHA

Allen had a job after school stocking at a bar. He saved up and spent all the money buying me a necklace with a bird carrying a banner that said THINKING OF YOU. My mom asked me about it, suspicious, like maybe I had stolen it.

"No, Mother, it's from Allen."

She beamed. "Oh, it's lovely."

"And by the way, Allen and his family are coming over tonight. We're going to tell you something."

My mom smiled at me, like she already knew. But she couldn't have. Because then she would have said something, right? At the very least she wouldn't have been smiling.

She cooked meat loaf, which I've always hated. She knew that. She baked a pie too but all I could smell was the meat loaf. The smell of it took up all the air in the house and made me sick. I couldn't help it. I didn't come out of my room and I breathed out of my open window.

Allen and his mom and grandma showed up, all freshly scrubbed, I'm sure. My dad talked nice to me through the door, trying to sweet-talk me into coming out. Then he lost it and started to yell and threaten and bang his fist on the door. My mom got flustered and said I wasn't feeling well. Allen's mom said of course, she understood, and then the grandma said something and there were chuckles all around.

I laughed too. A different kind of laugh, though. I flew my bird and its banner around my room.

They stayed on and had dinner. I opened the door, just a little, just enough to hear what they were talking about. Just normal adult stuff, not anything about me. They laughed a lot, but the stuff they said wasn't funny. Allen didn't say anything except when my dad asked him about a radio he had built. Then they moved to the living room to have dessert and I couldn't hear anymore. I guess that's when Allen must have told them. So why didn't they come and get me?

The next day I said sorry to my mom.

"The meat loaf smelled especially delicious," I told her.

"Why, thank you, dear! It was certainly nice to meet Allen's family." We looked at each other. She didn't say anything more.

I ate the leftover pie.

"See, Gary, she was just feeling sick!"

"We're glad you're feeling better," my dad said into his coffee cup. His eyes and nose were rimmed with red. He cleared his throat. "Though I think I may have caught your bug."

We went to church and pretended together. People smiled at me and my belly; I smiled back as best as I could without gagging. After the service Allen came up to me. He was glad I was feeling better.

"Thanks."

"So everything's all right?" he trailed off.

"With what?"

"With everything." His face was so red I couldn't look at him, which was easy enough because he was looking at the ground. "And us."

"Sure."

"I'm gonna be good for you, promise." He darted his eyes up for a moment. His mouth was twitching, fighting to keep his smile from bursting his whole face open. I knew he meant it, about being good.

I swallowed a mouthful of bile. It burned as it tore down my throat. "Thanks."

Then my mom saw us and hurried over, clasping her hands to her chest the way she did when birds ate out of her birdfeeder. I hugged Allen. It took him by surprise and he fell into me, and his mom and grandma sort of appeared out of nowhere, and then my dad too and they all formed a circle around us. I took a deep breath and held on tight to Allen and pretended and pretended and pretended, thinking to myself, I guess this is how everyone else does it.

MISSUS

That first date of ours, at the Home Improvement Expo, Mister explained how everything worked, the pumps and wells and toasters and what have you. He could tell, somehow, just by looking at things. He knew more than the salespeople. He was so serious, so focused. I was impressed, naturally, though I didn't really pay those gadgets much mind. I just watched him.

I knew, one day, he would bring his boy here. Our boy. I felt in my bones what a wonderful father he would be. How desperately his son would look up to him. Named after his daddy. What a wonderful man that boy would become, because of who his father was.

"Do you remember, dear, our first date?"

We were sitting at the kitchen table together. Stella was upstairs, playing with her dolls.

"Of course."

"I remember watching your face, and I had this feeling, like, one day, when the expo came to town, years later, that you would bring your son, and explain all the things to him." Mister could sense my pain. I knew he felt it too, he just couldn't acknowledge it.

"We can always bring Stella." He looked at me with such love. But Stella would never care about any of those things. Only a son can really understand his father.

I wiped away a tear. "I just, I felt it so strongly, like I was having a vision of the future, utterly accurate and certain."

"If we've learned anything, it's that you can never be certain of God's plan."

"Of course." I put my head on his shoulder. "But watching your face, you had this knowledge, and this passion and curiosity and I felt in my heart that you were destined to be the father of a boy, to make him into the kind of man that you were. And still are, of course."

I went on, "It causes me such guilt, such pain, because it's me that's broken, you know. The doctors told us, there's nothing with you."

"There, there, now." He held me close. "There's nothing wrong with you either."

"Please don't patronize me. We both know it's me that's flawed, that I've kept you from being that father to that little boy, teaching him all those things, teaching him how to be a man."

"You haven't kept me from a thing."

"You say that, but I know, I know it's all my fault. I had that vision of that boy; I know I've taken him from you."

"You've taken nothing and given me so much. I remember that fair too, you know. I remember the looks from all the other men, wondering how a poor farmer got the prettiest girl in town to go out with him."

"Stop, we both know I'm no beauty."

"You're my beauty."

"Stella, now there's a beauty."

"She's only a child."

"And her beauty is already striking. Don't pretend you haven't noticed."

"Both my girls are beautiful. I'm one lucky man."

"You can't actually compare us, though, she's a true beauty. Imagine what she's going to grow into."

"She'll be lovely, like her mother."

"Like her real mother, I'm sure, but not like me. Please, dear, please just let's have a little honesty between us." I lifted my head from his shoulder so I could look in his eyes. It was so important to me that he be honest. "We both know Stella's nothing like me. I'm not upset about that. The only thing that upsets me is your insistence that somehow I'm a beauty like her, when we both know it's not true."

"I didn't mean to upset you. That's the last thing I wanted to do."

"I know, I know. Just, please, for honesty's sake, then we won't speak of it again, please just admit that Stella is a true beauty."

"I've never denied that."

"Not like me. Please, dear, just admit it and we'll lay it to rest."

"That's just plain silly. Don't make me say that."

"I just need to know you can be honest with me, even when it's hard."

"I will always be honest with you."

"You can promise me that?"

"Absolutely."

"Show me." I held his face in my hands. We held each other's gaze as if we were balancing something heavy and precarious between us. "Now."

"Stella is a true beauty." He paused.

"Go on," I whispered.

His eyes widened. He looked so alive. "Not like you."

I kissed him, the way we did when we were young.

LUCY

Mister drives me. We have silence together. But the ends of his mouth, they are turned up making his cheeks into apples. It is a nice way for his mouth to be. In my stomach little parts of me are flying like the moths around the lightbulb on the porch because I might find my words with Rodger Marvin. And if I find them, who will I say them to?

The car stops driving. Mister hands me two things, one empty book and one book with writing. The letters on it say *BIBLE*.

"This is your Bible. This is for your studies. Some think you're not worth trying to teach. But not Rodger Marvin. He thinks you're worthy to witness the love of the Lord. Do you understand that?"

"Yes, Mister."

"Right. I'll be back in one hour." So it is time to get out of the truck.

A basement means it is a place that is underneath a house. This basement is underneath the church. There are the stairs that lead to the underneath. There is the first step which is lower from the ground than any step I have ever stepped, and then there is the next step, which is lower from the first step than I have ever stepped, and that is because of how low we are going. Then we can't go any lower. Here there are chairs and walls with colored paper in pretty shapes I wish I had made, and Rodger Marvin and a lucky girl. I know she is lucky because her dress has heart buttons all the way to her neck. It is lucky to have so many little hearts on the outside and also a big heart on the inside.

"Good evening, Rodger Marvin," I say, and sweep myself toward the ground.

"Why, look who's here! Lucy!"

He sounds as happy as Mister when he is waiting for it to rain and he hears it on the roof at night and yells out because without the rain all the living and growing on the farm will stop.

"I requested to the Lord that he lead you here and I'm happy to see he agreed with me that this would be a very special, very good place for you. Though you know, it was probably the Lord guiding me to bring you here all along." Rodger Marvin smiles and shakes his head, but not in the way of his not understanding about me. It is a shaking because of how smart the Lord is. "Not the other way around."

Well, I can't say anything except with my smile because of the nice way his words snuggle in my ear.

Then Rodger Marvin holds my hand and the hand of the girl, so even though I am not touching her, I can feel her. She is smaller than me but I can tell she has strength. It shows in her eyes that don't look away.

"This is Lizbeth Elizabeth," Rodger says. "She is a true daughter of the Lord, the one who insisted, demanded, we start a meeting of all the young ladies of the congregation who still thirsted for the community of church even after Sunday had passed."

"Hello, Lucy. My name is Lizbeth Elizabeth." She is a true daughter of the Lord like I am the true daughter of Mum mum and Stella was the true daughter of Missus. Even though Lizbeth is a special girl to have the Lord as your family it doesn't make her smile. But it does give her a lot of nice words and she gives them to me. "I hear you're dumb but I want you to know I don't care about that. Jesus was the only person who was ever perfect and he was half-God, in a way, so you can't hold it against someone if there is something wrong with them because there is something wrong with everyone."

"Yes," I say. I know she is right. She sounds very smart like Rodger Marvin, who knows a lot about a lot of things and so then he is respected around here. "I don't have right words for things and I have no good behavior."

"Really, though," Lizbeth says, "none of us has good behavior, since we're always sinning. But the Lord loves us anyway. That's what I'm trying to tell you."

Rodger laughs with all his big belly going into the laugh at once. "Lizbeth might be onto something here. Now let's begin. Have a seat."

We have our seats.

Then Rodger Marvin talks about things the Lord wants us to know about. There are a lot of people that the Lord wants us to know about. Mostly the Lord told those people to do something and the people didn't do it so they got punished. But the Lord still loved them anyway.

I do not stop to say What does that word mean? and What does that next word mean? the way I ask Samantha, because I don't want Rodger Marvin and Lizbeth Elizabeth to find out all the words I do not know. I open my empty book and I put some markings in it. I try to remember what the *Lucy* word looked like but I can't remember any part of it, so I look at the Bible and make some of the letters in that book but I don't know what they mean. But I know that someday I will open the empty book and look at what I did today and know about all the meaning. I will do that and then I will think of Rodger Marvin and Lizbeth and the people the Lord punished because he loved them.

At the end Rodger Marvin and Lizbeth and me all hold hands. There is something like a fishing line going through all our hands in a circle. I can feel it moving from Rodger into me and across me and into Lizbeth. My eyes are closed. The fishing-line feeling brings my heat to them and their heat to me. Then Rodger says, "Good night, ladies, good night, ladies, good night, ladies, I hate to see you go." He says it with regular words but what it sounds like is a song.

I stand and smooth my skirt over my knees to hope it didn't get too messed up the way Mum mum hated for it to be. I sweep myself to the ground like a heavy branch of the tree by the river which is called a weeping willow. It is a sad tree because someone drowned in the river and then the tree was all alone, is what Samantha told me.

"Good night, Rodger Marvin, good night, Rodger Marvin," I try and sound like him to show him I have learned.

Rodger Marvin says, "Before you go, here's an idea for you. Open up a book and copy the words, even if you don't know what they mean yet. It will make your hand familiar with how it feels to write. Just any book. Just open it up and copy what you see on some blank paper. Do that and bring it back next week and we'll take a look-see."

"What is a look-see?"

"We'll look at the words you've copied."

"You will read the words that I bring you?"

"Why, yes, of course I will! What do you say?"

"I say yes." Yes, Rodger Marvin will be the first person to ever read my words, to help me get them ready for everybody else.

Outside is where I wait for Mister and the truck. All the stars live in the sky above the farm so here there are no stars. The light from the lamps floats around like orange smoke. Lizbeth Elizabeth waits with me and her heart buttons twinkle orange. She says, "So you're one those farm girls, working for Mister and Missus."

"Yes. I am one of those farm girls. I am Lucy on the farm and

I can't ever leave the farm because or else Mum mum won't know where to find me."

"I've known them my whole life because of church. They seem strange. But they must be good people if they take in you girls that nobody wants to deal with."

I don't know if that is *you girls* or *good people* so I don't say.

Then Lizbeth says, "Well, you must know Samantha then. She was my neighbor before she went away."

"Samantha! Samantha! Samantha!" With orange hair and white hands and her eyes are the prettiest place in the kitchen.

"So you do know her?"

"She takes care of me and knows how to quiet me when I'm loud and make me move my hand to draw things."

"I didn't play much with her."

"Samantha loves to play but her skin blushes in too much sun."

"I heard it took a lot to make Samantha blush."

"Oh, no, Samantha blushes quick, like if a grasshopper wants to get to another leaf."

"That's pretty."

"Samantha is pretty."

"No, just the way you said it. The thing you said about the grasshopper." Lizbeth's hair is tight against her head so it doesn't get messed up like my skirts during bad behavior. "Anyway, we all knew each other from the neighborhood and church, but she hung around different kinds of people than me."

Then I use all the my thinking at once to say something that Samantha would say if she could have come with me if she didn't have to stay in the downstairs bedroom to keep the baby from bouncing.

"What about Allen?" Getting all the words from the corners of my insides to come together just right. "But did you ever know Allen?"

It is the best thing I have ever said. It is a perfect way. I know because of the way it sounded like a person with all their words. It is the best thing I have ever said because of how happy Samantha will be to learn about Allen.

"Sure, I know him. I saw him this morning. We live right near each other. Samantha too." Lizbeth looks at me with her eyebrows pointing down toward her nose. Her eyes want to make sure they see me look back at them so they don't blink. "All the same people have lived here forever and nobody will ever leave. That's the kind of boring old town this is. What about you? Where did you come from?"

"Tell him where Samantha is! Tell him Samantha is at the farm."

"Tell who? Allen?"

"Yes!" Yes!

"He knows." But Lizbeth does not look happy to talk about Allen, the way Samantha would be.

"Tell him, because he is trying to find her but doesn't know where to look." I know how it feels. I know how it feels to look and not to find.

"Lucy, he already knows." Lizbeth nods. Which means yes. But I know what she says can't mean yes. "Everyone knows."

"No! He doesn't know!"

But then a car comes and it is the car for Lizbeth because she calls good-bye and she gets in and I can't say the other things I need to say and Lizbeth and her car are already driving. I wait and wait for Mister but I'm not lonely because I'm talking to the moon, telling him the things I learned and asking please for him not to forget in case I need to ask again and then Mister finally comes and I can't wait I can't wait I can't wait to tell Samantha about what I have learned. Because I, me, Lucy, learned something, even though it's not about my missing words. It is even better than that.

But when I get home Samantha is sleeping even though the lights are on and Mister won't let me wake her up. He says, "If you ever have the blessing of being with child, you'll understand how much rest you need." Then he turns off the light so her dreams will know it's time to come out.

I nod to show him I understand how much rest you'll need. But now I need Samantha to tell her I know about Allen. Because she thought that Allen was sent away but really he is living on the same street in the boring old town.

In my room I look at the words I made in my new book and it feels like the little balloon in my chest is getting breathed into.

Missus comes into my room. I close my book like Samantha when someone comes in and she is writing. Except when it's me and she leaves it open.

"Lucy, we need to speak about something." She sits next to me. "I noticed a putrid smell coming from your room. For days I tried to ignore it thinking maybe you hadn't been bathing or it was from soiled clothes. But it was getting worse and worse and finally I went in to look."

Missus breathes deep. She pulls my head towards her and I am smashed against her. She is very sad. I can hear from the way her heart beats at me.

"I know you thought your job with the eggs was special. But after that night, Mister was right to keep you away from them. They are our livelihood, after all. But you were clearly upset. And for that I am sorry.

"But what you were doing with the eggs in the dresser is dangerous. Unnatural. Do you know what happens to the eggs if they aren't eaten?"

"Yes." Missus thinks I do not know but I do know. Because

Samantha taught me. Samantha, she knows because there is something growing inside her. "They are born into baby chickens."

"Only if they stay underneath the mother hen will they turn into chickens. Not if they are taken away from the coop."

"I know that the eggs will turn into baby chickens. You don't know because you and Mister eat them before they can be born."

"We have plenty of chickens, plenty of baby chickens too. You know that you can always play with those baby chickens, Lucy." She puts her hands on my shoulders but I won't let them stay there. Her hands are the ones that have eaten the eggs before they turned into baby chickens. "But that isn't the point. The point is you cannot keep raw eggs, or any eggs, in your dresser drawer. They go rotten, and rotten eggs are vile and disgusting and danger-ous. You can get very sick from eating something like that, some-thing rotten like a rotten egg. Don't you know that?"

"I will never eat those eggs. I am taking care of those eggs so they will become alive and I will be there since the beginning of them and care for them after that and until a long time after that."

"Whatever was growing inside the eggs died once you took them away from their mothers and into your room."

"No, those are not dead eggs."

Then I know. I know that Missus is trying to take my eggs because she thinks I am not right to be their mother. She thinks because I don't have all my words yet that I won't know how to take care of the eggs because Mister thought I couldn't have the job around the eggs anymore. He did not know how gentle I was with the eggs and now Missus does not know anymore consistency either.

"They were dead, Lucy, they smelled horrible. One was broken all over your nice sweater. I don't know how you were able to sleep in here. The whole house smells now. But you didn't know better. I'm trying to tell you so you will know better."

"One wasn't broken!" I look at them every day and kiss their noses and cover them with the softest sweater from Samantha because their shells are thin as a blade of grass. "Never was one broken."

I rush to the drawer. It is open like a gash in your knee. There are no eggs and no sweaters. Inside my mind I see the chickens in their shells with their heads cut off and Missus is there with scissors because that is what she used to cut off their heads and there are bloody feathers floating and sticking to her face.

"Where are my eggs?"

"Lucy, please calm down. They've been disposed of. In the compost. Do you know what that means?" Missus comes to touch my shoulders again but her hands are stuck with bloody yellow feathers. "They'll go back into the earth and help other things grow."

But it was me helping the things grow. I was stopping the things that were stopping the growing. I was helping the growing which is a secret. Most people do not know it but I do.

"Where does that mean? Where are my eggs?"

"They're in the compost, I just said that. Now let's please get some things straight."

"Give me back my eggs." I take Missus's hair so she can't get away without bringing them back. I shake her head up and down so she can feel I am holding her hair and she knows not to run.

"Let go," Missus whispers.

"Give them to me, go get them."

My babies are calling to me but I don't know from where. They are saying, Lucy, you have let us get hurt. We would not have gotten hurt except you let it happen. Lucy, we picked you because we thought you could be our mother, but a real mother wouldn't leave her babies.

"I didn't mean to," I yell for them to hear.

"I know you didn't." Missus eyes are wide and getting wider like a spill spreading. It starts small and then it fills up everything. "It's not your fault you were made the way you were."

I see them. The chickens, they are trying to pull their shells over their heads but too many pieces are missing and the chickens are drying up. I will go and try to put them in my mouth to keep them safe and not dry up.

"I am your new shell. Stay in here and I will keep you safe."

Missus is trying to get all her arms around me and I still have her hair in my hands. "Shhh, shhh, shhhh," Missus is saying. "Quiet, dear, quiet, dear, quiet, dear."

"I will save them, let me see them. I will know how to save them because I will be their mother. Bring me there."

"They're gone, Lucy. They're in the trash, in the compost. They're decomposing."

When I used to be little and Mum mum saw me do a bad thing she would pull on my hair and then I would know I was supposed to stop. Then I got too big and she couldn't pull on it anymore but I remember how it hurt. So I pull Missus's hair away from her and towards me. She bites on her lips and her eyes look like a pond that used to be still but then a stone got thrown in and makes waves and waves to the edges all around. But she doesn't scream. And if she doesn't scream, then it doesn't hurt her enough to take me to my eggs. I pull more.

"They're decomposing," Missus whispers. There is no more voice inside of her, only just the littlest bit left. "You took them from their mothers. They aren't eggs anymore."

"Take me there, we need to save them, they can't live without their shells until they know it's time to come out. They told me so."

"I'll show you," Missus says, and I let go of her hair so she can show me and she makes a loud sound that she swallows down before it is all the way out. "Come, Lucy, I'll show you how they are helping the farm grow."

Outside the light is from the sky and the little light from the house that doesn't shine very far. That light is orange and the light from the sky is white. We walk in the night. Missus is walking fast, more fast than I knew she could walk, faster than me, even though it is always me that is the fastest. It is away from the house, away from the river. It is towards the woods. And then we are there.

It is a little mountain with fuzzy edges, made out of soft dirt with twigs and leaves sticking out like a bird's broken feathers. It smells like the black moss that grows in between the rocks by the river.

"This is the compost. This helps fertilize the things that grow here. Here is where the eggs are. They were rotten. They were dangerous for people but they will help the plants grow. They will be a special part of what grows here, but you can't watch them grow in your drawer. That's not natural. Nature has its own rules. You can't fight it."

"Here is where my eggs are?"

"Yes."

"I will find them here. They are hiding under the dirt, keeping warm because their shells got broken."

"No, they're gone. They are becoming the earth. I wanted to show you that they went somewhere special."

"I will find them here." I put my hands in and start my looking, feeling for the eggs, and the dirt is soft and alive like a woman's belly and my insides are the melted sides of a candle dripping all over the mountain. Then I look with my fingers and the spaces in between my fingers and listen for their voices but they do not come. They do not come and I find a piece of a shell and another piece and another but nothing, nothing, nothing, on the inside.

There is no inside anymore.

Missus grabs my arms. "Lucy, come. Enough. Get up."

But I won't get up. I won't come with her. I will stay with them and tell them sorry, sorry, sorry. The eggs thought I was good enough to be their mother, but I wasn't. Because when you are the mother, you don't let bad things happen to the babies. Missus wanted to get rid of my babies. Because Missus was Stella's mother, but not anymore. Missus wasn't good enough to make Stella stay where she could find her, like Mum mum can make me stay on the farm. Mum mum will always know how to find me, but Missus didn't know how to find Stella.

Now Stella is gone and now all my eggs, they are gone too.

SAMANTHA

After church the next Sunday Allen came to greet me. He had sat a few pews behind me during the service. I had felt his eyes on my neck the whole time, trying to burrow inside me and down my spine, control my nervous system with his goodness.

He was fumbling with something in his pocket. I went cold. I covered my ears and tried to run, fighting against the sea of people streaming from the pews, heading back into church to the bathroom. He was following me, calling my name, smiling and fumbling. That fumbling was going to choke me. Or his kindness would. Or his blushing, or his gentle, freckled arms. I knew that now. I had pretended I hadn't known it all along. But the fumbling had shaken the pretending loose, and it had toppled over and shattered on the floor.

All he wanted was to marry his sweetheart. And I would be so terrible to him. Every day, more and more terrible to him, until I hated myself more than I even hated him and the thing inside me.

"Samantha!" His voice was strong and bright, rising above the streaming heads of our congregation.

I couldn't let him get to me. If he did, if he pulled out what he was going to pull out, in front of all those people, then he was going to get bigger and bigger and I was going to get smaller and smaller until he could smash me with his thumb, if that was what he had the urge to do, or keep me in the tiniest cage, if that was what he wanted to do. Or just love and be kind to me and the thing inside me, if that was what he wanted to do.

He was stronger than me because he was a good person. Something powerful inside him made him want to do the right thing. And he was also strong because he probably did love me, maybe just in a teenage way, but that counts as love, maybe counts even more because of its naïve conviction that it matters so much more than it does. I didn't have any love, or any goodness or anything to give. Just something I needed to get rid of. I couldn't fight him, I could only run and hide and never see or hear him or think about any of the good things about him ever again.

I ran into the bathroom, locked myself in a stall, and put my head between my knees. I tried to breathe. Maybe the air was safe there. I tried to suck some back in. But every time he called my name, he inhaled the air straight from my chest. I covered my ears.

Lizbeth came into the bathroom. "Allen's looking for you, Samantha."

"Don't tell him I'm in here."

"He already knows."

"Tell him to go home."

"Why don't you tell him?"

"Don't let him find me."

"I just said, he already knows you're in here."

"Please tell him to stop. I'm gone. I'm already gone."

"He won't buy it."

"Tell him I went out the window."

LUCY

The light uses feather hands, tickling my eyelids, itching so I have to open them. My cheek is on the compost and my hands are dug inside, holding tight. The belly is crawling with ants and other lives.

"Hello," I whisper to my used-to-be eggs. My whisper, it is dry and cracked because it wasn't getting any water when it was inside my throat. "I have to leave you here. Make the farm grow big and strong."

The things here, they will help make the farm grow, but Samantha, she is the real secret of growing. She is trying to keep her secret of growing until it is ready. And the other secrets of growing, the eggs and the secret of growing, those are secrets people yell when they find out about them. They take them away. Maybe that is why Stella is missing. Maybe Stella got taken away because Stella had the secret of growing. Mine is all gone and dead and into the ground and doesn't belong to me anymore. It got taken away and I couldn't save it, but me and Samantha, we will save her secret of growing and never let it get taken away.

Inside, Samantha says, "Lucy, you smell disgusting. And where were you last night? I was looking for you."

"I was looking for my secret of growing."

"What does that mean? Let's take a bath and you can tell me about it."

Samantha gets the bath ready and then I sit inside and she sits on the floor next to me. She puts a hand in the water to feel the warmness I am feeling all over.

"I tried to keep my secret of growing but Missus found it. She killed it in the compost."

"What do you mean? What were you growing?"

"I was keeping the eggs warm to be baby chickens and not eaten."

"Did the eggs go rotten?"

"No," I say. "None of them went rotten and none broke until Missus took them."

"Missus doesn't get it. Beause her body is damaged. Do you know what that means?"

"No."

"That means broken and ruined. That's why she can't have her own babies." Samantha gives me the soap. "Here, you gotta use this too."

Samantha says Missus never had a baby, but Missus said she was Stella's mother and you can't be the mother unless you are the first thing the baby sees, and are the first thing to see the baby. But even though I am missing words, I still know when Missus called me Stella that she was saying the truth. Her eyes and her voice told me it was the truth. That she was the mother. But not anymore, Missus said. But I am always Mum mum's, and the baby is always Samantha's. So why not Stella?

"You know the secret of growing, Samantha?"

"Yes."

"Because you are the secret of growing. That is the baby and how every day it gets a little bigger but you can't see it but you still know it's there."

"That's right."

"And you are there from the beginning of the baby and that is why you are its family. You and Allen. And when I go into the town next time, then I will find him for you and bring him back."

"But, Lucy, I already told you. He's not in town anymore."

"But Lizbeth said she saw him."

"She's lying to you, because she knows you'd believe anything."

"I wouldn't believe anything. Just the true things. I will ask Lizbeth to show me because she saw him just the other day."

"See, I told you people were going to lie to you. That's why I didn't want you going to that Bible study. I tried to warn you." Samantha shakes her head. "Look, Lucy, I know Allen's not in town. I'll show you."

I get out and Samantha she gives me a towel and we go to her room even though I don't put any more of my clothes back on.

"Look, these are all from him."

Samantha hands me the letters. They are opened and covered and full of words that Allen made. Not words like Samantha's, which are open and wide like the vines that grow up the porch. His words are little and then big and little again. Like the pretty edges on the inside of a rock, if you hit it with another rock to find out what's inside.

"All about how far away he is, and how he's trying to save up money to come find me."

"Where is he?"

"He's far away."

"But what is it called?"

"You've never heard of it."

"But I need to learn its name so I can help find him, so he can be there on the first day."

"You won't be able to find him."

"You have someone that is trying to find you because of how much he loves you. But Mum mum, she knows where I am but she still doesn't try to find me."

"When I leave, you can come with me. You don't have to wait for your mom."

"Yes, I do. I mustn't ever ever leave the farm or Mum mum won't know where to find me."

"No, you can't stay here. You'll come with me."

"Where?"

"We'll find somewhere to live after the baby is born."

"Where will it be? With Mum mum?"

"No, just us. Down along the river somewhere. We'll plant really high flowers so we'll have privacy, and grow vegetables and do whatever we want all day long."

"And the baby will grow there."

"The baby will be fine."

"Because you will always take care of him."

"The baby will be taken care of, don't worry about him. And we will take care of each other. So you won't need to wait here for your mom. You'll come with me."

"But Mum mum will be so scared when she comes to get me and I'm not there."

"No, she won't," Samantha says. "She's fine without you, why else would she dump you here?"

MISSUS

The boy haunted me. Mister's son. Sometimes it was hard for me to be around Mister, he reminded me so much of the son we didn't have. The devotion with which Mister studied the Bible, the determination that coaxed any plant to thrive, his agility with a saw or hammer; would those be qualities our son would have? Would he be as tall or as thin? Would he honor his family above all else?

A man as good as Mister deserved to see himself live on through blood. It was sacrilege to say, but without blood to survive you, your memory dies when your body does. But if we had a child, a blood child, then the world would be blessed with another man as good and strong as Mister. We would leave this world knowing we had given the world something good.

The guilt was more than I could bear. To think that it was my body, keeping him from all he deserved. And to make it worse, he refused to blame me. I had to force him to acknowledge that it was my body and not his that had caused us such sorrow. That I was broken; that he was still whole.

More and more often, I didn't make it out of bed. My heart was heavy as an anchor, making it impossible to go through the motions of the life that had once been so full of joy and hope. Mister made Stella breakfast, drove her to school, took her shopping, made us dinner. Each night he brought me mine on a tray.

"There's no reason to feel this way," he tried to tell me.

"I have no choice."

"I have everything I could ask for," he mollified. His kindness was crushing.

"You're only trying to appease me."

"It is the truth."

"I know a man's nature. It's not natural to be satisfied without having a blood child."

"Then I am an unnatural man, but I am satisfied, I promise you. All I want is for you to share in that happiness. Please, just eat a few bites of supper." He held up a fork.

"I can't, dear." Being so close to food made my stomach churn.

Eventually he put the fork down.

"We miss you," he told me. "Our daughter needs a mother. Let's take a walk tonight. Just a few minutes."

"You take her, darling. Be there for her, the pain is too much for me tonight. Being outside will just make the world seem that much more empty that he isn't in it."

"There is no *he*," implored Mister. "There is only us. Why isn't that enough?"

"There is a he. I can feel him. But you go. Show Stella that she is loved. Please."

I watched through the bedroom window as they made their way to the woods. The sunset against the bony silhouettes of the trees set a beautiful stage for their stroll. Seeing them together gave my heart some peace. At least they had each other. I brushed my hair, put on my dressing gown, and made it downstairs for the first time that day. I cleaned the dinner plates and put on some water for tea.

"How was it, my loves?" I asked.

"Cold," said Stella. She stamped her boots and rubbed her mittened hands together.

"I hope your daddy kept you warm."

"He's a wimp! I had to keep him warm." She put a freezing hand against Mister's cheek. He yelped and we all laughed.

"It was beautiful," Mister said. "Tomorrow night you'll come with us."

"Something to warm you up." I set their tea in front of them.

In Mister's grateful face, I saw a glimmer of his former innocence; innocence my failings had taken from him. The same innocence his son would have. To see his son's wide, dark eyes would be to restore Mister's childhood's eyes. If only he could look into his son's face, Mister would be able to feel the world as it was before I took his future from him.

"You need to get some fresh air," Mister pleaded the next night. "You haven't left the house in days."

"Please, don't waste your time up here with me, go be with Stella."

I took a few bites of food so he would leave me be. He needed to be with Stella, not me.

For a while the house was still. The emptiness was a vessel for all the things I lacked. For the life and family my body had stolen from me and my husband. The house surrounding us was as barren as the missing half inside me.

Then I heard them plunking out a duet on the piano. Her weekly lessons and our constant praise didn't seem to be effective; Stella wasn't any good. But to think that despite my guilt and shame and broken body the house could still be filled with life made the music as exquisite as if it had been practiced to total perfection. And above the music floated a sound that had become foreign in our house. Laughter. It harmonized perfectly with the clumsy piano playing. It beckoned me downstairs.

They were sitting at the piano bench together, their legs touching. Looking at them, her olive complexion and dark waves, his pale skin and thin, gold whips of hair, you would know in an instant they weren't related. Mister hit some terrible chords, perhaps on purpose, and Stella pushed his shoulder to chide him. He pretended she had hurt him. She petted his injury. More laughter.

Then Mister looked over and caught my eye. He took his hands off the piano and stood up. I know he wanted me to join them, sit in between them, pretending we were complete. But I put my finger to my lips and motioned for him to stay put. The laughter, the levity, and the warmth were all too precious to disrupt. If I joined in, I would surely ruin it. Sometimes the best thing you can do for your family is to stay away from them.

"Stay," I mouthed. And then I smiled, full and wide. It had been so long. It felt as new and exhilarating as a first kiss. Mister smiled back. He trusted that I knew best. He sat back down at the bench.

"Well, what do we play next?" He tickled Stella's side.

The music and laughter. It was clear she could offer him more than I could. She could offer our family more than I could.

LUCY

"You're gonna come with me, right?" says Samantha. "After the baby is born, like we talked about. Because it's going to be soon."

"But I have to wait for Mum mum."

"Lucy, I need you more. I don't have anybody else but you. And you can't stay here alone."

"You will have the baby and you will have Allen. I will ask Lizbeth where he is."

"Please don't ask her. She doesn't know. Just leave it alone."

"She knows. She saw him the other day." I saw in Lizbeth's face that it was the truth.

"I'll need you, Lucy, just you. We'll buy a little house and plant vegetables."

"You don't like vegetables."

"We'll plant the ones I like. And we'll only eat the things we grow, and that way neither of us will have to get a job. I used to have a job scooping ice cream in the summer, and it was so boring." Her words are slower now, like how the river moves when the winter starts to come. The moving slow is how you know it's coming. "The ice cream gets really hard, because it's so cold, and then it's hard to scoop. So it makes your hands hurt. You've got to come with me or else I'll have nobody."

"I have to wait here for Mum mum or she won't know where

to find me. But I will find Allen for you. You won't be alone, Samantha."

Then I don't have to say anything else to Samantha because she is asleep even though her feet are still on the floor and her head is hanging heavy with all her orange hair and she is still in her clothes. I put her feet on the bed and her head on the pillow because that is where those things should go if you are sleeping. I go to my room and get my blanket and put it on top of her and then I get in it too and I am careful not to make any moving so that she doesn't wake up because when you have a baby growing inside of you, then you need lots of rest, more rest than I know about.

The door opens. It is Missus. I squeeze my eyes shut so she will think I am sleeping and let me stay.

"You mustn't leave us, dear," Missus says, very very quiet. "Not like she did."

I promise, Missus, I say in my mind. I will stay here, where Mum mum can find me. I won't leave. Not like she did.

PART II

The Secret of Growing

LUCY

The sun is already wide-awake and hanging in its high place in the sky. But where is the gonging, which means it is time to get up? Now Missus is taking me out of Samantha's bed, which is where I stayed all night. Missus says her words as small and quiet as anyone could ever say words.

"Lucy, come." She takes the blanket off my side. But where is Samantha? When I fell asleep she was here, but now when I am awake she is not here. Did her dreams take her back to where they hide during the daytime? I slip off and we slip out. Missus puts her hand on my back and pushes me soft up the steps to my room.

"Lucy, get some clothes together. We're about to leave for the hospital."

"But where is Samantha?"

"She's eating breakfast."

"What about my breakfast?"

"Rodger Marvin will feed you breakfast."

"Why the hospital?"

"Because that's where Samantha will have the baby. Personally, I can't see what's wrong with a home birth, but we promised her parents."

"The baby is coming?"

"Yes, the baby is finally coming! Isn't that exciting? Samantha won't have the burden of keeping that baby alive anymore and her life can go back to normal."

"Why isn't it normal?"

"Now she's stuck here with us, a couple of old folks, that isn't fun for a young girl like Samantha. Young, pretty girls want to be free."

"I will come to the hospital, to help Samantha."

"You're a sweet girl, aren't you? But, no, you'll be going to stay with Rodger Marvin. Now hurry, get your things."

Not just her mouth is smiling. Her eyes and her cheeks and her ears are all pointing up towards the sky. That is where you look when you think of the Lord. And that is why when you are happy your mouth goes up towards the sky, where He lives and happiness is made.

She gives me a sack to put some things in. What she wants is for me to get some things from inside my room and come downstairs. I want to go downstairs to be with Samantha and the about-to-be-born baby but I can't go yet because there is nothing in my sack. I open my drawer. Inside there are only things I do not need. I put in my book and a pencil and dress and sweater. But the sweater is a lie because it is too hot. It is the time in the year when everything is melting. Under my arms and behind my knees always part of me is melting.

I put all those things back so they can stay in the I-don't-need-them place. Now I will go downstairs.

But I can't.

I can't because of the shaking. It is a shaking of all the things I put back. The sweater and the dress, they are shaking and I do not want them to fall apart. I do not want them to fall apart and become things that are not together anymore. My heart it is beating fast to try and keep all the things together. I put my hands inside to hold the things together but the shaking is stronger than my hands. And then I feel one small thing inside my hand. Where did it come from? It is one small white piece of a thing. It is a piece of a thing that shines with its white, even in the dark. It is a piece of the shell I tried to keep safe and went rotten and broke. It is the one small piece that Missus did not bring to the compost.

And then I feel another small thing. It is another small white piece of a thing. And then I feel another small white thing, and another and another. Every time there is a shaking there is another small white thing in my hand.

Until there is no shaking. I take out the sweater. I take out the dress.

And then I see underneath, there is something there. It is not one of the things I do not need. It is something else. It looks like a ball of something wet and smashed. I touch it with my finger. It sucks you in like mud. It is very small and very warm and breathing and beating.

All my inside air is sucked out of me and out of the room and through the window. I put the ball in my hand and then my hand becomes a heart that is beating hot beats to my whole body. I know what it is because it talks to me when I dream. It has one black eye that opens, and it has another black eye that opens, and it looks at me, me, me, who is there since the beginning of it. Since its first day, which is today, which is now, which is still happening.

Hello, Lucy, it says.

MISSUS

Not all parents were like us. Not all parents were willing to give so much of themselves in service of their child. Stella was lucky. Beautiful, long-limbed, and lucky. Blessed. She had been blessed to be given to us. To be welcomed by a mother who was willing to sacrifice so much. The guilt I could never shake, that was a sacrifice I endured for her. Each breakfast, each hand-sewn dress, each night I had spent sleeping next to her crib, each was a sacrifice. All the afternoons I let Mister stop working as soon as Stella returned from school; always choosing her over the farm and seeing our profits suffer because of it.

Stella was lucky to have us. Of course, we were lucky to have her. But I believed Stella was lucky in another way. Blessed in another way; she would be given the chance to repay us. I knew Stella should have wanted that chance. Because didn't I trust her to be good? And what good person, when given so much, doesn't hope for the chance to repay what has been given to her? What good person isn't moved to action by the power of their gratitude?

From the kitchen window I watched as Mister and Stella raced between the tomato plants. Stella rushed into the house, into the home that always welcomed her, sheltered her, comforted her. The home that had taken her in when nobody else wanted her. Her face was flushed, bright with happiness and victory. So alive. Her life a part of so much life on the farm. Her growth part of so much growth. Just as we offered what we had to her, she could offer what she had to us. Her beauty, long limbs. Her luck. Our luck. I was her mother, and as a mother, you fight to ensure your child has everything. Every chance. It was my duty to make certain Stella had her chance to honor her family, to serve her family. To repay her family. To repay her father and mother. To repay me.

LUCY

Hello, Lucy.

But I cannot answer.

I know you tried to save my brothers and sisters.

Yes, I did.

I hid from Missus and stayed warm under your sweater.

You are very brave, I think.

What is your name? I say.

That's for you to decide.

But sometimes babies whisper what they want their names to be.

So put my mouth next to your ear.

I lift it to my ear and it almost fits inside.

Jennifer, she whispers.

I'm Lucy.

I know. I've known about you forever, since you first came here and talked to us and tried to save us.

I have to go to Rodger Marvin's now.

Keep me close.

I will.

Put me in your pocket. And get me something to eat. Some bread crumbs and some grains of sand. It's good for my digestion.

I put her in my pocket. She rubs against my legs in the place where the eggs used to rub and it would make me remember things but forget them before I got them into words. Now I feel Jennifer beating and breathing against my legs and I am doing the remembering again. Just because words don't come with it doesn't mean it isn't remembering.

Downstairs Samantha is at the kitchen table alone. Like a family is how we eat breakfast, which is together with everyone present. We aren't a family, but nobody says that part. A family, they are there from the beginning of each other. But we all got here at different times and now we are leaving at different times.

I sit by Samantha. I put some of her grits in my pocket. On Samantha's face there is hurting. I know because of the way the parts of her face are moving, her eyes and mouth. They move to places in her face they usually don't go to. They move in hurting ways to hurting places.

"Samantha, are you hurting?"

"Yes." She holds herself over her belly. I put my hands where she holds herself to be her extra holding. "It hurts. Bad."

"Are you sick?"

"No, it's just the baby."

"The baby is sick?"

"No, it's not that. It just hurts."

"Oh, Samantha, don't be hurting."

It's okay. Jennifer's mouth is full of grits when she says it. It's normal.

But Samantha's eyes look scared.

"You'll be here when I get back, right?" says Samantha.

"Yes."

"And don't let Lizbeth tell you any more stories."

"Yes."

"And you won't do anything stupid to get yourself in trouble?"

"No."

"Good. Because I'm gonna need you to help me. As soon as I get back, we're outta here."

I put my hand on Samantha's belly. There is something underneath which is like the dirt, you can't see the underneath. But the underneath is the reason there is so much life up top.

"Look how big I am." She lifts her face up. "Jesus, I'm huge. I can't wait to get skinny again."

She is smiling now. The hurt is still there but her smiling is stronger. Samantha puts her fingers in the cracks of the table and runs them back and forth, back and forth. She tries to breathe all the hurting air out of her body.

"This used to give me splinters," she says. "When I first got here, I liked feeling the splinters because I wasn't as mad when I had splinters. But I've done it so many times, now it feels smooth. Like metal. Feel."

She takes my fingers and runs them back and forth, back and forth. I feel all the times Samantha has moved her fingers in this way. It feels like a stone from the river, it feels like what happens to the dirt when you run up to the house in the same way every day. It feels how something changes just a little every day until one day when you look it is the opposite of what it was. When it was nothing and now it is something. When you couldn't watch even if you wanted to. When you couldn't see, even if you were watching. Then, that is the secret of growing.

"Crazy, right?" Samantha says.

"Right." This time I know that what she says is right. It is not just a thing that I am saying.

Then she cries and holds her belly, then holds her back, like a horse bucking.

"Samantha!"

"No, no, I'm okay. Shhh, don't be scared."

Then Samantha, she is standing up. Her arms around me is the bark around a tree and her belly makes it so big that all of me can't touch all of her but there is so much life and blood in her belly that I feel more of her than I ever felt of anybody else.

She whispers, "I'll be back, I'll come back after and find you here and we'll all be together again. We'll go to that special place where we all belong. With trees and a river and a beautiful house and lots of flowers and sunshine. Just you and me. You know?"

"I know."

"So be good. Practice your writing. Practice writing me a letter. I'm bringing my diary, I'll write down everything and show you the words when we're back. Learn as much as you can, and get ready to have an adventure with me."

And the baby, says Jennifer.

"And the baby," I say. "I'll learn things with Rodger Marvin so I can teach the baby. And then I'll go find Allen and you can all be together from the beginning until the end. You and Allen and the baby. That is what a family is."

"You have to come with me," says Samantha, and she falls over her belly. I pick her up with my strength. "We have to find somewhere to live together. I'd rather die than go back to my parents' house."

Then Missus comes.

"Ready, Lucy?" Missus's eyes are big, big eyes like they have filled up with more eye than before. "Ready to enjoy some more time with Rodger Marvin?"

"I don't want to leave Samantha. She is hurting."

"It's only natural. Nature has it own rules, remember?" says Missus. "Now come along."

She moves me toward the door, which means it is leaving time, which means good-bye, Samantha.

"Bye, Lucy, be good," says Samantha, but her voice is not her all-the-time voice. It is her hurting voice and I hate the way it sounds, like inside my blood there are splinters. Missus says it is time for me to go with Rodger Marvin and time for Samantha to go to the hospital. But how can I leave if Samantha's hurting, even if Missus says nature has its own rules? How can I leave even though Samantha says it is okay, don't worry about me? What if the okay kind of hurting turns into a different kind of hurting?

MISSUS

"Daddy, come look what I can do." Stella pulled Mister's hands away from the dishes he was clearing. "I've been practicing for weeks. Mrs. Cache says my pirouettes are the best in class. Daddy, come see!"

Mister laughed. "With such a glowing review, I can't wait to see. Go ahead and show us." He took a seat at the kitchen table.

"No, I have to do it in front of the mirror, in my room. I'm gonna put on my shoes, come." Stella skipped out of the kitchen.

"All right, Missus, let's go to the dance recital in Stella's bedroom."

"You go on, dear. I know she'd prefer you all to herself."

"I think that's the age," said Mister.

"Daddy's little girl." Though Stella was hardly a girl anymore.

"Come on, Daddy!" Stella hollered from upstairs.

"Now go on, don't keep her waiting," I told him. "Go find out what beautiful new things she can do."

"Was Daddy handsome when he was young?" Stella asked me the next day. She pranced up to me as I was taking laundry off the clothesline.

"Of course, dear." I folded a sheet by keeping one edge pinned to the line. Stella didn't offer to help. "He's handsome now, don't you think?"

"Mary from school said he is."

"And what do you think?"

"Isn't it weird if I do?"

"Every girl is sweet on her father," I explained. "It's perfectly normal."

Stella twirled around. Perhaps she was demonstrating the pirouette she had performed for Mister the night before.

"Daddy says his mom loved to dance, like me, I wish I could have met her. I wonder if we look alike too."

"No. You don't look like her."

"How do you know? She died before you married Daddy. I thought you never met her."

"I didn't. But, Stella, she wasn't really your grandmother."

"What do you mean?"

"You're not related. Not by blood."

"But . . ."

"Families are made in many different ways, dear." I took the last sheet off the line and carried the basket inside. "Talk to your father about it."

Mister and Stella were on the front porch after dinner, taking in the dusk and impending sunset. I watched them from the open kitchen window. Stella was alternating stretching and standing on toe-tip, ostensibly practicing her dancing.

"Daddy, Mrs. Cache at school says I have a dancer's body. Because my legs are so long." Stella stretched a leg up toward the sky, almost vertical. "What do you think?"

Mister didn't answer, didn't even glance at her, just stared off on the property. Stella spun in a circle and then grabbed Mister's shoulders and dipped herself to the ground. "Well?"

Mister's eyes were darting, as if he were drowning and looking for something to grab on to. Then he saw me through the window. I nodded at him, smiling reassuringly.

Stella dropped her hands from his shoulders. "It's okay, Daddy, it's just a question."

But Mister was quiet, frozen.

"Daddy, say something!" Stella demanded, her hands now on her hips. Our poor daughter, seeking her father's approval of her talent, beauty, and body, only to be stonewalled by him, for no good reason.

The screen door slammed, even louder than usual. I tried to intercept Stella as she ran through the kitchen, but she tore past me. I stormed onto the porch.

"Mister, how could you leave her hanging like that? Please affirm her. She's becoming a young woman, she's seeking male approval."

"You're her mother, you can teach her about these things."

"No, dear. It won't do any good coming from me. You're the man of the house, and some things just have to come from a man. Don't you understand, after all this time?"

His face hardened stoically. I stood on my toes and kissed the tip of his nose. "Go on, now. Show her that you still love her, even though she's not a little girl. Show her that growing up is a beautiful thing."

I took his hand and led him inside. Once I heard him knock on her door, I climbed to the top of the stairs. I could see just enough to make sure he followed through.

Stella was sprawled on her bed, on her stomach, her colt legs up in the air, wearing pink linen shorts she hadn't been wearing at dinner. Mister sat on the edge of her bed.

"Stella, sweetie, I didn't mean to suggest you're not a beautiful dancer. My mother loved to dance—"

Stella cut him off. "Oh, don't give me that. Mom told me already. I know she's not my real grandmother."

"I didn't realize your mother had spoken to you about that," said Mister, taken aback.

"Yeah, she did." Stella buried her face in her pillow.

The room turned stiff, fragile as cracked glass. I wondered if I should step in, put a hand on my daughter's head, take my husband's hand, warm the icy room so nothing would be broken that couldn't be put back together. But before I could, Mister spoke.

"You were always ours, Stella. No matter who gave birth to you. Nobody could love you as much as we do."

Then Stella flipped onto her back, propping herself up on her elbows. Her eyes were narrow.

"What?" Her pretty mouth was tight, almost smirking. "I'm not your kid? Is that what you're saying?"

"No. That couldn't be farther from what I'm saying." His voice was strong and sure. "You are more ours than if you came from our bodies. Out of everyone in this whole world, the Lord chose you to be ours."

He put his hands on her shoulders. They were silent, their faces barely an inch apart. Mister's strength softened Stella's face. Her eyes grew wide, her mouth fell slightly open. But she wasn't in the room anymore. Perhaps she was unearthing some impossibly distant memory of that young lady who gave birth to her, nursed her, first swaddled her, rocked her. Or events that transpired even longer ago, between the young lady and some unknown man, whose blood Stella shared.

Slowly, Stella broke into a sly smile. I felt Mister's relief in my own chest as we both exhaled; he audibly, I silently into my hand.

"Okay, so I'm yours," she said. "I'm just not your kid."

Mister began to speak but Stella cut him off.

"But you never answered my question. I've got a dancer's body. It's just a fact. It's nothing to get all stuffy about." She extended a leg and put a foot in Mister's lap. "Don't you think?"

He didn't respond.

Stella stretched her other leg over him.

Abruptly, Mister grabbed her ankle, pulling her closer to him. He reached her ankle up to his face, widened his eyes, blinked a few times, and looked closely at it. He grabbed her calf in both hands, studied it, then took her thigh in both hands and brought his face down to meet it.

"Well?" Stella maintained a serious expression, awaiting Mister's response.

"After thorough inspection, I'm going to have to agree with Mrs. Cache," he said, smiling.

"Gee, thanks." Stella giggled. But her laughter subsided as she softly, gingerly, called Mister by his first name. I had never heard her address him that way before. We all seemed a bit surprised, Mister still holding her leg, me in the hallway, even Stella herself. Then she sat up taller, looked in his face, said it again, bolder this time, as if she dared him to disagree with her. Now it was her word to use as she pleased, and it was more fun, more exciting, more adult, than *Daddy*.

LUCY

"I know you will behave yourself, Lucy," Mister says.

I know there are words that are caught on the back of Mister's tongue, but he doesn't say them to me.

"Mister, Samantha is hurting."

"She's going to have a baby. We're taking her to the hospital."

"The hospital, it takes very good care of Samantha's baby?"

Mister nods. "That's why she's having it there."

"Mister?"

"Yes?"

"Tell her Lucy says don't be scared. Tell her I will help her when she gets back."

Mister squeezes his cheeks like he is trying to make them fit inside his mouth. He looks through the window. It is covered with dirt like the glass over the pictures at the farm and then Missus asks me to wipe them. Underneath are the pictures. Now me and Mister, we are the picture inside and if someone wanted to see what we look like they could use their hand to wipe away the dirt.

"It is not in our hands," he says. "It is in His hands now."

Then he reaches over and I don't know why but then I know it was to open the door next to me. So I could get out. So I could leave. But while he was still reaching I thought maybe it was so he could touch me. To say good-bye.

Rodger Marvin is in the underground of the church and

Lizbeth Elizabeth is there too. Her eyes are closed. She makes sounds I have not heard before. They are the beginning of one word stuck to the end of another word. She is opening one hand to one side of her and opening one hand to the other side of her like maybe she thinks a bird will come rest there.

Rodger Marvin puts his fingers on his lips. That means quiet. But just for me, not for Lizbeth. Lizbeth is allowed to make more sounds, and Rodger Marvin likes the sounds that she makes. I know because of his smile. She makes more sounds, faster and louder. Her legs melt because the sounds have become so big and heavy she can't carry them. The top of her falls in front of her to the floor and Rodger Marvin watches. He doesn't help her up. I put my hand in my pocket and Jennifer kisses it to let me know it is okay that Lizbeth is on the floor. It looks like regular falling but it was a special kind, and Rodger Marvin is watching to make sure she doesn't get hurt.

Lizbeth opens her eyes and looks at Rodger Marvin. She looks scared and she stays on the ground. Rodger Marvin smiles and makes a yes with his head. Lizbeth she stands up shaking like a baby horse and touches her braids and looks quick at me and what she says is nothing. Except with her eyes she says, Hi, Lucy, very quiet.

Then Rodger Marvin says we should all spend some time praying for the healthy delivery of the baby they're having over on Mister and Missus's farm. We hold each other's hands like a tall and beautiful tree grew in between us. I feel the thread between us, from Rodger Marvin to Lizbeth to me to Jennifer to Rodger Marvin. It is the same when you do your mending. The thread takes away the space inside the holes and what used to be apart, now becomes together.

Pray that the baby's healthy, Jennifer says. So I do.

Pray that he's big and pink and plump and all the things babies are supposed to be, says Jennifer. So I do.

The thread that runs between us goes hot.

Then Rodger Marvin says, "I know you feel that power of these prayers, Lord. You've been hearing the power behind these folks' prayers for years and years, and I don't believe you're going to stop now. I know you're not going to stop now. I can hear you assuring us you're not going to stop now. I know you are going to continue to listen to our prayers until our time of judgment when we come to be one with you in heaven. Lord, we ask for the delivery of a healthy little boy so that he can have the best that his time on this earth has to offer, and that with his life he might glorify you and that he be delivered not only by the steady hands of the doctors but also by the all-powerful hand of the Lord."

Pray that Samantha isn't scared, says Jennifer.

Please, please, Samantha, don't be scared, I say with my thoughts.

The thread between us is red and hot and beats at the same time as my heart which makes it so there is something moving through the thread, something that pumps from one part of me another to another to another, and then to all the parts of Rodger Marvin and Lizbeth, and each time it gets to another part it gets stronger and hotter.

Pray it doesn't hurt too much, says Jennifer.

Please, Samantha, don't hurt too much.

Samantha, you know you are strong, I pray. Remember how strong you are because your belly is so big and that is where all your strength is, from the baby that is the secret of growing. And I will find Allen so you won't be alone. I will help you find the place by the river that I will know when I see it and I will help you grow the plants as high as you want them and won't let the weeds take the life away from those plants, even if the weeds are pretty.

"That's some mighty prayer, ladies," Rodger Marvin says. When he says words he makes them take a longer time than they should and it lets them shine their own little bit. His eyes are pressed down hard. There are drops of water on his face like on the grass in the morning. He raises our hands together toward the sky. "I know that baby and his new family are going to be grateful to you for the vigor and the intensity of your prayer tonight. We thank you, Lord, we thank you for your open ears and open heart and your love I can feel running through us all tonight. Ladies, can you feel it?"

"Yes," we say.

Rodger Marvin lets all his air escape and drops our hands. He wipes his head with the corner of his shirt. The thread between us goes cold and then dries up and becomes the same as the rest of the air.

"It's the young sisters of the Lord that produce the most vigorous prayer," he says.

"But the Lord considers everyone's prayer equally," Lizbeth says. Her words are small. She puts her arms around her special book and her chin is on top of it to let her head rest on all the strong words the Lord wrote.

"I have no doubt that's true. Some of us just become more physically impassioned while doing it. Nothing is more beautiful than faith in the face of a young person." Rodger Marvin uses his fingers to touch his hair and touches his shirt and breathes in a lot of the air in the room then breathes it back out again. Now it is hotter and the air has drops of wet in it.

"Lucy," Rodger Marvin says, "there is a lot you want to learn, isn't that right?"

"Yes." Yes, it is right. Ever since the beginning of me there has been so much that I have wanted to learn.

"But there is a lot you already know."

"Only some things."

"What are some of the things you already know?"

"Well, the best thing I know is the secret of growing."

Rodger Marvin sits in a chair and me and Lizbeth also sit in chairs. He holds all of our hands together like a bouquet of hands. He holds them tight, tight. He wants to squeeze something out of our hands, something that will drip on the floor and then he will finally see what it is.

"Tell us about the secret of growing, Lucy." He squeezes our bouquet of hands. Nothing comes out. Then maybe I feel something, something like when you find a word you didn't think you knew and it was the perfect word, the only word. It fills the open space with no gaps and no cracks.

"Well," I say. "It is about how the world is really turning, but you can't feel it."

"Faith," says Rodger Marvin. "It's what lets you believe in the things you cannot see."

"And it is about stones getting smooth every time the water goes over them. That is the secret of growing."

There was a meat with black and green on it like the back of a caterpillar and I put it in one of my shoes in the closet so Mum mum wouldn't throw it away. Because Mum mum, she yelled when food turned different colors. She called it rotten and she said that it was wasted and if the refrigerator was open, it was me that made it so there was no more good food for us and Mum mum didn't have any money to buy us more.

A lady was there to see Mum mum but Mum mum was gone and so the lady said there was a horrible smell coming from somewhere in the building and she thought it was from our home. But I didn't smell it and I said I don't smell any bad smell. I smelled the smell of the secrets of life and I saw the caterpillar growing.

"No, Mum mum is gone," I told the lady.

"When do you anticipate her coming back?"

"Do you anticipate her coming back?" I said, and closed the door and went to the closet. I looked in the shoe and there were tiny white beans dancing around in the caterpillar meat and I watched them and laughed. Those white beans were alive and they were so happy to be alive and all of it was because of me.

That was when I first found out the secret of growing.

Then it was later. Mum mum came home. She cried and cried. "There is something dead in here! Have you killed something?"

There was a man with Mum mum and he was Monte and he said again and again it's probably just a dead rat. Don't get hysterical, he said. Then Mum mum cried and cried and asked questions I didn't have the words for and she shook my shoulders and I shook my head and she shook her head because I couldn't give her anything that she wanted which were answers to her questions. So I shook my head more.

"Where is it, Lucy? I know you know. Think. You need to tell Mum mum so I can help you. Is it the cat?"

"It is not the cat."

"But, Lucy, you loved that cat! Is it the neighbor's cat? Have you killed the neighbor's cat?"

"There's nothing dead, Mum mum. Nothing is dead here. Everything is alive here. You and me and the secret of growing."

"They'll evict us and take you away if you don't tell me what you've done."

"Tell me about the secret of growing," the man said. "What is it?"

His name is Monte and his car shines like a prize, which is what you get when you win. I could see it from the window under the lamp when Mum mum would run outside to meet him.

"This is the secret of growing."

I ran to my shoe and showed them. We wanted to watch the secret of growing together. That was what I thought. That was why I showed them.

"You can't leave her alone like this," the man that is Monte said.

"Don't pretend you have any idea what this is like for me," Mum mum said.

"I don't pretend anything. I just know you can't leave her alone like this anymore."

"All these people, all these people think they could do a better job with her. They wouldn't last a day. Not a day."

"You aren't a weak person. It's not about being weak. It's about realizing your strength. The strength inside you, to do the right thing."

"What choice do I have in all this?" Mum mum screamed. "I didn't ask for this!"

It was the loudest thing she had ever done and me and the secret of growing went to be in the closet where the hanging dresses covered our faces and so all we could see was colors and all we could feel was soft. But we could still hear everything else.

"Camille, you're a proud woman, but I know this is not easy for you. Let me try to make it easier for you. My friend Rodger has helped people with their kids when they can't manage alone anymore. He owes me a favor. At least let me ask him if he has any ideas. Let me help you. Don't you want someone to help you?"

"Of course I want help! Do you think I asked for this? Why would anyone ask for this?"

"Then let me help you through this. She'll be happier somewhere else, you'll be happier here."

Then Mum mum was crying and yelling loud because she was so mad about me being a bad sort of girl and because she hated the secret of growing and Monte was saying things to her, and maybe they were the right things because then the crying was over.

Rodger Marvin tells us to go upstairs and wait for him, he says that later we are going to have a party with some boys from church and I always love a party, even though my dress is not a party dress. But first he has to lock up the basement.

Outside it is the time of day when the sun is turned on the brightest.

"Are these lessons helping you feel closer to the Lord?" Lizbeth asks.

"I am learning about what the Lord likes for us to do."

"Yes, that's important too. But is it making you feel close to him? Like, really close to Him?"

"How close is really close?"

"Really close. Like He's inside you. Almost like you're the same person."

"Like when a baby is still inside its mother?"

"Yes, that close."

"I don't remember when I was that close."

Lizbeth she puts her arm around my arm and we walk under some trees that drop white flowers on us which are not snowflakes but look the same. It is very warm and the insides of our arms are getting stuck together like dough before the oven. There is a seat made out of wood where an old man sits and he pushes his hat towards us when we walk by. Then he closes his eyes, puts his hands together in his lap, and lifts his face towards the tops of the trees. Putting your face that way is the best way to feel the sun and have the white flowers with no weight drop on your face. So I put my face like the old man and wait for a flower with no weight to drop on my face. Because even with their no weight, I feel them where they land and that part of my face feels brand-new again.

"The summer. I hate it. It's so hot it makes me feel like staying inside with the fan on and the curtains closed."

"Why?"

"The sun makes everything so slow and sticky."

"I like the sun. It dances on you if you take off your clothes," I say, but then I remember. "But you mustn't ever take off your clothes in front of other people."

"Well, before the original sin there was no other way to be.

People went around naked all the time and nobody thought anything of it because we didn't have shame or lust. Those are the things that make it so you have to wear clothes." Lizbeth looks at me, trying to dig her eyes inside my eyes. "Did you know that?"

I tell her, "One time I learned a game. It was a game with no words and it was the only game I knew how to play."

MISSUS

I have a memory of Stella that has remained so vivid that sometimes I swear I can reach out and touch her shoulder as she perches at my vanity, captivated by her reflection. It was the night of her first school dance and she was so delighted, so cheerful, it would have been impossible to imagine that in only months, she would desert her family and abandon the only home she had ever known, a home we offered her when nobody else would.

Stella flung open the door to my bedroom. For weeks, she had spent her evenings on the phone, discussing every detail of the much-anticipated event with her friends. And really, our whole household had eagerly been awaiting that night. There was no question; our little girl was a little girl no longer.

"I've got to use your makeup, Mom."

I was touched she needed me, in whatever small way, to assist in getting ready. Stella had specially requested that Mister drive her to the dance. "Daddy's more fun" is how Stella had presented it to me; when she wanted to make a show of her maturity, she used *Mister* instead of *Daddy*. And though I feigned hurt feelings at being excluded, I understood their special bond and wasn't surprised she wanted him to herself on this special night.

Stella sat on my vanity stool and riffled through the drawers, pulling out the necessary products. She made a serious expression in the mirror, then got to work. Using her fingers, she rubbed blush on the apples of her cheeks, paused to assess her heavy-handed handiwork, and applied more. Errant flecks of face powder stuck to her dark hairline and onto the collar of her white eyelet dress. Around her wide, dark eyes she applied thick black lines of eye pencil. She gathered her hair into a knot of the top of her head, sticking in every hairpin I owned. She drenched her wrists and neck in my long-forgotten perfume.

"Where's your lipstick, Mom?"

I went to my bureau and retrieved the coral lipstick from among my handkerchiefs.

"Here you are, dear." I handed her the lipstick. "You know, I wore that lipstick on my first date with Mister. I bought it especially for the occasion."

"Really? It's that old, huh?"

We both laughed.

"Yes, but it hasn't lost its magic. It's good luck," I told her. "Mister loves that color."

The lipstick was the only product she knew how to apply properly. She rolled up the tube, stroked it tenderly against her lips, and pressed her lips together. The color glowed against her olive skin. Then, her work complete, she stood up and did a spin for me.

"Well, how do I look, Mom?" she asked eagerly. She sounded as if she really wanted to know, that what I thought really mattered. My heart swelled.

"You are breathtaking," I told her.

And she was. The garish pink smears and already toppling bun were powerless to detract from her beauty. Her cheekbones were high and proud. Her golden shoulders emanated an almost physically perceptible warmth. Her full, coral lips demanded attention, and her dark eyes glistened with youth and excitement.

"How could anyone resist you?"

We held each other's gaze. I remembered what it had felt like when Rodger Marvin handed her to me for the first time. The weight of her in my arms, in my chest. The heaviness that was all her.

Then she rolled her eyes at me and flounced out of the room, leaving the vanity in disarray. I sat on the stool and put everything away.

The moment was over. It had been brief, but I was grateful for it. I hoped not to forget it. How could I have guessed the memory would come packaged in pain, not joy, each time I unwrapped it in the years to come?

"Thank you for taking her tonight," I told Mister. We waited downstairs for Stella to complete her finishing touches. I know how special she wanted to look. I remembered the feeling. I had prepared for my first date with Mister by braiding my hair and applying lipstick for the first time, relishing each moment.

"This is a big night for us," Mister said, sounding apprehensive.

"Don't sound so nervous. You'll make her uneasy. It's all part of growing up, and she's fully grown."

"She is, isn't she?"

"Yes, dear, of course. She's not a little girl anymore. One look at her and anyone could see that."

"I suppose you understand these things better, being a woman."

"Yes, but I think you understand too." I wrapped my arms around his neck. "She'll be fine. Trust me."

I kissed his stoic cheeks. The man of my family, the head of my household, my provider. It was he who gave me hope. It was he I trusted to lead our family into the future.

LUCY

I knew the boy because sometimes he was in the hallway and he liked to wave. And I liked to wave too. That is how branches dance with the wind. So when he waved, I waved. But he never said anything, just went behind his mother when she was walking out.

Then Mum mum and me were in town. She went inside somewhere and then came right out. The skin around her eyes was scared.

She said, Lucy, this is an important meeting with a lawyer about receiving the finances that are entitled to us, to you, from your father. You sit on this bench and you'd better behave yourself because this is your future I'm trying to secure for you. You can't come inside. There are things inside that you can't hear and you can't see and there is nobody to watch you. You have to stay outside and be well behaved.

Do you understand me? Lucy?

Yes, Mum mum.

Sometimes that was what I said when Mum mum said too many words that I did not have but I did not want to hear her say the same words again.

Yes, Mum mum.

I'm trusting you, Lucy.

Yes, Mum mum.

You behave, Lucy, because I'm doing this for you.

I was on the bench and the sun was playing a lot because it was extra hot. It was using the leaves to make shadows on the ground and the top of my head was bubbling like a ready skillet. I lifted and lifted the end of my dress to let in the sun underneath. The sun was dancing along my legs and it felt better that way and I was happy to stay on the bench and behave.

Mum mum was gone and gone. And she didn't come back and didn't come back. Then it was later and she still didn't come back. I got off the bench and walked over to the trees and looked at the sun through the trees and it made me so I couldn't see because of the big spots on my eyes. Then I went back to the bench. Then I got off. Mum mum was gone and gone. And then she didn't come back. I laid on the bench and tried to be good and not to leave and not mess up anything or take anything or do anything of the things that Mum mum says I mustn't ever do. But it was too hot. So I forgot everything except it was too hot and I lifted up my dress over my belly and all the way over my face because the sun was getting my eyes more and more spots on them.

"Hello," said the boy.

I took my dress off my eyes so I could see who was making the words. And it was the boy from the hallway. He had more color on his face than I did and his eyes were blue which is the same color as the sky when it is day and there are no clouds or weather. I liked the way that his eyes made a shining place on his face and so that was where I looked.

"Hello," I said.

"What is your name?"

"Lucy. Do you live in my building?"

"I am Eduardo. My mother works in the apartments of the people who live there. But we don't live there."

"Where do you live?"

"We live with some other people that have come from my country, until my dad comes and builds a house for us."

"Where does he live?"

"He lives far away but soon he will come to be with us."

"Do you go to school?"

He said yes.

I asked him, "Do your words get better at school?"

"Yes," he said. "But not good enough."

Then he looked sad. When you are missing words you do not want to tell anything more. Because the other people do not like to hear wrong words and then know how much you are missing.

Well, then I told him he didn't need all his words to play a game. I told him that I knew about a game with no words.

"It will be a good game for you," I said. "It is a good game for me too and I am missing a lot of words."

He sat on the bench with me and I put my hands by his pants and I put his hands up by my knees. He started to laugh and take his hands back to himself. But I said, No, no, it is a good game, it is a good game that you will like, I said. So I moved my hands and he moved his hands. We were playing a game even though we had no words and it was a good thing we played together. I wanted to say, See, it is a good game, but it was the game with no words so I couldn't say anything.

Then he stood up. I thought he didn't like the game anymore. I thought the game was over. I didn't want the game to be over. The last time I played the game with no words it was over so fast I couldn't show how good I could be at a thing. But he took my hand and I knew the game wasn't over and I was happy the game wasn't over.

We went to where the trees were and he put my dress up near my shoulders and his hands near my belly and pressed himself against myself so we got close like when you hold hands and there is no air in between your fingers anymore. That is how close. He was breathing his air on my face. It was hot and it weighed more than regular breathing air. He was making other noises but no words. I didn't know if that was okay during a game with no words. Then there was his mouth. It was the hottest thing I had ever felt. His mouth crawled inside my mouth like a worm and I was trying to swallow his mouth or spit it out. I didn't know. I wanted to laugh but I couldn't because I couldn't spit out his mouth so there was no room for my laugh.

Then he took his mouth away and he was saying words. They weren't any words I had heard before but I still knew they were words.

"This is a game with no words," I said. "It isn't the right game if you use words and I don't know how to play the one with words."

He made a noise of all s's. *Sssssss.* But I didn't like him using words in a game with no words. I said it again and he crawled his mouth back inside my mouth and pressed up tighter and moved my hands down but it wasn't the same kind of game I remembered anymore.

Then Mum mum was not gone. She with outside with the man that was Monte. At first she couldn't see and then she saw. When she came over to the tree it was too loud to remember.

After that Mum mum didn't bring me with her anymore.

MISSUS

I keep her letter in the top drawer of my dresser. It's grotesque, I realize, to keep such a thing. It's not as if I take it out and read it, as a way to remember her by. But to throw it in the garbage seems, well, I suppose these things are family matters and should stay with the family. Even after everything, I feel the motherly impulse to protect Stella from herself, from the chance the outside world might ever discover her betrayal.

Her room was neat and cold. His piles of little clothes were lined up in the crib and on the dresser. Her clothes hung straight and obedient in her closet, which had never been anything short of a disaster. Her shoes were lined up in pairs, not their usual pile. The bed was made with tight corners. I wasn't even aware she knew how to make a bed that well.

And the letter was on her pillow.

Good-bye Mother, Good-bye Daddy,

Mother, you are too kind to me. If you knew the truth about me, you wouldn't be. You would punish me like I deserve. You wouldn't tell me I could have anything I wanted after he's born. Because all the things I want are bad. Because that's just the type of person I am.

Daddy, if I were you, I wouldn't love me anymore, either. I wouldn't want to be around me. I know you used to love me when I was your daughter, and I'm sorry I stopped being that. I thought I didn't want to be her anymore but I'm sorry I took her away and I wish there was some way I could be her again. But I know I can't. I know she's gone for good, which is why I have to go now too.

Thank you, Mother, for being so good to him. But he has to come with his mother. He'll just remind you of me and the bad things I did. Even if you know it's not his fault. It's not fair to you to be reminded. And it's not fair to him, either. I got him into this and I'll get him out.

The letter went on and on. It was so painful to read her troubled words. And what hurt us all the more is that she signed the letter, *Love, Stella.* It was the last lie she ever told us. Had she loved us, she could never have done what she did. Though she was right about one thing: we would have done anything for her, if she had stayed. And instead, we can do nothing. Nothing but remember, and try to forget. We have kept her room just the same as it was the day she left. Only God knows why. The heart works in mysterious ways. We were made in His likeness, after all.

LUCY

"Well, it's not your fault you are the way you are," Lizbeth says. "The Lord made you like that on purpose."

"How come?"

"I don't know, but He made you that way. There's got to be a reason."

Where we walk is under the trees and then the trees end and there is a road.

"So where do you wanna walk to?" Lizbeth says. "We could go into town and get an ice cream. Except I don't have any money. Maybe they would give us one for free. Or we could just sit under the trees."

Jennifer beats a little harder. I put my hand in and she touches my finger with her mouth.

Tell her you'd like to see where she lives, Jennifer says.

"I'd like to see where she lives," I say.

No, no, Jennifer says. Say, I'd like to see where you live. She said she saw Allen last week. Same stupid town, remember?

"I'd like to see where you live," I say.

"It's only right down that street there." Lizbeth points to a street. "Nothing out of the ordinary."

We want to see it, says Jennifer.

"We want to see it."

Lizbeth opens her mouth wide like a cat. "Okay then. We can just sit inside with the fans on and get cool."

"It's nothing out of the ordinary so I'd like to see it."

"I guess when you work on a farm a boring street in town is out of the ordinary."

"Yes, it is out of the ordinary, that is why I want to see it."

Good, Jennifer says. That was good. She hops and her toes dig in between the threads in my pocket like my hands in between the tomato roots.

The cars wait for us while we go across. When Mum mum and me lived in the city that was how many cars I saw every day. On the farm I don't see any cars every day. The sound of planting and growing is a better sound than the sound of that many cars.

The sun is sinking and when it sinks it starts to spill. That is when the sky gets orange. That is what is happening. The street has houses painted colors and each one has grass all around and there are big, tall lamps that are going on and they have light the same color of the melting sun so once the sun is all done melting there will still be orange melting colored light for the cars.

"This is my house." Lizbeth stops. The house is white. There is a tree in front and a car outside and windows with pink curtains. "Want to come inside?"

Ask her which one is Samantha's house, Jennifer says.

"Which one is Samantha's house?"

"The end of the block." Lizbeth points.

"Can we see that too?"

"Guess so. We have some more time before we need to get back. I know Rodger Marvin is going to bring us to that potluck tonight with the boys' Bible study. He doesn't realize I've known those boys since I was three and I've never been interested in any of them and I never will."

"Will Allen be there?"

"No. He's not the church type."

"What type is he?"

"He tags along with the other boys. He likes to build things. His dad died when he was little."

"What things does he build?"

"Like model cars and airplanes. Radios."

"He's smart so he can build so many things."

"Eh, not really."

We walk past a house and grass and a car and a house and grass and some flowers and a car and a house and grass and a car and some flowers and I pick one of the flowers but Lizbeth says no, that isn't allowed here in town. I tell her that the farm is a place for growing and then picking. She says people will get angry if they see you picking their flowers because it's hard to make them grow here. Not like on the farm.

"Well, this is it."

"This is Samantha's house?"

Lizbeth says yes.

It is the same shape as Lizbeth's. But Lizbeth's was white and this is a dirty color of being old. It smells like being old. All the newness sucked up by time and sun and air. The leaves on the tree have dust on them. That means the tree is sick. I know because Missus told me when I was trying to wipe some leaves to see what was on the other side of the dirt like when I wiped off the glass and then I could see a picture underneath. You can't wipe off that dirt, Missus said. It means the tree is sick.

There is a gray car that has no more shine. Monte, he has a blue car that shines a lot. He is special to have a car like that because it looks like a prize and he is always petting his car with a cloth to make it shine. Then Mum mum can see her face in it and she loves to see her face shine. But this car would not let Mum mum see her face smile back at her.

Outside Samantha's house there is a rope tied to the steps with nothing on the end of it. Sometimes I know there are dogs that are tied on the end of a rope. So they don't run away anymore. But there is no dog or no anything else. The tied-up dog was sucked up by time. The grass is brown and sharp but there are some yellow flowers still in between. I walk onto the brown grass and pick a yellow flower and put it in my pocket. Jennifer holds it in her mouth. They would not be mad at my picking because of how much Samantha loves me and what you do when you love someone is let them pick your flowers.

"Her parents are old, so they have trouble maintaining everything."

"How old?"

"Very, very old." Lizbeth's words weigh a lot in the air. I am afraid they are going to make her fall down again like her words made her fall in the basement.

"As old as Missus?"

"Older. Some people say they are really her grandparents. But my mom remembers when Samantha's mom was pregnant. She says nobody could believe it. People at church called her a witch and said things behind her back. I don't believe any of that, though, Samantha's parents are very devout."

"When you are old you don't have babies?"

"Usually not. Except sometimes you can. The Lord performs miracles every day, so just because something doesn't usually happen doesn't mean it never will."

Say, Which one is Allen's house? says Jennifer. His is the house we really need to see.

"Which one is Allen's house?"

"It's on the side other of that fence. You can see his roof, barely. See, the red one." Lizbeth stands on the ends of her toes and points over the fence. I stand on my toes and see his red roof, barely.

Jennifer rubs against my leg with her mouth. It feels like a thorn that catches your dress because it doesn't want you to pass by. It wants you to stay close.

We gotta get over there, she says. Tell her you are good at climbing fences. Say, I am good at climbing fences.

"I am good at climbing fences."

"What's the point? It's just the same dumb old house as all these. Let's go to my house. I have some paper dolls I haven't cut out yet."

I'd like to see it anyway, Jennifer says. Allen's house. She is making a lot of moving inside my pocket because she wants me to listen to her.

"I'd like to see it anyway. Allen's house."

"How come?"

Say, Because Allen is very important to Samantha.

"Because Allen is very important to Samantha."

"Hah." Lizbeth laughs but not because a funny thing made her do it.

"It's not funny, it's for real."

"That is funny, and it's not for real."

"I'm serious." Being serious is how you get people to listen to you. Serious is what Mum mum became when I had no good behavior.

"Did Samantha tell you that?"

"Yes."

"What did she say, exactly?"

I try to remember all Samantha's words very carefully. They made marks on my brain like pressing your finger in the dirt before you put in the seed. I can still feel the marks because of how deep they went.

I tell Lizbeth, "Loving him was like wanting something out of the blue and then it is all you can think about."

"What a liar!" Lizbeth says, and stops walking to make sure her words don't get too far ahead of her steps. "Lucy, listen to me. Samantha was not being honest with you."

"Why?" I do know the word *honest* and I do know that Samantha is always that word.

"Because she was very unkind to Allen when she lived here." Lizbeth's words are slow and heavy sinking to the ground.

"No, she wouldn't be. He is the father of the baby."

"She told him it wasn't even his!"

"It is hers."

"Yeah, but it's his too. Everyone knew it was his. He was the only person who ever spent any time with her."

I don't care what Lizbeth says, says Jennifer. We have to get to Allen's house. Say, Can I see his house?

"Can I see his house?"

"But, Lucy, there's honestly nothing to see. Just another boring house and we'd have to climb over that fence and then go across a ditch that's always full of mud and leaves and things. Just take a look at any of these houses and imagine I'm telling you it's his."

I take a look at any of the houses. But I know that none are Allen's because Lizbeth said it's over the fence and across the ditch and none of these have a red roof.

"Look, that one across the street, right there, it's Allen's." Lizbeth laughs and closes one eye quickly. That is called winks.

But Jennifer knows. She knows his has the you-can-barely-see-it red roof. She says, No, it has to be his. Tell her it has to be his.

"No, it has to be his. It has to be his house."

"I promise Allen didn't mean anything to her. She humiliated him after everyone found out she was having a baby."

"What is *humiliated* him?"

"She made him feel stupid because he wanted to have the baby and get married and be a family."

Tell her Samantha's not like that, says Jennifer. She doesn't make people feel stupid. She is hopping up and down and her words are bouncing inside my pocket.

"Samantha's not like that. She doesn't make people feel stupid."

"Maybe not you. But it was the way she was to him. Why would I lie to you?"

"She is going to find Allen but she doesn't know where he is. As soon as the baby comes, then she is going to find him and I am going to help her."

"Allen hasn't moved since the day he was born." Lizbeth pulls on her braids like she wants them to grow longer, like a wish you make with your hands. "Sorry to disappoint you. I'm just telling you the way it is."

"The way it is is, we have to go to Allen's house."

"No, it'll take too long. The only place we have to go is back to church. You can bet that Rodger Marvin will reprimand us if we aren't back by the time he's done. Do you know what *reprimand* means?"

"No."

"It's like punishment."

I do know that nobody will be happy if I make trouble for Rodger Marvin. I know because Mister told me and I am trying, trying to remember not to make trouble for Rodger Marvin. Because listening to Mister and Missus is what I always, always must do so that I can stay on the farm and Mum mum will know where to find me.

But now I am also trying to remember something else and that is that I have to find Allen because Samantha loves him and he loves Samantha and that is why they made a baby so when the baby opens its eyes on its very first day it sees its family. Which is Samantha and Allen.

"We have to go to Allen's house." I know I have Mum mum

coming for me. I know where to wait. But Samantha doesn't have anybody coming for her because Allen doesn't know where she is, and Samantha doesn't know where he is.

"No way. Let's go back." Lizbeth takes my arm and so she can bring us back to the road. "Maybe you'll like one of the boys at the party and he can show you his house. Since you're so interested in who lives where."

Lizbeth smiles. I want to smile back because that is a thank-you for smiling at me. But I know I can't, because smiling is only for happiness, and Samantha cannot be happy without her family together.

Don't let her pull you away, Jennifer says, we have to go to Allen's house. We have to find Allen for Samantha because she thinks he's gone far away, when really he's right over the fence. We're so close. Samantha needs us to go just a little further.

Samantha will be so grateful, Jennifer says. She can't leave the farm to find him, but we can!

Grateful. That is what we are to the Lord.

Exactly.

And that is what Samantha will be?

Yes! She will be so happy if we find him for her.

She will love us even more if we find him for her?

Yes! She will love you even more.

Even more?

Yes! That's what I'm trying to tell you!

Now I know where we have to go and that is to Allen's house. That is over the fence. So I pull the other way from where Lizbeth's pull is trying to take us. I am stronger so my pulling is doing a better job than her pulling.

"We have to go to Allen's house."

In my pocket, Jennifer is beating very fast and very hot. Yes, yes, she says. We have to go to Allen's house. We must must must.

"We must, must, must," I say.

"Lucy, no! Absolutely not! You come with me."

I get my arm away from Lizbeth and I go to the fence. The fence is made of wood up and down and put tight together which means there are no holes or steps or things to pull up on. Those are some of the things you need to do climbing. I know that from being Lucy on the farm and climbing over the fence to give the pigs their slop. I put my hands all over the fence to try to find how I can climb.

"You're not gonna get over by yourself," calls Lizbeth. "You need someone to give you a boost. Only I can't give you one because you are going to get all dirty and lost and Rodger Marvin is going to blame me. He told me to look after you."

Make her help you, says Jennifer.

"Help me!" I say.

No, no, says Jennifer, go over to her and make her help you. You know how.

How?

Make her pay attention.

So I grab her hair and Lizbeth screams. She melts towards the ground like a wilting flower and tries to get my hands away. What do screams mean? They mean scared and hurt. But if it doesn't hurt she won't help. Sometimes that is how you make people help you. Sometimes people, they don't listen to you unless they are hurting. Hurting opens their ears up straight to their brain, which is the place where your thoughts are born.

"Help me."

"Let go! Let me go!"

"Help me," I tell Lizbeth. I know I am using the right words but she is still not listening.

"You know better than this, Lucy, I know you do. You have a kind heart. I've felt the goodness from your good, kind heart." She puts her hand on my hand, which is on her hair. She is trying to take back her hair.

"Help me get over." I pull harder, pull the hairs away and she tries to bring them back.

Lizbeth, she is crying. Her face is red and bubbles. I do not like red bubbles because they look like being stuck. I hold the hair hard as my hand can hold and walk to the fence. I shake the hairs which makes her head shake and then she screams again and then I let them go.

"Help me get over."

She is crying now when she says, "You are being very very bad. Just like people at church say you are."

"Get me over."

"I told them we should try to help you."

"Help me over."

"I thought they were wrong but they weren't."

"Give me a boost." A boost is what you need to get over. You can't get over by yourself.

"They said the devil made you but I told them God made you and loves you just the same as he loves the rest of us."

I grab her hair again. I know it hurts her because she is crying and red bubbles are bubbling on her face. I am tired of hurting her. It makes my arm heavy like swinging too long on a tree branch. I want to let go. But I know I have to keep pulling until I get a boost.

She shakes her head in the way that means no. "I won't listen to anything you say, I won't listen to you, it's the devil making you do this."

So I have to pull and pull and pull and pull and pull and pull and try to get her hair far away from her head. I push my knee into her back to help my pulling and she shakes and then can't stand and is on her knees down to the brown grass which is dead, it has sharpness, not like grass that is alive and wants to be touched.

Then she says let go and let go and that she will help me, just let her go.

Let her go, Jennifer says. She will help you over.

I let her go. But Lizbeth does not help me over.

She runs. She tries to run fast. But I run faster because I am always the biggest and the strongest. Bigger than Mum mum, and Samantha and Lizbeth. Sometimes you are scared of being the biggest but sometimes you need it, like now.

Lizbeth's hairs are flying behind her like they are chasing her face and I catch her hairs in my hand and pull. She falls on the brown grass and dirt and I almost fall too. Because we are attached which means I have her hair and so when I go where we need to go she has to come too.

She turns to me and her eyes are getting bigger like they might pop and I don't want that because your eyes are what lets you see and I want Lizbeth to always be able to see but I need her to boost me.

"Do it," I say. "Help me over."

"Put your foot in my hands, grab the top of the fence, and swing over," she says, and after every half of a word she has to cry before she can say the next half of a word. Every half of a word is stuck behind some of her crying. I put my foot in her hands. I grab the top of the fence. Now I know what a boost is, and I will always remember.

I go over. The top bites up my inside leg. That is called splinters. I go down. Then I am on the other side. It looks like the other side except without Lizbeth and there is some mud and sticks and leaves.

"Lucy, you are going to be very, very sorry!" Lizbeth cries to me. Her scream makes all her words smash together so they aren't words anymore. It is what happens when there is too much inside of you to make into words and you have to get it out before it turns rotten and starts to poison you.

Tell her you're sorry you have to go to his house because it means a lot to Samantha, Jennifer says. She says it quick because she wants to get to the next part, which is when we find Allen and Samantha will love me even more.

"I'm sorry," I call through the fence. There are hairs stuck in the corners of my fingers and I know who they came from. That is Lizbeth. I put them in my pocket with Jennifer. She will keep that part of Lizbeth safe. "I am sorry, Lizbeth. I have to find Allen."

MISSUS

And then, a miracle came to our humble house. It was a few months after the excitement of Stella's first dance. Stella had been our blessing and now she was being blessed.

She needed the comfort of her mother to help her see it that way, though. But that was understandable. I had been young once. I had felt the thrill and promise and entitlement of youth. I tried my best to persuade her she could still have it all.

After Stella stopped going to school, she spent all her time in her room, curled in a ball on top of the covers, looking out the window. I dragged my rocking chair from the porch to her room, next to her bed. I stroked her hair and talked about the things she had always been so excited about: her love of dancing, the promise of going to college and living in the city. I reminded her what a beautiful dancer she was, how impressed her teacher was, how jealous her fellow students were, and how she could look forward to advancing her skill after the baby. I racked my mind for the few experiences I had had in the city as a young woman and embellished them, telling her about restaurants that served exotic foods, glamorous shops with imported clothing, and nightclubs that stayed open until morning. I recited passages from her favorite books, telling her how much she could learn in college about literature and poetry, music and dance and theater. I tried to keep her dreams alive for her, though it was impossible to tell if it was doing any good. Nothing I said brought even the faintest glimmer to her languid eyes.

"Dear, there is nothing your father and I won't do for you, after the baby comes. All your dreams, we want them to come true. We will work to give you every opportunity."

No response.

"We'll get you a wonderful little apartment, and you can devote all your time to school. You'll be a true, modern city girl, like you've always wanted."

Silence.

I sighed and stroked her hair.

The miracle inside her grew. It was clearly a boy; she was carrying him so low. My mother had taught me to recognize the signs, and she had never been wrong in predicting a baby's gender, not once.

Mister left us women alone to tend to the business of the baby. He chose to stay out late working on the farm, and I kept his dinner warming in the oven for him. Stella would sit at the dinner table, eating her food slowly so she could wait for him, but no matter how late she waited, he never seemed to come in until we retired upstairs.

One night Stella got up from the table in the middle of our dinner and ran out the door. I didn't try to stop her, just followed behind. She headed to the stable, where Mister was feeding the horses.

Stella grabbed Mister's elbow as he lifted a bale of hay into a stall. "Daddy, come to dinner."

He shook her off. "Stella, go back inside."

"Daddy, come eat with us."

"Stella, it's not right for you to be out here."

"But it was all right before."

"Not around the horses. Not in your condition."

"Why are you mad at me, Daddy?" Stella cried. Her voice cracked.

Mister thrust a bale of hay over the gate. "Leave me be," he said, his voice thick and husky. "I've got work to do. I have to keep this family fed." He strode out the other door of the barn. Stella fell to the ground, sobbing.

I knelt next to her, gathering her in my arms, lifting her up. She was limp as a newborn kitten.

"There, there," I soothed her. "Dear, he's a man. He isn't cross with you, and he knows this is a blessing. He just doesn't understand these things the way women do."

"He does understand," she whispered through her tears. "He understands more than you do."

"Shhhh, he'll come around, just give him some space for now."

I helped her out of the barn with her arms around my shoulders, her legs dragging behind her as if they were both broken. We labored up the stairs into her room. I put her into her nightgown and tucked her into bed, just as I had done when she was small.

"Darling, being with child is much more important in His plan for us than being Daddy's little girl. You understand that, don't you?" I lifted up her chin to look into her eyes. "You can see how this follows His plan."

She had stopped crying. Her dark eyes were blank as stone. Her tear-streaked face was slack.

"You have to accept the consequences of being a woman. It's all part of His plan. Stella, you must understand how important it is to follow His plan." I wiped the stagnated tears from her swollen cheeks. "For now, it's what He wants from you that's important. You can focus on yourself again after the baby comes. Tell me you understand, please."

She blinked at me as if she didn't recognize me or had just woken from a dream and didn't know where she was.

"Sure," she said amenably, though almost inaudibly.

I clasped her to my chest. "That's my good, brave girl."

And the miracle inside her grew.

LUCY

The other side looks like the other side. That means the street and houses and some trees and lamps. All in a line and the line doesn't change. I don't remember which house was Allen's because before I could only see a little bit of the top. Now all the tops they are the same like the letters you can't tell which is which.

But Jennifer, she knows.

It's that one over there, she says. The one with the red roof. See?

I start to walk.

I go through some mud and sticks and leaves. My shoes have some new mud but that is okay because the old mud on them will not be alone anymore. Then I get to where the ground is flat and hard and where the house with the red roof is.

I walk up the steps and to the door but Jennifer says no.

You can't knock on the front door. Once they catch wind of where you came from they aren't going to let you see Allen. Samantha said they are trying to keep them apart, remember? Let's try and get his attention and he can meet us out here.

Okay.

Go look in the windows and try to find him that way.

There are some windows in the front of the house so I look in them. I see some things that would be in a house but no boy that would be Allen. So I go to one side of the house and find some more windows. I look in them and there is a bed and some things that would be in a bedroom but no body that would be Allen. And then I go to the other side of the house and find some more windows. I look in them and see some things that would be in a house but no body that would be Allen.

I tell Jennifer there is no body that would be Allen or any body that would be anybody else.

Go all the way in the back, Jennifer says. Go look in the backyard.

But there is another fence with tall, long wood and no cracks or holes and there is only me and Jennifer and she doesn't have the hands to make a boost for my foot like how I got over the other fence.

Go back to the front of the house and pick up the metal bucket, Jennifer says. Turn it upside down and use it as a step.

I didn't see a metal bucket, I say.

But Jennifer says it's there. I go back to the front and there is a metal bucket stuck in the mud by the front steps and I do what she says. I turn it so it looks like a tree stump and climb on top and swing myself over. Only this time the top tears even more on my inside legs and I am bleeding and ripped open once I get to the other side.

But even though I am over on the other side there is no boy here. There are dead plants. That means they did not do the weeding. The weeds, they take the life from the other plants so the other plants can't live. Then the only plants that live are the weeds and you end up with a box full of weeds and this is what they have. There are more fences too. Fences that make us in a big box made of fence. There is a thing made out of wood that looks like a little house with a big hole in the front instead of a door.

Maybe Allen is inside that little house. Maybe he is hiding from something inside that little house.

No, that's a house for a dog, Jennifer says.

Maybe it is a house for Allen to hide.

No, it's not.

So I go look in the hole. There is a dog who fills up the whole inside. He is a brown dog with gray spots and long ears. He looks asleep but then he opens one eye at me. It is a yellow eye. If it were a thing shining on the ground I would pick it up and keep it in my pocket. Now I am afraid he will yell in his dog voice and then people will come and send me back to the farm once they catch wind of who I am. But the dog just opens both his eyes and uncurls a long tongue very slow which is how he says hello.

Ask him if he knows where Allen is, Jennifer says.

"Do you know where Allen is?" I ask.

But he doesn't answer.

Well, let's go look inside these back windows, Jennifer says. So I go and look inside these back windows but inside these windows there are just some more regular house things and no boy that could be Allen.

Maybe I will knock, I say. After you knock then someone opens the door and you get to go inside and maybe that is how I will find Allen for Samantha so she can live in her special place with him while I wait on the farm for Mum mum.

No, no, you can't knock. Let me think for a minute, Jennifer says.

I put my head down to look at my inside leg that is bleeding. I bend down inside my legs to suck off some of the blood. It tastes like rust, which grows on the old horseshoes after it rains. It feels like needles because of the tiny pieces of wood that are stuck inside. They are trying to bury deeper so they can't get sucked out and they can live inside me forever.

Then the yellow-eye dog comes over and he licks some of the blood. It hurts but it feels good too which is a special kind of a hurt and a special kind of feeling good. It is a feeling I don't want to end. I touch the dog on his back. His tail moves back and forth, fast, like the arms that wipe away rain from the window of Mister's truck. I put my arms around the dog and put my face close and I like what the world smells like close to the dog. But then the dog moves away fast and leaves. My eyes prick all over and I don't want the dog to leave even though I do not need to find a dog and I do need to find Allen.

"Come back," I say to the dog. "Let me pet you some more, before I need to go over the fence again."

But the dog doesn't come back. He moves fast over to the fence and then stops and looks at me. I walk over to him and get on my knees and put my face by his face and I like it again, the way the world smells close to a dog. He lifts his paw and bangs on the fence.

He wants out, says Jennifer. Open the gate for him.

But I want him to stay.

He needs to be let out. Open the gate for him.

Give him a boost?

No, just open it. The latch is in the high corner up there.

Jennifer is right. I open the fence and the dog runs. I walk back to the front of the house to look in the windows again and there is the dog. He looks at me and I look back. I want to put my arms on his neck but then he runs away. Good-bye, Yellow Eye Dog, I say. I look in another window and move to another window and then back to the front of the house to the other side and there is Yellow Eye Dog.

"Yellow Eye Dog, why are you back?"

But he doesn't say anything. He looks at me and then runs away. I look in the window and it is the same. I look in another window and it is the same. Then I go to the front of the house to wait for something to change.

And here is Yellow Eye Dog at the front of the house. He looks at me and then he runs down the street. Then he runs back to me and licks my hand. I wonder about my taste. Then he looks at me with his yellow eyes. And he runs down the street again.

Aren't you going to follow him? Jennifer asks.

No.

Well, you should. He knows something.

Okay, I say, and I get up to follow him, which means to move at the same time to the same place. But before the following happens there is a noise. It is the sound of a closed door becoming an open door.

"Who let Rusty out? Allen, is that you? Did you leave work early again? Boy, I'm always saying you needn't feel like you have to do that on account of me. I'm perfectly capable of sitting around the house all by myself."

It is an old woman with white hair holding a stick so she doesn't fall over like a tree when the inside of it has died. Yellow Eye Dog runs to the old woman and breathes on her and then runs into the house.

"Get that dog out of the house!"

Don't say anything, says Jennifer.

"Allen! Get that dog out of the house!"

We don't say anything.

"Allen, is that you?"

"No," I say. "It is not Allen."

Don't talk to her, we're going to get in trouble, says Jennifer.

But I know that we won't. There is something missing with this woman like there is something missing with me and that is why I can tell we won't get in trouble. Because she won't be afraid. She will know about the sameness of us and not just the difference.

"Who is youse, then?"

"Lucy," I say. "And Jennifer."

"Have you come to help with the house? Maggie said she was going to try and find someone to help with the house. Swear it grows itself each and every day. Nothing never where I left it."

Yes, says Jennifer. Say yes.

"Yes."

"I say, why didn't youse knock? Or youse did and my hearing's going too? Wouldn't come as no surprise. These days I've got to thinking the Lord wants me all to Hisself, He makes it so nearly impossible to communicate with another person. It's flattering but a bit lonesome."

"I didn't knock."

"Well, that's a bit of relief, let's come on in. What did you say your name was? Lucianne? What kind of name is that? My days are numbered, Lucianne, I don't have the breath for a name like that. No offense to your mother. Now let's go on in. And take that dog outside."

And we go on in.

MISSUS

We have been waiting so long my mind has lost track of the time. But not my heart. My heart knows the time has come.

God knows why Samantha's parents insisted on her delivering at the hospital. There is nothing wrong with a home birth. It's safer at home, no needles and machines and drugs, no strangers telling you what's best for your own child. Samantha has been hidden away in some room for such a long time, and they haven't told me one single thing. But it doesn't make a difference what anyone does or doesn't tell me, I know it's time. I can feel it inside me. It's time.

"Excuse me, sir, please show me to the baby," I tell the man at the desk. "It's been quite long enough."

"Ma'am, the baby isn't born yet," says the attendant. "The girl is still in labor."

I can see in his face he's lying, and calmly I tell him so. The man turns his back to me and pretends to file some papers.

"Excuse me, sir. Please bring me to the baby."

"You're going to have to wait a bit longer, ma'am."

"That just can't be. We've been waiting all this time. Mister! Tell them to bring the baby here."

"I know it's been a long time, but it's just going to be a little longer," says Mister. He puts a hand on my shoulder. "I know we can wait a little longer."

They are trying to make a fool of me. But I can see through it.

"You don't think I know? You don't think I can tell it's been born?"

"Not yet," the man says through mean, clenched teeth. "Nurse just came by here, said not yet."

What possible reason could they have for wanting to keep me from him? It's too much for me to bear, but I keep my composure. I have been through so much, I will not be broken now.

"Now is the time," I explain slowly and carefully. "Please listen to me, and you bring that baby here."

"Ma'am, did you hear what I said? The girl's still in labor."

"Bring him here this instant."

"You'd better calm down, ma'am. You're not going to like it if we have to ask you to leave."

"Let's walk, let's walk outside till it's over," says Mister.

Somehow he steers me outside. But he can't keep me out here. I'm going back in. I've been waiting so long, it must be time. He made us both a promise. We couldn't both have gotten it wrong. My body knows He's made good on that promise. He knows I couldn't bear to wait any longer. He wouldn't make me wait any longer.

LUCY

The inside of Allen's house is made of old, beautiful things that are still beautiful. Usually old things are broken with their cracks and dust but these old things shine like new things. But I know they aren't new things. They are just the kind of things that used to be and someone loved so much they got kept.

"Where do you want to start?" says the old woman. "I'll make sure to stay out of your way while you work."

Ask her about Allen, Jennifer says.

I know.

Then do it.

"What about Allen?" I say.

"He's not home. Don't need to worry about him getting in your way."

"Where is he?"

"At his job. He works pretty hard, my grandson, helps with the bills. Works as much as kids these days should work. It was different in my day. Kids had to stop schooling by the age of eight or ten to take on jobs. Me, I was lucky enough my daddy made enough money I was able to finish.

"He's too sweet, my grandson. Naïve. Comes across like he's younger than he is. His father, God rest his soul, wasn't like that. He was tough. A little bit mean. He was one of the boys throwing rocks. Allen gets his sweetness from his mother. But he's a hard worker. Goes to his job and keeps up with his school. Love that boy more than I probably loved my own, terrible to say."

Ask her where Allen works, says Jennifer.

"Where does Allen work?"

"He works at That Place."

"Which place?"

"That Place is the name of the place. Don't you know it? By the coal mine. Place where the miner can get a meal or a pack of whatever they prefer. Sit at the bar and get off their feet. Allen sweeps the place and unpacks the boxes. I used to go there, long time ago in the past I used to meet a miner there, sometime in between the passing of my late husband and now."

"Where is That Place?"

"I already said, don't I? It's by the mine."

"I don't know about by the mine."

"Well, Lucianne, may be best you keep it that way."

"What is the mine?"

We have to go there, says Jennifer. Stop talking about the mine and let's go.

"Sweet young girl like yourself don't have any business hanging around any coal miners. Though it's not my place to make that judgment. A long time ago I used to meet a man there, a miner. A very handsome man. My late husband wasn't a looker like this man was. Me and the miner, we knew there would never be a future for us, but that didn't stop us from our meetings. Lasted years, until he got too old to work at the mine and moved away. He was my very own sweet thing, the only real secret I had to myself. I'm not an emotional woman, Lucianne, but my heart hung heavy after he left."

"I know that feeling," I say.

"Love is hardest when you're young, isn't that the truth? And this man made me feel young. That's why it pained me so to have him leave. There was no future for us, but that was cold comfort when he left. I didn't care about the future anyhow when I was with him."

Lucy, we know where Allen is, Jennifer says. That's why we came here in the first place. Now let's go.

But I want to stay with her. She is missing something the same size as what is missing inside me. Her heavy heart, it pulls the same as mine when Mum mum said, You mustn't ever, ever leave the farm or I won't know where to find you. Her cold comfort, it is the same on my skin when Mum mum said, Always call Mister and Missus Mister and Missus. You must always obey them or they will send you away and I won't ever find you.

We know where he is! says Jennifer. We have to leave.

She grabs on the inside of my pocket with her mouth and I feel the pulling on my skin.

I open the door. The outside feels empty. Inside is full of words and old things kept safe and beautiful. But we know where Allen is, and so we have to leave. We have to leave the woman. Her heart hangs heavy. Her skin pricks with cold comfort. But she has all her words and her talking fills the room and she doesn't hear that we are gone.

SAMANTHA

I told Lucy I would write it down.

It went something like this. Hours and hours of screaming and pain and anguish.

It was my screaming. But it was still awful and tedious to be subjected to. I wished my head really could have been screamed off so I wouldn't have ears to listen to it with. So there was the pain, and the pushing of course, and the screaming, with nothing breaking it up but the doctor checking in every hour and saying it wasn't coming yet, and the nurse trying to keep Missus out of the room.

Then, finally, I heard it. New screaming. His screaming. The siren, the alarm, the ringing bell, the sound that meant it was all over.

I should have been exhausted, considering what I had just gone through. All I should have wanted was to sink back into the pillows and straight into sleep. But instead I wanted to go flying toward the exit door, laughing all the way. I was victorious. I was empty. He gasped for breath in between short, insistent cries as the nurse wiped him off and wrapped him up. His crying meant I'd made it. It had felt like it was going to last forever, that I was going to stay fat, pregnant, and stuck forever. Listening to his screams, I loved myself for getting through it without killing myself. For the first time in a long time, not since the night with his father, it felt so, so good to be alive, and I had myself to thank.

Then he got put in my arms.

I couldn't breathe because his little hands were too small, and each finger had a matching too-small fingernail. My heart stopped beating because his little eyes were trying to open. He knew there was a world out there, and he wanted to see it.

He wanted to see me.

I burned with shame. I was the lowest human being on the whole planet. There were slugs with bigger hearts than mine. He had come so far and was fighting to open his eyes to finally see the face of the person he had spent all these months with, the one person he knew in the whole world, only to find that person couldn't wait to be gone from his life for good. This morning, an hour ago, a minute ago, I'd have been skipping out of the hospital, celebrating my freedom and emptiness. But thank God that person I had been, even one minute before, was gone. She was dead and buried without one final prayer or fond remembrance, but her last words rang in my ears: *I changed my mind*.

Her last words and her best words.

She made me promise to write them down here, so there's a record her heart knew what to do, the only time it really mattered.

I changed my mind. He's mine forever.

I cried and cried and cried and cried. My tears streamed down and matted his hair. I tried to brush them off but they just kept coming. His poor little head was all wet, covered in his mama's shame.

"I'm sorry for even one minute of your life you had a mama like that," I whispered to him. "But I'm different now."

The nurse took the hospital gown off my shoulders. "Babies ain't usually hungry right when they born, but let's try."

But he was. I knew he would be. I knew because I am his mother. He was so tired and hungry from the ordeal of being born, and who in the whole world knew how to feed him except me? I had been feeding him this whole time, all these months. And when he was away from me, getting born and wiped off and wrapped in a blanket, he was terrified. Every one of those seconds, he didn't how he was going to be fed. He wasn't inside me anymore and he didn't know about the new way to be fed in the outside world. I was the only person who could show him how.

The nurse showed me how to show him. I fed him and the tears kept coming. All my insides seemed to be flowing out of me at once, but that was okay with me. I let them come. They weren't tears of shame anymore. Nothing shameful would come out of the new me, except memories of the old me.

"Hush, girl, hush, girl," said the nurse. She put her arms around both of us. "Things'll be all right for you both."

She was right.

Because I was never going to leave him alone again. Not even for a second, not even to get wrapped up and wiped off after being born. If I could do it over again, I would stay with him even during that part, and for every other part there on out.

He finished his first time eating in the outside world. I lifted his face up to my ear so he could whisper his name to me, but he was too worn-out. He smacked his lips together and went to sleep, his first sleep in the outside world.

"When you're ready, you can tell me," I told him. "I'm your mama. Now. And forever."

LUCY

Get in the car, says Jennifer.

I can't.

Of course you can! This man will take us to where Allen is.

But I can't.

Why not?

I can't get in the car because I remember.

The car door is open and a man is inside waiting for me because he said, Going someplace? And I said yes because I was going to That Place. But not anymore. Now I have stopped going. The car is breathing hard like a wild animal when it stops running. I know when the car is done catching its breath he will be gone again and then there will be nobody left to take us to where Allen is.

But still I can't get in the car because of what I remember.

I remember I am farther away from the farm than ever since Mum mum said never to leave the farm. Except now I have done that. I have done what Mum mum said never to do.

I hear Mum mum. She says, You mustn't ever, ever leave the farm or I won't know where to find you. I hear Samantha, she says, I heard Allen got shipped off somewhere, I don't know where he is. I hear Jennifer, she says, Samantha will love you so much. And all the reasons to never leave the farm and all the reasons to get in the car, the words of all of them are coming apart and mixing making new words. The new words are twisted together. They make a rope that is tying me tight to where I am.

But I start to pull. I pull against Mum mum's words, Samantha's, and Jennifer's. I try to only hear me, and my words, and pull with those. The pulling breaks the rope into pieces that melt into the air like snow in your hand.

The rope breaks. That is how I get into the car.

When the car stops moving then it is full dark, no orange stripe of leftover sun in the sky anymore. Where he stops there are other cars stopped in the dirt. The air here has more weight than air does when it hangs in other places. When I open my mouth the air has more weight on my tongue and more tastes than other air, like when there is a fire the tastes of what the burned things used to be become the air. When I breathe it down inside of me the air lands heavy on my insides like dust.

The dirt that was underneath the car chases behind. The dirt doesn't want to be left behind. It liked the feeling of something touching it from above. It doesn't want that feeling to leave. But just because you a want a thing to be yours doesn't mean it stops being able to leave.

Inside That Place is light but not the kind that makes it easy to see. It is the kind of light that melts everything together so nothing is its own thing anymore. Everyone is sitting except one person who is the person that brings people things. Like Mister when we sit for breakfast and he puts our breakfast in front of us like a father except he wasn't here from the beginning of us, just from the beginning of Stella. There from the beginning of her, but not with her anymore.

Go ask someone about Allen, Jennifer says.

I pick a person to ask. He is a man with dirt on his face. I want to ask him because I know about having dirt on your face. So even though I do not know his name I know something about him and he knows something about me. There is no place to sit next to him because there are already people sitting next to him but I go behind him and say, "Where is Allen?"

"Who's that?" His eyes are tired. Maybe because he is looking for missing things. Maybe he is tired like Missus, because of Stella never being found. Your eyes can never rest then.

"He is the father."

"And why would I know where he's at?"

"This is his job. To work here."

"Is he the boy that sweeps up here?"

"Yes."

"Ask Mark. Behind the counter." The man points.

The man points to another man who is standing all alone. That means behind the counter. Then there are two people behind the counter and one is me.

"Girlie, you can't stand back here."

"But I need to talk to the person behind the counter."

"That's me. The man behind the counter. The one and only."

"But I need to find Allen."

"He's gone home for the night."

"He's home?"

"That's what I said."

But we were just there, says Jennifer. And he wasn't there!

"But I was just there."

"Don't know what else to tell you. Allen went home early tonight. I think he's getting ready to ship off somewhere. Now get going. You can't stand back here. You shouldn't be here at all."

And since there is no Allen there I do get going.

We have to get back to his house, Jennifer says. Maybe if we go fast we can catch up to him. Understand? We have to move fast. We have to move even faster than he moves.

But how fast does he move?

However fast it is, we have to be faster.

MISSUS

It couldn't be possible, what our daughter was trying to do, not after the love and comfort and understanding we had extended during these months that she had needed us so. We offered her compassion and care, and this is how she repaid us? Committing the ultimate sin, under our roof, in the only home she had ever known, and available to her only because we had taken her in when nobody else wanted her.

I brought up her breakfast, but her room was empty. Since she had stopped going to school, she had spent her days in her bedroom, curled up on the bed.

"Stella?"

No answer. I left her breakfast tray on her bedroom floor.

"Stella?"

She was in the bathroom.

"Stella, no! Give me that!" I wrestled it away from her and she collapsed on the floor.

"Stella, how could you?"

She didn't say anything. She had no expression on her face. Her arms hung limp at her sides like vestigial organs.

I shook her shoulders. "Stella! Answer me! How could you?"

She pressed her lips together. "Okay," she said finally.

"Okay, what?" I demanded.

"I'll tell you how. Mom, I can't have this baby."

"Of course you can. You can and you will."

"It isn't right."

"It's the Lord's will, how can you question that?"

"It's not His will, Mother. Listen to me, I'll tell you why." She got up onto her knees. Her eyes were coming to life again, her voice was excited. "I'll tell you why. Listen."

I stood up, pulling her up with me.

"No, Stella, you listen to me. I'm your mother, and I will do anything to stop you from doing something terrible, something you will never forgive yourself for doing. But I won't listen to your excuses."

I tried to pull her out of the bathroom. She pulled back. She tugged on my arm the way she had when she was a young girl passing by candy in the grocery store.

"Mother, Mother, just listen and you'll understand. I want you to understand." She pulled my arm. The socket was burning.

"Stella, that's quite enough. I won't hear any excuse for sin."

"But, Mother, please, it's about that, that's exactly what I have to tell you." She pulled on me even harder. I yanked my arm free. The release of the tension that had built between us caused her to lose her balance and stumbled backward on the floor. She looked up at me, stunned.

Clearly I couldn't leave her to her own devices. Things had to change, to protect Stella and the baby. When we slept, I locked the doors. In the morning I brought her breakfast. I made sure she ate all her meals. For exercise we took walks by the river. I explained to Mister she was sick. And she was. And that the pregnancy was a dangerous one. And it was. And that she couldn't be alone outside of her bedroom without my supervision. I told it to him in this way because it would have killed him to know the truth about what she had tried to do and would have found a way to do had it not been for me. He trusted I knew best. He has always trusted me.

I was hardly keeping Mister away from Stella, but rather Mister had become so busy lately, refocusing his attention on the business of the farm, just as Stella and I were now focused on preparing for the baby. But every day Stella begged me to bring Mister to her room, saying Daddy knows, knows what I mean. She even had the audacity to claim he wouldn't make her keep it.

"Dear, your father and I have spoken about this. I know where he stands on this," I tried to explain to her. "Trust me."

"You don't understand. Please just let me talk to him. Please, Mother. Then you'll see. Please, Mother, please get him to come up here."

"All right, Stella. We can talk to him."

I called him in. He took off his hat when he entered the room. He stood at the foot of her bed. There was a moment of silence while they looked in each other's faces.

"Mister, Stella has something to ask you."

She didn't say anything.

I put my hand on her shoulder. "Stella, go ahead. What did you want to ask your father?"

"Talk to Mom, please," she said softly, searching his face. Then she said his name. I had heard her call Mister by his name before, but always playfully, always with a twinkle in her eyes. Never imploringly. Whenever she had wanted something from him, he always became *Daddy* again, but not this time. "I know you won't talk to me anymore, but just talk to Mom."

"Your mother knows what's best for our family," he told her.

"But she doesn't understand." Her eyes were wide and swimming.

"Your mother understands better than any of us." He looked at the hat he held in his hands.

"Please, if Mother knew," Stella whispered. "If Mother knew, then . . ."

She sat up on her knees and reached out for his hand, the one that held his hat. He flicked his wrist and put the hat back on his head.

"Trust your mother," Mister told her, and left the room.

Stella looked as if she might cry, but clenched her jaw and didn't. I thought that meant she was getting stronger.

She stopped asking for Mister after that. At some point she stopped speaking to me altogether. I read her favorite books to her to keep her mind active, though she gave no indication of listening.

I knew she was having a boy, and Mister bought the loveliest blue fabrics from town. Stella and I sat in her room together and I sewed. But Stella took no interest. She didn't help me with any of the clothes I made for him. She didn't do anything, just stared out the window. Sometimes it seemed she went minutes without even blinking.

"Are you expecting a visitor?"

She didn't smile. She didn't even flinch.

"Oh, darling, I'm just trying to lighten the mood."

Silence.

"Here, darling, help me with these clothes."

Silence.

"Stella, this is a blessing."

Silence.

"Aren't they just adorable, these little clothes? What's sweeter than baby clothes?"

But she didn't move her eyes from the window.

I did all the work. I made all those tiny clothes. Thousands of perfect, even stitches.

One morning I unlocked her door. The room was immaculate, and freezing, and empty. She had disappeared. Out the window. The wind was howling, like a siren trying to alert me, trying to stop her.

But a siren triggered too late. I screamed. I dropped her breakfast. Mister came up behind me. He ran to the window. I crumpled to the floor.

"How could she? Mister, how could she have?"

She was just gone, gone, gone. And worst of all, she had taken him.

LUCY

Outside it is cold now. I put Jennifer in my pocket.

No, no, leave me out.

But it's cold.

Leave me out.

Which way to go?

Back to the road.

Which is back to the road?

That way.

We go away from the light of That Place. We are walking on dirt. A car goes by us.

Get away from the road when a car goes by.

Why? I thought the cars were our friends, like the one that took us to That Place.

We don't have any friends.

What about Samantha?

You know what I mean.

No, I don't.

Quit playing dumb, we don't have the time.

I'm not playing.

Then the dirt becomes real road and there are too many cars to get away from the road when a car goes by.

This way, that way, Jennifer says.

How do you know the way to go?

Because I was memorizing the turns while we were in the car.

And this way and that way are the ways we go.

The road becomes a smaller road and goes through a town with stores with lights off inside. There is a sign that says DEPOT. We walk until there is no town anymore. Then there are houses and houses.

Do you know where we are? Jennifer says.

No.

This is the fence! We just need to get over the fence and then we're back at Allen's house! Remember? Look, you can see the top of the church, just right over there!

Yes. We need Lizbeth to give us a boost. That is how you get over a fence. I remember.

It doesn't have to be her, it can be anyone.

Where is anyone?

They aren't here yet.

What do we do?

Wait. Someone will be by soon enough.

I know how to wait. That is what I am doing at the farm, until Mum mum comes back.

Good, says Jennifer. So start waiting.

Dear Lucy,

A funny thing came over me today. I was in town doing my shopping. Monte let me take his car, and I don't know what possessed me, but after I left Miriam's I drove straight out of town and down that long country road until I found myself at your farm. And the whole time I was driving there I didn't even tell myself, Now I'm driving myself to that farm where Lucy lives, or I'd love to see my daughter right now, or anything like that. Well, it was as if I didn't even know where I was taking myself until I drove right up to that house and then there I was!

I got out of the car, touched up my lipstick and fixed my hat and walked carefully up the dirt path to the front door, and I must've knocked for five full minutes and not a sound, not a peep came from inside. And I walked around the porch and peered in all the windows like a regular detective woman and didn't see a soul, only some kittens underneath the porch.

So I figured you were on an adventure! Was I right? On a wonderful adventure either in the faraway mountains, maybe some farm business in another county, or maybe you all were just doing your errands in town. All I knew was, it was something exciting! You always enjoyed traveling a bit, seeing somewhere you'd never seen before, things like that. And then you get to come home and play with those kittens, and you've always loved animals so, haven't you? How special for you.

I felt close to you, being where you've been, seeing what's become familiar to you. And I felt happy knowing you were having some change of scenery, traveling around a bit, seeing some of what else is out there. Riding in cars. Remember how much you loved Monte's convertible, sticking your head out the window, watching the world go by?

Then I went home. I cooked Monte some dinner, my cooking has greatly improved, and after he took me out for a drink at the Gin Joint, and I went to sleep with the feeling of having had a fine and satisfying day settle over me. A high-quality kind of day, part of which I felt I had spent with you, Lucy. We did have ourselves some good times, didn't we?

Love,

Mum mum

MISSUS

Hello, my boy. I have been waiting for so long. It has been so long, but I never doubted. I never doubted you. I never doubted Him. I never doubted Mister.

I knew it would be a boy. We asked for Rodger for a girl carrying a boy. He told us it was too soon to tell, but when I saw Samantha, I knew. She was carrying him so low.

Here he is finally. Finally. The nurse hands him to me.

Here he is. His eyes are open. My eyes are open. We are memorizing each other's face. My boy, it's been too long. I have been waiting so long, but, yet, I have also known you for so long. Just like the boy Stella took from us; I knew so many things about him already. I knew he would put family above all else. I knew he would have a way with animals, a way with melodies, big hands but a gentle touch.

My boy's skin is so soft. The softest fabrics don't compare, because unlike silk, touching him isn't a feeling that happens against your skin, it's a feeling that happens inside your skin. Like the first time someone you have been praying would touch you reaches for you. It's an extraordinary feeling. When Mister kissed me the first time, it was his mouth touching mine, yet the feeling was all inside me. The rest of the world has had countless chances to burn and sting and blister the outside of me. But only my boys have been able to reach inside.

Samantha is shrieking from her delivery room. But this is what she wanted. She was the one who came to us, who approached Rodger Marvin, begging for his help. Our help, our Christian charity. She was no prisoner. She's a young girl and she has her whole life. There is time for all her dreams to come true, just as there was time for Stella. But there isn't any time left over for me. It is all used up. The only time I get is now.

Samantha will forget these moments at the hospital, just as I am certain she will forget her entire stay on the farm. When you have your whole life, you will forget about lots of things. Samantha has years to do her forgetting. But I am too old now to forget anything. I am destined to remember everything that has been taken from me, by God, by my body, by my own daughter.

Samantha has years and years to become a mother.

And finally, I have my son.

LUCY

A man with a hat is shaking me like he is the wind and I am an arm of a tree against the window. And Jennifer is screaming like the feeling when you hit your elbow against the open drawer. She is as hot as a black stone by the river all day. In my mind it was a quiet place but out here is it a very loud place. When the whole world is full of words and you are not, sometimes you want to stay inside yourself where it is quiet.

"Is something wrong?" says the man. He has a face but it is a hard-to-see face because night has come and is laying its darkness all over.

"Yes," I say. There is something wrong.

No, yells Jennifer. What are you saying? Ask him for a boost!

"You in some kind of trouble? Are you lost?"

"Yes," I say. I am in some kind of trouble and I am lost. The only place I need to wait is on the farm for my Mum mum.

No, yells Jennifer. A boost, a boost!

"Where did you come from and where are you trying to go?"

"The farm." I came from the farm and I am trying to go to the farm.

"Which farm?"

"The farm with Mister and Missus." The farm with Mister and Missus, which I was never supposed to leave or else Mum mum could never find me and now she never will.

"Mister and Missus who?"

"Mister and Missus, that is their farm." Always call them Mister and Missus is what Mum mum told me.

"You ran away from there?"

"No. I would never run away or else Mum mum could never find me. That is why I mustn't ever, ever leave the farm." Except then I did and now Mum mum will never find me.

Stop feeling sorry for yourself, Jennifer says. We have to get over the fence. Try, try to get over, Lucy, try, this is our last chance. We're so close and we're not going to have another chance to find Allen. He's back at home, that's what that man Mark said. It's just right over this fence.

"Who's Mum mum?"

"She is my Mum mum."

Listen to me, I don't hear Jennifer say. Because some things that people say, I don't hear them. There is no place inside of me for them to fit.

But I do remember this. I do remember Mum mum said never leave the farm and I did. I do remember if you want someone to find you, you should never leave that place where you are. But I did leave the farm and that means that Mum mum won't be able to find me. Maybe she is at the farm looking for me and she is saying, Lucy, Lucy, where are you? I told you! You mustn't ever ever leave the farm but you have disobeyed me just like you have so many times before and now I will never find you, you will always be alone, as alone as when I was locked in the room and Mum mum didn't come back.

If I were there I would say, No, Mum mum, I had to leave because nobody was there to look after me when everyone went to the hospital. Monte will be able to tell Mum mum that is why I am not on the farm. Because Mum mum lives with Monte in the city and I will tell him that Samantha had to go to the hospital to have her baby and there was nobody there to look after me. That was why I left the farm but I did still want to be found by Mum mum. Always.

But that is too much to tell Jennifer so I don't say anything to her.

I say to the man, "And Mum mum told me I wasn't ever, ever to leave the farm. That is where I live now and wait for her."

He takes off his hat and puts his hand in his hair. When Samantha puts her hands in my hair I know there is a thread that runs down into the center of the earth and on the other end of that thread is me.

"You live on this farm," the man says. "Not with your mother?"

"Yes. On the farm is where I wait for Mum mum to get me."

"You got chickens on the farm?"

"Yes, lots."

"What color is your farmhouse?"

"Yellow."

"It's the chicken farm, about ten miles outside of town?"

No! Say *no*! says Jennifer. We'll figure it out ourselves, let's get out of there. Forget the fence, just run, run, Lucy, please, I'll show you how to do it fast, just start running, don't say another word.

"Yes," I say.

"I can drive you back there. We're not too far."

No, says Jennifer. I haven't done wrong by you once, have I? You have to trust me, that's why you saved me all along, so that here, right now, right now at this minute, you would run away and find another way to get over the fence and find Allen. Samantha is going to have nobody if we don't find him for her. That is why you picked me, Lucy, don't you see that? This moment, that is why you picked me! You could have picked any of the others but you picked me!

"Mum mum, she said never to leave the farm. That's what Mum mum said and she is the one I always must listen to and nobody else."

"We'll get you back safe," he says. "It's far but it's not too far. I know the way. My wife is in my car. You stop worrying now. You're safe with us."

When we drive, the wife touches my hair and holds my head by her shoulder. Jennifer says things but I don't hear what they are because of the way that touching feels on my head and that is how we drive back to the farm, back to where I can wait for Mum mum, back to the place I wasn't ever, ever to leave and I will never tell Mum mum that I ever did.

LUCY

"Lucy, this is him!" Samantha says. "Can you believe it?"

Now Samantha is upstairs, more upstairs than even before when she was upstairs. Samantha and Baby. Up the stairs until there are no more stairs, that is called the attic. There is a bed but it is not a bedroom. Samantha used to have a bedroom but now she has the attic. It is a place for all the things that don't have places anymore, not even in the trash or the compost. There are broken pictures of a girl and baby clothes with lots of holes and old dresses on the floor, not nice like Mum mum would put me in, and silver shoes that have lost their shine. And dust. That is what the attic is.

Baby looks smashed like something is pressed against his face and he can't get it off. His favorite thing to do is hold my finger and cry and not open his eyes.

"How perfect is he, Lucy?" Samantha says. "Can you believe I made something so perfect?"

But I forgot about what the word *perfect* is. So I cannot say if I believe it.

"I'm waiting for him to tell me his name, like we talked about. Remember?"

"I didn't find Allen," I say. Needles fall behind my eyes so I can't close them without the hurting. "I couldn't find Allen, Samantha, even though I looked."

"Oh, Lucy!" Samantha's arms come up toward me but they do not come all the way to me because Baby is in the way. I want Samantha to put down Baby so her arms can come all the way. "Don't worry about that! It doesn't even matter."

"It does matter."

"Everything's fine!"

"Where should I look now?"

"Don't worry about Allen!"

"But you can't be a family."

"We'll be a family together."

"But where will you live?"

"We'll figure it out. Now I know what I have to do. Look at him."

I look at him.

"Just look at him. Now, can't you see that everything is going to be fine?"

I forget what *fine* is. So I do not say anything.

"Isn't everything going to be fine, my little sweet baby?" Samantha asks Baby. "I get it now. We're gonna be together forever. And doesn't that mean everything's gonna be fine?"

But Baby doesn't say anything. He doesn't know what those words mean consistency either.

"Come down the stairs, Samantha.

"Come down the stairs to where we have breakfast like a family where everything is there from the beginning of you, and Baby can have his place with us and we can be there from the beginning of him too.

"Come down the stairs to the outside where we touch the dirt and plant the plants and the dirt pulls the plants down deep inside it to keep them safe."

"Soon, soon I will," says Samantha. "There are so many stairs and I'm so sleepy all the time."

"Why are you so sleepy all the time?"

"That's what happens with you have a baby. You have to work twice as hard at keeping you both alive." She stops her words so she can suck in extra air which is called yawning. "I'm really just as happy lying around up here with all this weird junk, getting strong for when we leave together."

She puts her finger in Baby's mouth and they smile at each other like it was a joke that I didn't understand and I wish they would tell me why it was funny so I could smile too because my mouth misses my smile.

"Samantha, if you don't come down the stairs, how will we find Allen and get the house and the place to live and the other things that you need to have another life together that isn't your life on the farm? The ways things are supposed to be, you said."

"They'll come in time. When the universe is ready to send those things our way. The most important thing is that we're all together." Samantha she smiles so I see that it is the most important thing, that we're all together.

Then Missus comes in. When the door opens the dust gets up to do its dance around the room. It burns my eyes and chokes my throat.

"Is he done feeding?" says Missus. "Is the little one sleeping now?"

"Let him sleep with me, Missus, we can fall asleep here on my bed together," says Samantha.

"You need to rest. Look at you. You have no color. You won't get proper sleep with the baby sleeping on you. And they say about sleeping with the baby, it isn't good for either of you. The baby's to be put to sleep in his crib."

Missus picks up Baby.

"The mother next to me at the hospital said that it's for bonding, that you sleep with your baby." Samantha sits up tall in bed and reaches her arms out.

"Bad habits, sleeping with the baby in your bed," Missus says.

"Please, Missus, let him stay." Samantha sounds like Missus is hurting her, but Missus is not touching her. Hearing Samantha sound like hurting is the same as me hurting.

"Nonsense," says Missus. Now Baby is sleeping on Missus's shoulder.

"The other mother, she's had four kids. She told me about bonding so I would know. It's important for a new mother to know." Then Samantha's voice sounds tired again. Her voice is coming from buried inside her and buried under the covers. Her head sinks into the pillow. "That's what the woman at the hospital said. And she's had four kids."

"Samantha, I'm sure you realize I know what's best for the people in my house. Now, Lucy, what are you doing with the afternoon?" Missus says but doesn't look at me. She is looking at Baby who is sleeping and not looking at anything.

Say you're visiting, says Jennifer.

"Visiting."

"Stay up here, then. It's fine. If Mister needs you, I'll come get you."

Missus shuts the door.

"Samantha, why don't you ever write in your book anymore?"

"Mmmm." Samantha is almost sleeping. "Because I don't have secrets anymore."

Now Samantha is sleeping. I am not ready for any sleep but sometimes if you want to be with a sleeping person then you need to meet them in their dreams. Under the covers is warm and smells like milk and salt and oranges. Our smells come together and then it is not the smell of either of us anymore. It is a new smell. I have never smelled it before but I know it. Jennifer's eyes they close and it feels like the wind blew a blade of grass across you.

I am not ready for sleep, but sleep comes to me.

But there was another time. A time when I wanted sleep and it wouldn't come.

———

Mum mum went away and I stayed in the bedroom. She made it so the door couldn't open. I knew the sound. There was a window and it didn't open either.

She ran to Monte. He was in his blue car. I watched through the window.

I watched through the window all the cars that didn't bring back Mum mum. I used all my strength to open the door but my strength wasn't enough. Then it was night and I didn't sleep because Mum mum was who held me during my sleeping and told me she loved me and called me Dear Lucy. That's how I knew it was safe to be sleeping.

I watched through the window all the cars that didn't bring back Mum mum. I used all my strength to open the door but the door was stronger than me. There was a cake and a glass of milk on the dresser and I ate it and I was still hungry.

I watched more through the window. None of the cars brought her back. I licked the frosting off the box. I sat in the closet and looked up at all the dresses. I was part of their rainbow but I didn't have the rainbow feeling. Then it was night and I didn't sleep again.

I put on Mum mum's shoes even thought my feet were too big and her necklace and her lipstick.

"Lucy, I'm back!" I said.

"Mum mum, you're back!"

"My Dear Lucy."

And I held my pillow tight and then I fell asleep.

LUCY

"Go get in the truck, Lucy," Mister says. "It's time for your lesson."

"Okay," I say.

But Jennifer says no.

Why no? Rodger Marvin shows us new words and new ways to love the Lord.

Because we're not quite ready yet.

Why not?

I have an idea, says Jennifer. Go to Samantha's room, her old downstairs room.

I go to her downstairs room.

Look, that hole in the floor. Reach under it.

I put my hand in the hole. Under the floor is where the kittens like to sleep but they aren't there now. But what is there now is a book.

Samantha's book. Why is it under the floor?

She hid it there after she got back from the hospital.

But how will she write in it?

She doesn't anymore. Remember, no secrets?

I will ask her.

No, she's sleeping. If she was awake she would say it's okay to bring it. I promise. Just bring it with us. It will help us find Allen. She might be too sleepy to try and find him, but we aren't. Who is going to look out for her and the baby unless we find him for her?

So I take her book and put it in my pocket. Jennifer holds it tight against her and safe. Each feather is a fist that keeps holding on.

"Let's go," Mister calls to me, and we go.

Good, this is good, says Jennifer. We'll show it to Lizbeth. When she reads what Samantha writes about Allen, she'll see how bad we needed to get over the fence. She'll see we needed her help then and we need it now.

Then Lizbeth won't be mad anymore.

Exactly, says Jennifer. She can't stay mad when she reads how much Samantha needs to find Allen, and sees that we were only trying to help.

MISSUS

Here are we are, Mister, me, and our boy, sitting together on the porch, watching the orange sun sink behind the skyline of the farm, the barn, the silo, the fences, the blades of grass. Our family. Complete.

Our child, yes, but not like Stella. Though holding him, feeling the rise and fall of his breathing, so delicate but so powerful, I am reminded of her. I am reminded of that first night with her, how happy and at home I was sleeping on the floor. I am reminded of the flush of her cheeks, her natural glow fighting through the face paint on the night of her school dance. I am reminded of the beautiful swell of her belly, as the miracle grew.

Most of all, I am reminded of the son she took from us. Though he was still inside her, he must have been so scared when she took him away from the only people who loved him. I shudder and hold our boy tighter, shushing him, as if my memory of Stella could have frightened him as well.

"There, there, nobody will ever take you away from us," I whisper to him.

Not like Stella. This boy will grow to be a man, a person of character, who puts family first. He will be loyal, a provider, like Mister. Because whom have I been able to count on during my earthly life but Mister? When I was weak, it was Mister who gave me strength. When I stumbled, he lifted me up. When I couldn't eat, he brought me my food. When I couldn't be there to take walks, play music, with Stella, he was. What I couldn't provide for our family, he provided for us.

I reach over and put my hand on Mister's arm.

He smiles faintly into the distance.

"We're finally all here," I say to him. "After all this time."

"His path for us was not always easy to understand."

"We are here because of your strength. Because you never gave up, and because you have always done what's right for our family. You always trusted me, even when it was hard."

"Well, you have always known what's best."

I laugh and kiss our boy's head. "A mother knows best, it's true."

I waited eagerly for Mister to return from dropping Stella at her dance. I embraced him as soon as he opened the door. His eyes were dull and tired. The skin around his eyes sagged, as if it had lost its will to stay taut. I knew his day had been long and hard. Part of that was due to the onset of the planting season, but I also knew he struggled to accept that Stella was fully grown. It hurt to say good-bye to the bundle Rodger Marvin had brought over during dinner many years ago. But it was necessary. And where there had been a girl, now there was woman, and that was nothing to mourn.

"Thank you," I told him, "for taking her. You know I would have done it if I could have. Thank you for always being able to make up for what I have lacked."

"Has it ever been enough?"

I held him tighter. "You have given me more than I will ever be able to repay."

"Please do one thing for me."

"What is it?"

"Let me rest tonight. You pick her up."

"You do seem tired, my darling." I stroked his creased face.

"I am." His eyes softened and warmed. "Will you come to bed with me?"

"Dear, have you forgotten already?" I laughed. "I have to pick up Stella. I can't go to sleep."

"Then come upstairs and sit with me. Please."

Before I could oblige him, he continued, "We are family. We should be together. Family is everything, isn't it?" He was agitated. Our farm had never been easy work, but today he woke even earlier than usual to begin planting the corn. He had spent the whole day seeding and then stayed out escorting Stella. In a meager number of hours he would have to wake again. "That's what you believe, isn't it? Isn't that what you would have me believe, all these years?"

I put a finger on his open mouth. "Of course, dear. Shhhh."

"*We* should be together," he said quietly. His shoulders slumped. "*We* should be a family. Why wasn't it enough?"

"I am always your family, even if you are upstairs resting and I'm downstairs in the kitchen. No matter what separates us."

"Why should anything separate us?" he said, his voice rising again.

"Oh, my poor, tired Mister. You never let me give up hope, did you? You're the only reason I have any hope at all in this life." I led him toward the stairs. "We'll say a prayer, like we did every night in the old days. Remember when you used to pray for us, for the both of us, when I didn't have the strength?"

He nodded as we climbed the stairs, side by side, holding each other's hand.

"Tonight I'll say the prayer. For the two of us. For our family. That tomorrow you won't be as tired and things won't seem as hard."

We reached the top of the stairs. I didn't let go of his hand.

"I'll pray that tomorrow our family will be stronger. That tomorrow we will be fulfilled. That tomorrow all those seeds you planted today will begin to grow."

SAMANTHA

I want my parents to know they were wrong about me. They thought I would never make a good decision on my own, but look at me now. I'm going to write them a letter, saying they can meet him once we're settled in our new place and ready, and once I've decided to forgive them, but I hid my journal in the bedroom downstairs after I got back from the hospital, after I changed my mind, after I wrote down her last words. I thought because I don't have any secrets anymore, it meant that I didn't have any reason to write anything down. I didn't know that when you're happy, you want everyone to know, that it's the best thing to brag about.

But I'm sure I can find something to write on. This room is stuffed with junk. The closet is full of old dresses and shoes that I can't imagine Missus ever wore, and the dresser is packed with terrible homemade baby clothes that Missus insists we dress him in, not that I have any other options. And though he looks sweetest in just a diaper, Missus never lets me keep him like that. She says lots of love went into making those clothes, it wouldn't be right not to use them.

A faded pad of yellow paper is in the top drawer of the dresser. Just the top ten pages are used. On each page is written the same thing, almost exactly, each draft different by just a word or two. Each word picked so carefully, written so carefully in small, neat, even handwriting.

She was trying to get it perfect.

I know who she is before I even see her name. I know she was real before I see her name. I know Lucy was right. I know she was up here, like me. I know the clothes were hers. And whom all the baby clothes were really for.

Good-bye Mother, Good-bye Daddy,

Mother, you are too kind to me, I can't stand it. If you knew the truth about me, you wouldn't be. You would punish me like I deserve. You wouldn't tell me I could have anything I wanted after he's born. Because all the things I want are bad. I want what isn't mine. I don't know why. That's just the type of person I am, I guess.

Daddy, if I were you, I wouldn't love me anymore, either. I wouldn't want to be around me. I know you used to love me when I was your daughter, and I'm sorry I stopped being that. I thought I didn't want to be her anymore. I wanted to be something else. Now I'm sorry I took her away. I'm sorry I made you come to the dance with me. I wish there was some way I could be her again, but I know I can't. I know she's gone for good, which is why I have to go now too. There's no room for the new me here.

Thank you for being so good to him. I know you did a lot to make sure he'd come out okay, and I'm sorry you'll never get to see what he looks like. But he has to come with me. He'll just remind you of me and the bad thing I did. Even if you know it's not his fault. It's not fair to you to be reminded. And it's not fair to him, either. I got him into this and I'll get him out. I just have to fall the right way so we go out together and I don't leave either of us behind, all alone in my body.

You said I could have anything I wanted, afterwards. But this is all I want: bury us in the woods where Daddy and

me used to walk. There's a tree where we put our initials. I
named him after Daddy, after his Daddy, so that can be our
marker.

Daddy, maybe since we're really gone for good, you'll be
able to come around me again. We hope you can visit us
under the tree because we miss you already. We have missed
you this whole time.

Love,
Stella

I run my fingers over the pad of paper. The layers of words
leave impressions on the paper like wrinkled skin. I feel what happened to her. Mister did this to her. Missus let it happen. I go to
her closet. I touch her clothes. In the far end of the closet, ostra-
cized from the rest of the clothes, there is a lonely white, eyelet
dress, with a small, embarrassed brown stain on its seat. I know
that stain. It was on the back of my dress too. Her father did this
and her mother didn't stop him. That's why Stella had to leave.
She didn't abandon them. She was saving her baby from them.
Saving him from what had happened to her.

I tear off the top draft, fold it up, and put it in my pocket. I
grab him from the crib. As soon as we leave the room, I know I've
forgotten to put on shoes but I don't go back.

Outside the ground is damp from a light rain and soft enough
to run. We run through the stalks of corn, the leaves whipping at
my shoulders, until the woods start. The stones and twigs stick in
between my toes and I trip forward but catch myself. He bumps
his head against my chin and starts to cry.

The tree could be anywhere. We go deeper into the woods.
Each step forward doesn't look any different from the one before it,
and I have to slow down and gingerly maneuver my footing through
the underbrush, until there's a path, overgrown but clear enough to
follow. I pick up our pace. My feet hurt all over now, but it's easier

to ignore because the jabbings and stickings and prickings have stopped coming as surprises. The path ends at a clearing.

The sky is indigo and the first eager stars are fighting to be seen against the last of the daylight. In the middle of the clearing is a gray sycamore, alone, as if he has been waiting for people to gather around him, reaching his arms out and up, beckoning. The grass is soft here and I walk painlessly to the tree, to their tree. I feel as if I were being escorted to a regal gentleman who wants to make my acquaintance.

Stella and Daddy. I run my hands over the scar, like the one my baby's father made for us. A scar on a tree to mark a wound on the inside that will never scab, never heal. Baby stops crying. I set him in the grass. He looks up at the branches. They wave to him. His eyes are wide and alert, as if he were studying the branches for something in particular. I get down on my hands and knees. I run my hands over the ground around the trunk like a prospector at a riverbed.

"Stella?" I whisper. I put my ear to the ground. "Are you here?"

I move around the perimeter of the tree, digging my hands into the dirt now, feeling for something. He is quiet now. The rustle of leaves is the only sound.

"Good boy," I tell him, and keep looking. My fingertips study the blades of grass, the dirt, the stones, the tiny white bugs, the fallen leaves. "Good baby."

Then, halfway around the tree, he starts to cry. I put my palms flat on the earth, my ear to the ground.

"Stella? Are you here?"

He cries louder. Warmth swells underneath my palms. My love-line, my lifeline, are charged like electrical wires.

They are here.

My baby is screaming, choking on himself, sputtering. But it is loud, strong and pure.

"You found a way out, didn't you?" I whisper to her. "You got away from them. You were good. You were a good mother. Stella, I'm gonna be good to him too, I promise."

I crawl back to him and bring him to Stella. I let him wail. I let them wail to each other, and although it is only him I can hear, I know what she is saying.

Go now.

And I will. We'll leave from here. Right now. I can find the river in the dark. The river surrounds the woods. I just have to walk straight in any direction, keep straight, and I'll hit it. If I follow the river long enough, I'll have to come to one of the bridges. I'll bring the letter straight to Rodger Marvin, I'll show my parents, I'll show the police, I'll show whomever I need to. I'll show everybody, so the world can know what they did to you and protect itself against them.

I will help you.

We stand up and begin to run. Thank you, Stella, for bringing me here. Thank you for leaving your letter for me. I didn't believe in you at first, but you didn't give up.

Keep going.

The woods are thick and the sky is getting dark, but we are able to move through it as quickly as if there were a lighted pathway to the river. I'm not running to the river, my legs aren't carrying me. I'm being willed there.

Save him.

But a pit in my stomach grows with every step. Finally the pain is so strong I have to stop. I breathe deep and dig my fingers into my side, trying to work out the pain, but it darts like a frightened mouse, into one organ and then another. I run through it for a few more steps. But I have to stop again.

Don't stop.

I try, but I can't put one foot in front of the other. I know why. I didn't want to think about it, but now that I have, I know I won't be able not to. I know I can't leave her.

This could be your only chance.

Lucy, who loved him before I did. Lucy, who promised to take care of us when nobody else would. Lucy, who promised I would never be alone. Lucy wouldn't leave us, I can't leave her with Mister. We have to wait until she gets back. It's just a few more hours. Stella, you'll keep us safe until then. I turn back toward the clearing. I sink a palm into my stomach and kneel over it. The mouse smashes against my spine, trembles for a moment, and then goes still. The pain subsides.

No! Save him.

We walk through the clearing, follow the overgrown path. We reach the edge of the woods that border the farm. We stop for a moment, where we are still hidden by branches and the darkness, before we step out into the moonlight and walk through the corn to the house.

Please come with us, Stella. Help us wait for Lucy. If you knew her, you would have waited for her too. Then we'll all go together.

I hold my breath so I'll be able to hear her reply, so I won't miss a sound, so I will be able to go back to the house strong and brave, knowing she'll help us.

Please, Stella, I wouldn't be able to forgive myself if I left Lucy here with them. You must understand, you know what they did. You wouldn't leave someone you loved with them. That's why you took him with you.

I strain to hear her say that she'll wait with us, that she will keep us safe until Lucy comes back and then she will shepherd us away, that she found a way to save her baby, and she will find a way to save us.

But the woods are silent.

LUCY

In the basement today there is no Lizbeth. I know why there is no Lizbeth. Because she is scared. She is scared of the time I needed her to give me a boost so I had to pull her hair. I am sad there is no Lizbeth. If you need to get over a fence, you need a boost. But I scared her for a boost and now there is no Lizbeth to read what Samantha writes and then not stay mad.

But there is Rodger Marvin.

"Lucy, Lucy, Lucy. What are we going to do with you?" says Rodger Marvin. He does not sweep himself to the ground like the heavy branch of a tree. That is the way he usually says hello to me and the way I like for him to say hello to me. Because when he sweeps low it blows warmth on my cheeks. But now his hands are on his hips like Mum mum when she sees bad behavior. "Have a seat."

I sit.

"Now tell me why you hurt Lizbeth." Rodger Marvin holds my hands together hard so they can't do any more pulling of Lizbeth's hair. "She is your friend, a fellow daughter of the Lord, and you abused her trust in you."

"Because I needed a boost."

"Why did you need a boost?"

"To get over the fence, to go to Allen's house."

"And why is it you needed to get to Allen's house?"

"To tell him things."

"What sorts of things do you need to tell this boy?"

"I need to tell him where Samantha is. He doesn't know where she is and she doesn't know where he is. If I don't find him, then Samantha will be alone."

Show him the book! says Jennifer. Rodger Marvin will understand why they need to be together. Everything is in there. How much Samantha loves him and why she needs him. He'll tell us where we should go to find Allen. Then Samantha and Allen and the baby can be a real family.

"This says all the reasons why," I say, and I show him the book. The outside is soft from all the times she opened it to go inside and closed it to keep the insides safe. "These are the sorts of things I need to tell Allen, when I find him. So they can be a real family."

"What is this?" Rodger Marvin taps the book with his fingers.

"This is the book Samantha writes in."

"Her diary?"

"I am the only one she ever shows."

"Did she give it to you?"

"No. She put it under the house and I found it."

"And why did you bring it here today?"

So he can read it to us.

"So you can read it to me. Because you will understand why they need to be together and then help me to find Allen. Because I cannot leave the farm to live in the special place Samantha wants for us. I have to wait for Mum mum and never, ever leave the farm or she won't know where to find me."

"Okay, well, let me have a look here," Rodger Marvin says.

Good! This is really good, says Jennifer. He will tell us the places that Allen might be. Maybe he'll even take us there. Good, Lucy.

My belly smiles because of the good thing that is happening. Rodger Marvin reads Samantha's book. We have silence together. Silence is the best place to read someone's words. Because then the words can grow as big as they need to with no sounds in the way. When Mum mum read her papers, I said, Tell me, tell me, and Mum mum said, Shhhhhh, be quiet, I'm reading.

Jennifer beats hard and fast in my pocket. Every time Rodger Marvin turns the page Jennifer gets a little hotter because she knows every time means we are closer and closer to finding Allen. Every page is a step that goes one in front of each other.

Rodger Marvin shuts the book. He looks hard at me. So hard Jennifer feels it through my pocket.

"Lucy, thank you very much for bringing me this book. It was the right thing to do. I am disappointed that you hurt Lizbeth last week, but this helps make it right. Do you understand what I am saying?"

"That I did the right thing." Now the smile in my belly is smiling all over.

"Yes, that was very good. Now I am going to take you back to the farm."

"But now you tell me what's in Samantha's book."

"All in good time, child. For now we must go back to the farm."

"But when will you tell me? Will you tell me in the car?"

"Next time I will tell you everything you need to know."

"But now I have to go back to the farm?"

"Yes. We have to go right now."

"And next time you will tell me?"

"Yes."

No! Jennifer says. This isn't right! He has to tell us now. We can't waste any more time. The baby is already here. Samantha has to find Allen, she can't stay on the farm. It's not her home.

But I must always listen to Rodger Marvin, I tell Jennifer.

No, now.

No, Jennifer, I say. Nobody will be happy if I make trouble for Rodger Marvin. He will tell us the next time.

Jennifer is bouncing in my pocket. It feels like my guts are trying to escape. I put my hand in to stop the bouncing. She bites my finger. I wipe the blood on her because I do not want Rodger Marvin to see the blood and think Jennifer is making trouble.

No! No! No! yells Jennifer. He knows and he's not telling us! He knows where to find Allen and he's not telling us! This isn't right! Something's wrong!

Where to find Allen is important. I know. But the most important thing is to listen to Rodger Marvin. Mister told me that nobody will be pleased if I make trouble for Rodger Marvin. When I don't listen to Mister then I don't get breakfast and I don't get to do my favorite jobs and I have to feed the pigs instead and they knock me over and ruin my dress and then I have to do stitching. Which is something I can't do because of how small the needle and thread is.

Rodger Marvin's car is big and shines like Monte's. Inside the car the seats are soft and hold your body in the perfect way so I feel as light as the white flowers that float forever in the air when you blow them off the stem. We listen to music about people singing about how much they love the Lord and Rodger Marvin tells me how good I am and how right of a thing I have done by bringing him Samantha's diary.

Next time he will tell me all the things I need to know about how to find Allen. Next time Samantha will love me more when she sees that I have found Allen. Next time happiness will grow inside her and maybe even spill out of her eyes and I can catch some on my finger and put some of her happiness on my tongue and taste it, next time.

Don't worry, Jennifer, I say. Next time.

We drive over the bridge. In between the bridge and the farm there is nothing and we drive through the nothing. Then we are at the farm. Rodger Marvin and me go inside together. Mister is surprised because he is the one that usually gets me after my lessons, except this time Rodger Marvin was so proud of me that he brought me home.

"This is a surprise," says Mister.

"Mister, let's step outside," says Rodger Marvin. He is holding Samantha's book. He pats the book with his hand because he wants to tell Mister about how good of a thing I did by showing him the book. "There is something you need to know."

I run up and up and up all the stairs to find Samantha. I put my hand on her door and suck in some air. The air is to carry my words to her. To tell her everything I have done. I have brought her book to Rodger Marvin. Next time he is going to help me find Allen. Samantha doesn't know where Allen is and Allen doesn't know where Samantha is. But I will. Not now. But next time I will know, because of bringing her book to Rodger Marvin.

Don't you dare! screams Jennifer.

But she will want to know.

She's sleeping in there! It's late.

But I will tell her Rodger Marvin is going to help us find Allen.

She'll still be here in the morning. You know how much rest she needs.

So I don't dare wake her because of how much rest she needs. Her body is working two times as hard. I take my hand off her door.

I go to my room but sleep won't come. There is no room for sleep. My thoughts are taking up all the space inside of me. The thoughts are the things that Rodger Marvin will tell me next time. The things from Samantha's book about where to look for Allen and how much Samantha will love me because I found him and that is called grateful. Grateful she will have Allen just like I have Mum mum. And so I do not sleep and do not sleep. The moon shines through the window. Then it trades places with the first white light of going-to-be-morning.

And in the not-still-night-but-not-still-morning time, I close my eyes and remember Jennifer before she was Jennifer. Even though a dream isn't real life but still just as close to you, I feel the way the eggs hugged on my legs and my legs were a special place for them that they had never had before. They were a special feeling for me that I never had. And even though they were our breakfast, even though they were living things for eating so that we could grow with their life, they weren't scared.

MISSUS

Mister told me what Samantha wrote in her diary. Afraid I would fall to pieces, he told me gently, cautiously. He remembers the bedroom scene when Stella left. But I remain composed. I tell him I would like to speak to Samantha alone. Mister looks a little uneasy but he understands this is women's business. Young girls can't be counted on for much, but they can be counted on to be fickle, mercurial. That's no reason to crumble. I go to her room to ask her about it.

But the attic door won't open more than an inch. Samantha has moved her dresser in front of the door. Frail though I may seem to some, one slam of my hip against the door shoves it open enough for me to slip through. It takes much more than furniture to keep a mother from her son.

Samantha is not only sleeping with the baby, which I told her not to do, but she is holding Stella's letter. Sleeping with the baby, and with Stella's letter pressed against her chest.

I blink to make sure I am seeing it correctly. There it is; Stella's uneven, unsightly printing on the sheet of yellow paper that I had bought for her myself. There's no mistaking it. And although it doesn't seem possible, it does not surprise me. I have been through too much in my years. There is no shock. There is no disappointment. Betrayal is no stranger to me. I know him intimately.

There is no time to be surprised. No time to gasp, to clasp my hand to my heart, no time to become weak in the knees. No time to wake Samantha, no time to raise my voice, no time for accusations. No time for anger, only action.

I put the letter in the pocket of my apron. I pluck the baby from Samantha's arms. Samantha doesn't even flinch. She sleeps the deep, peaceful sleep of a child, not the restless, ready, alert sleep of a mother.

Mister will drive Samantha home as soon as it's light out. Until then, thank goodness I still have the key to the attic. I always thought it would come in handy again to have a room that locks from the outside. It's proven to be useful in a life where nothing can be taken for granted.

Though if Samantha doesn't care to wait until the morning to leave, she can feel free to use the window.

PART III

What a Promise Is

LUCY

The sound of other mornings is the sound of the sun waking up and yawning. The sound of other mornings is the sound of the moon sinking into his bed between the mountains and the crickets putting away their music.

The sounds of this morning are not the sounds of the other mornings.

The sounds of this morning are the sounds of Samantha screaming. It is loudness that is everywhere, on the inside and on the outside. It is loudness in between the cracks of the floor and holding on to to each piece of dust that hangs in the sunshine and is stuck on the fingerprints on the mirrors and windows. It is loudness that has filled me all the way up.

Jennifer is shaking. Her mouth is tapping together like a branch against a window in a storm. I do not have time to even touch her or say, Do not be scared. We rush out of the bed but I get stuck in the sheets because of how fast I am. I fall on the floor and get free and run down the stairs. But down the stairs there is no Samantha. Not in the kitchen or the downstairs bedroom or anywhere. The loudness has moved to the outside. And then I hear more loudness and the loudness is calling my name.

"Lucy, Lucy, get up! They took him, they took him!" says the loudness. "He's gone, he's gone."

"Samantha!" I rush outside. Rush is to hurry even if you drop something and step on it and it cuts your foot, you can't slow down and you must keep rushing.

And what is outside is Samantha and Mister and the truck. The door to the truck is open. Samantha is outside the truck. She fights the open door like you fight a spiderweb you walked into. Mister is trying to make her small and fold her inside but she grabs the outside of the truck so that she can stay on the outside and not be on the inside.

Because what will happen when she is on the inside is Mister will take her away. I know because that is what people do when they put you in cars you don't want to be in. They take you to places you don't want to be and away from the people you don't want to ever leave.

"Lucy, Lucy, my baby is gone!"

Samantha turns to run to me. But Mister holds on and makes her too heavy to move. So I run to her. There are stones in between my toes but the hurting makes me faster. We put our arms around each other. We become two circles that don't have any beginnings or ends. Inside our circles she can be safe as the inside of the eggs.

"He's gone!" Samantha screams, and the screaming breaks open the inside of my ears. Now anything can get inside my brain.

"Lucy, get back inside," Mister says. He pulls Samantha away. I keep my circle strong.

"He's gone! He's gone! They took him."

"Who took him?" I say.

"He was gone when I woke up. Missus broke into my room. I was waiting for you, I couldn't leave without you. And I started looking for him and then Mister dragged me out here and it doesn't matter what I promised them, I won't go without him!"

"Who took him?"

"They did something to their daughter, Lucy, to Stella. I found this letter, they did something horrible to her, they've tried to hide it all these years."

"Stella? Missus used to be her mother."

"Exactly, but she died, and it was their fault!"

"Samantha, enough!" yells Mister. He lets go of Samantha so that he can grab me. My circle around Samantha is broken but I won't go back inside. Mister starts pulling me toward the house but he forgets how strong I am underneath my clothes and so I don't move. I am strong and still as the river frozen in winter.

"The baby's not safe, you have to go get him, Lucy, you have to get him."

"I will!"

"You have to bring him home to me."

"I will, Samantha, I will!"

"You have to go get him! Go now!" Samantha says.

Mister pulls and pulls me but I am making myself heavy digging my feet into the ground. Mister drags me by my arm, which is fighting to stay attached to the rest of my body. It wants to stay with the rest of me but Mister is trying to pull it away.

Samantha runs to me and we hold on to each other the same as if the wind was blowing us over and we were the only strong thing you could hold on to to stop from being blown away. Her hair smells the same but with the most sadness I have ever smelled on her. "Mister's taking me home but I can't go, I can't go without him."

"Don't go, Samantha. Don't go, you can't go without him."

"You have to find him, promise me. Promise me, Lucy. Find him and bring him home to me. You know where I live, right? Lizbeth showed you?"

"I do, I do, I do. I promise. I do."

Mister lets go of my arm. He throws Samantha over his shoulder. She screams, "Nooooooooooo."

The scream makes you become small. Then become smaller than that. Smaller than that. Smaller than that. Smaller than that. And hide where you can never be seen again. Because the thing that makes her scream is going to come and make you scream like she is screaming. Hurt you until you scream like her.

But I won't become small. I will stay big, big as me, for Samantha.

"It's time for you to go home, Samantha," says Mister. "There's no reason for you to be here anymore."

"I looked everywhere! Where did you take him?"

"You made us a promise, Samantha, and you have to keep it. We found out you weren't planning on keeping your promise. But that isn't right. We're helping you to keep your promise to us. It's what is right. We are doing what is right."

Samantha would always keep a promise. I know because she has always done all the things she said she would do. So that means Mister is wrong. Wrong that Samantha didn't want to do her promise. So why does Samantha have to go?

"You'll do something to him! Like you did something to Stella. I know all about what happened. I'm going to tell everybody, everyone is going to know what you did."

"We did nothing but love her too much," says Mister. "We gave her everything we had. She wasn't willing to follow His plan."

Mister holds Samantha tight and he folds her into smallness and puts her in the truck and the door closes.

"Samantha!" I rush to open the truck door so she can get out. But already Mister is in the truck on the other side. The truck comes alive and is driving away with the dust chasing Samantha trying to bring her back.

Dust, please, dust, bring her back! I beg.

And the dust listens. Because the truck door opens and Samantha falls out. She tries to run but she trips. She falls onto the dirt. The trucks stops. She stands up again. Her face is covered in dust.

I run to her. I run harder than to save myself from something chasing me. I run harder than to save myself from something that would take my life for itself. Mister is fighting to get her back in the truck. She is fighting to stay out of it and I am almost there, almost there, almost there, but he gets her inside and the truck goes faster and faster and faster and then I am not almost there. I am not almost anywhere. I am almost nowhere. Not here and not there.

Mister, Samantha would never not do a promise. I swear. Swear is the opposite of a lie, but even stronger. She would never not do a promise, so bring her back, bring her back, please bring her back.

LUCY

We wait until the night. Jennifer says that dark is the best time to escape from the people that don't want you to leave.

Walk along the river, Jennifer tells us. If we follow the river, we'll end up at the bridge that goes through town.

The baby is at the bridge?

No, but that way we'll be in town and can find the church and Rodger Marvin can tell us what was in Samantha's book. He promised he would help us the next time he sees us.

I've never walked to town before.

Me neither. But I know the river will get us there.

How do you know?

Because that's how bridges work.

They bring you to town?

Yup.

You can follow the river even in the dark. Because there are stones that you can feel with your foot and there is the sound which is the water and you can follow that too. And the moon shines light against the rocks and against the water. That is not the same as having morning light but also it is not the same as having only darkness.

Jennifer doesn't say anything. I know she is not sleeping because I feel her thoughts against my leg. They aren't the thoughts of someone sleeping which are called dreams. She is having awake thoughts that she isn't saying. Maybe they are about where we could find Baby and how we could bring him back to Samantha. I am glad maybe those are the thoughts she is having because the thoughts that I am having are about following the river to the bridge.

So Jennifer can have her thoughts and I can have mine.

Then we are at the bridge which lives above the water. Sunlight is melting the darkness at the places where the sky touches the earth. We climb up from the river to the bridge and I look down at the water and the rocks, and when I look down I know that Jennifer is right. In the darkness is the best place to hide.

Look, Lucy, there's the church.

I don't see it.

You can only see the steeple, that's the highest part of it, like a tower, do you see it?

Yes.

That's where we're going, says Jennifer. Rodger Marvin will tell us what was in Samantha's book, and then we will know where to look for the baby. The things Samantha wrote will lead us to the baby.

It takes too long even though we can see where we are going. Each step should take us closer but the steeple stays the same farness away and doesn't get any bigger which is what happens when things get closer. But the houses and the trees and the signs all get bigger and bigger until they disappear because they are behind us and the new houses and trees and signs all get bigger and bigger until we pass them too.

I do not like watching the steeple stay the same when everything else is getting bigger so I just watch the ground and I watch the cracks in the ground get closer and closer. I say, I am almost there, crack, I am almost there to you, until I am on top of it and

until it disappears because it is behind us and then I say to another crack, I am almost there, crack, I am almost there to you,
until Jennifer says stop.

And that is because we are here. We are there. We are at the
steeple but it is hard to see it anymore because it is so high and so
big and getting swallowed in the place it touches the sky. And that
is because we are at the church.

Rodger Marvin is outside putting water on the plants, which is
what you do when you want them to stay alive and grow. I am not
close to him yet. But I know what I need to say and my knowing
carries the words across the far-ness.

"Rodger Marvin, tell me what was in Samantha's book."

"Lucy! Goodness gracious! What are you doing here?"

"To know what was in Samantha's book."

"How on earth did you get here?"

"Followed the river."

"That's a mighty long ways to travel by yourself. Do Mister and
Missus know where you are?"

Say yes, Jennifer says.

"Yes."

"Mmmmm, are you absolutely sure about that?"

Say yes.

"Yes."

Now tell him why we're here.

So I say, "Now is the next time. Now is next time, so tell me
what was in Samantha's book. I need to know."

"There was something very important inside that book that I
needed to know," says Rodger Marvin. "It was a mighty brave and
good thing you did by showing me that book. You know that, don't
you?"

"I know it was a good thing. And now I need to know all the
thoughts Samantha had in the book and you said next time."

And this is next time, says Jennifer.

"And this is next time."

"Dear child, let me tell you."

"Tell me."

Jennifer holds her breath. She wants to hear only Rodger Marvin telling us the inside of the book and not the sound of her breathing. But she cannot stop the sound of her heart which beats loud and fast and strong.

Then Rodger Marvin says, "The book said how happy Samantha was following the Lord's plan for her. And from here on out she is devoted to glorifying Him with her life."

"No. The other parts. About where to look to find Allen. That is what you were going to tell me next time."

"Samantha and the father both feel secure at the place they are in their lives because they have given themselves up to the Lord's will and they are no longer trying to fight it. That's where they are, Lucy."

But where should we look for him? says Jennifer. Where should we *look*?

"But where should I *look*?"

"You should look to the Lord. Which means you've come to the right place. Come with me, Lucy, let's go inside."

We go inside the church. Inside the church is where next time is and where Rodger Marvin will tell me where to look. Inside means I've come to the right place.

Rodger Marvin gets down on the ground like when you do weeding but there is no dirt and no plants on the church floor.

"Join me," he says.

Tell us where to look, says Jennifer. We need to know what was in the book.

"I need to know what was in the book."

"Shhh . . . let us pray."

Now. We need to know now.

"But I need to know. Now."

"Quiet, dear child, let us pray."

In the quiet there are lots of sounds.

I hear the sound of eggs touching each other in my skirt, their shells touch and make a sound I can hear and their insides touch and make a sound that only they can hear.

I hear the sound of Samantha touching my hair. That is a sound like wind through the wheat.

Hey, says Jennifer, you're supposed to be praying. Pray that Rodger Marvin will tell us what's in Samantha's book.

I listen to myself but I do not hear any prayers.

I hear the sound of Samantha's pencil writing in her book. It is the sounds of the chickens' toes when you reach under them for the eggs.

I hear the sound of Mum mum's key opening the door to come in. That is the sound of your heart jumping up and down, up to your throat, down in your guts. That is the sound of your feet running across the floor and the sound of your arms through the air and wrapping around Mum mum. That is the sound of a cup of warmth that has spilled from your heart all over your whole inside body.

Prayers, says Jennifer. Focus.

I listen careful, careful to the whispers floating inside the quiet. Maybe some of the whispers are the prayers left behind by the other people. Deep, deep, deep, I breathe in the dust and the air and the quiet. All the secrets that were inside the whispers, now they are inside me.

But there are no prayers. There is only quiet, real quiet this time, real quiet and the sound the dust makes when it lands on all the inside parts of the church.

Rodger Marvin stands up. He gets the dust off his knees and so do I. He lifts his arms to the sky and so do I except there is no sky.

Now we are standing so it is time for me to say, "Rodger, now it is the next time. And it is after the praying. So tell me please. I need to find the baby for Samantha and her book has secrets which are answers to questions about how to find the baby."

Good, says Jennifer. Well said.

"Lucy, Lucy, Lucy my dear," says Rodger Marvin.

"Yes, that is me. The person you will tell."

"Your love for your friend is a beautiful thing. Beautiful to see, born from His love for us. I admire that in you, I truly do. But let it suffice to say that the baby is safe."

"Baby is not safe without the mother."

"He is safe. Safe enough. Uhhh . . ." Rodger Marvin stops talking before his words were done coming out. Rodger Marvin always lets all his words come out to find the right person's ears.

"The baby is safer. Safer than he would be being raised by a troubled, unmarried young girl. Do you understand?"

No, says Jennifer. How does he even know that? Ask him how he knows.

"How do you know?"

"It's not an easy situation. But I, we all do our best to see that these young souls have the best chance possible to grow and love in the name of the Lord and live a life that glorifies Him, despite the challenges and adversity they face."

"But where should I look?"

"You don't need to look anywhere, dear. Samantha's book said that she knows, because she loves her baby so very, very much, that the best possible place for her baby isn't with her."

The book didn't say that, says Jennifer. Samantha wants the baby with her. Only with her!

"The book didn't say that. Samantha wants the baby with her. Only with her!"

"Lucy, I know it's hard to understand, but Samantha knew the best place for her baby wasn't with her."

That's a lie! cries Jennifer.

"That's a lie!" I cry, but inside I don't know why Rodger Marvin would lie because the Lord hates lying and Rodger Marvin loves the Lord more than anyone in the whole world.

"It's the truth. Lucy, I'm sorry. It doesn't mean Samantha is a bad person. People are faced with decisions that aren't always easy. I know Samantha thought a lot about it, and even though she was confused after its birth, I had personally counseled Samantha and knew her wishes. She knew from the beginning she couldn't offer—"

But before Rodger Marvin is done, Jennifer yells, Stop! Stop listening! He is lying to us, Lucy!

But why would Rodger Marvin lie?

I don't know, says Jennifer, but let's get out of here.

And then I run out of the church. I run like if something was chasing me that wanted my life for itself so it could grow from it and leave me with nothing like an orange when you suck all the juice out.

I am running because Rodger Marvin is telling lies and lies are things you must not ever tell. I am running because I have to find the baby all by myself. It is the running that is teaching me how I am going to do it. Rodger Marvin throws the words at me from behind. The words he throws are *Come*, and *back*, and *Lucy*, and *Please*, and *I know it's hard to understand*, and *I will explain more*, and *Don't run off*, and *It's not safe*. And all those words, they get underneath my feet and underneath my arms and lift me up up up higher. And even though I do not know all the words, all the words know how to help me to get away.

I don't remember where the fence is.

Jennifer doesn't tell me where the fence is.

But when I run there is only one way my feet will go and that way is to the fence. And we run and run and Jennifer holds tight to the pocket and makes herself as light as she can like an eyelash that fell on your cheek and you didn't even know. And how light she is becomes how fast I go.

Then there it is. I stand close to the fence. There is no way to get to the other side which is where we need to be. There is nobody to give me a boost and a boost is how you get over a fence that is too high to get over alone.

Try to get over, Jennifer says. We'll start back at Allen's. First we'll find him and he will help us.

But I need a boost.

Just try.

But a boost is the only way to get over a fence.

Just try.

How?

Give yourself a boost.

A boost is not something you can give yourself.

Well, try! Find a way to pull yourself up.

I put my hands on the fence but there is nowhere on the fence for them to fit. I try to lift my body like if I was falling but the opposite, falling up into the air. Except I am too heavy to fall into the air so I stay where I am, hard and heavy on the ground.

I hear loudness. It is Rodger Marvin yelling, *Please come back, dear child, you could be hurt*, and the sound of the dirt flying when the words crash on the ground. I look behind me and he is running toward us. Not fast like me because he is too round but I know if we stay here on this side and don't get over even if he runs not fast like me, we will still be here when he gets here. When he gets here, I know we will be farther away from where the baby is than we have ever been.

So I put my hands on the fence again and my hands look look for something to grab, something to pull, something to lift me up like the opposite of falling. But there is only nothing, only the little bits of the wood that get stuck inside my hands which are called splinters and when I look look look with my hands the splinters inside yell and scream because of the way it hurts but I don't stop. I keep looking. The way I keep looking is pick a new place to look on the fence and a new place to look on the fence. But there is no way to lift me up.

Hurry up! yells Jennifer.

So I put my hand as high as it can go on the fence and my finger gets stuck in a hole. Getting stuck in that hole is what I need to pull myself up. It is a boost without another person. I use my one finger stuck in the hole to lift the whole rest of my body and the whole of Jennifer in my pocket. I feel that this is the most heavy my body has ever been and it is because of how hard it is, hard like difficult, what I am doing. My one finger pulls up my and Jennifer's whole bodies. My feet walk up the fence like the world tipping over and walking straight up into the air to where the Lord lives.

Then I put one leg to the other side of the fence. The top of the fence grabs on to my skin under my dress and tries to stop me, tries to get me to stay on the wrong side. The Rodger Marvin side and the farm-where-there-is-no-baby-anymore-because-the-baby-is-gone side. But I won't let the fence keep me on the wrong side. Because skin ripping isn't something that will last forever, even though the hurting tries to tell you it will. Then I say to my other leg, Come to the other side, other leg, come to the other side. And my other leg listens.

That means we fall. Jennifer holds on with her mouth and her feet. It is the hardest she has ever held on to anything, even her shell when she was still inside of it. All of me and all of Jennifer, we fall and fall and fall and now we are on the ground, which makes everything hurt. Jennifer is mashed up in my pocket so I take her out and try to fluff her up and use the wet of my tongue to clean off a little of her blood but she is all right.

I'm all right, she says. Ouch. But I'm all right.

Me too, I say. Ouch.

We are both all right. Because we are on the right side now. The good side. The baby side. The Samantha side. There are no lies on this side. This side has only promises, which are the truth.

SAMANTHA

——

I've told myself many times that I would rather die than come back here to my parents' home. But that was before he came along and changed everything. Now so many things are worse than dying that dying couldn't give me any peace. Like him being alone out there. I would never pretend to love someone only to turn around and desert him when he became inconvenient. I know how bad that hurts, thanks to my parents. So I will stay here until Lucy brings him back to me.

My parents call me to dinner, as if nothing's changed and six o'clock still means dinnertime, no matter what. When I don't join them at the dinner table, my mother brings a plate of food to my bed, as if it were the only distance from my bed to the table that was making eating an impossibility. I turn away from the food, lie on my side, and look around the room. I recognize everything, but only vaguely, as if this room were a place I visited once or twice, not slept in for fourteen years. Because none of the things in here are mine anymore. To own a thing you have to say to yourself, That's mine. Otherwise there's no difference between you, the thing, and anything else in the world. And I'll never say that about any of this crap. In the whole world there is only one thing that is mine.

I know now what I need to do. I need to get rid of all this teen-age junk. If I have all this stupid teenage junk lying around, he'll see it and think I'm still a stupid teenager, not strong enough to be his mother. He'll remember how I cursed him when he was still inside me.

He'll remember the fence.

When Lucy brings him, they'll see right away that I was waiting just for them. I won't have to pack anything or decide what to bring and what to leave or ask them to carry anything. There won't be anything left to keep me here, nothing to choose between, nothing to weigh us down.

He'll see it is only him. I only have eyes to look into his. I only have ears to hear him cry. I only have arms to hold him tight. He'll have to forgive me when he sees I've gotten rid of everything else. To show he's all that matters, the only thing I want to keep.

LUCY

The other side of the fence looks like the other side of the fence. That is what it looked like before. All the houses I have seen because I have been here before. Even though I didn't think about them after I left them, when I see them now I know I have been here before. And that is called remember.

Jennifer says, This is the way to Allen's house, this way, that way, but I say to her, I know. I know because I remember.

Well, good for you, says Jennifer.

I use the bucket and I undo the latch, and Jennifer does not even have to tell me.

Outside there is the little house where Yellow Eye Dog lives and I go inside to see him. I do not have to knock on his door and wait for him to say, You can come in, because I know he has been waiting for me. Then me and Yellow Eye Dog we are together inside the little house. It is the smell of the world next to a dog. He is lying with his head on his paws. He lifts his head. His eyes are yellow which is the color of the sun even though you can't look right at it. Even if you can't see it, it is still the color.

Yellow Eye Dog, I say, there is a girl named Samantha with orange hair. She had a baby but she went missing.

Yellow Eye Dog, have you seen the baby?

Yellow Eye Dog shakes his head.

I listen to the quiet to find my next question.

No, says Jennifer. He hasn't seen the baby.

Yellow Eye Dog, do you know where Allen is?

Then I tell him the reasons I am looking for Allen. I tell him about what a family is. I tell him about what a promise is. So he will know what I am doing is the right and good thing. And once he knows that, then he will help.

Yellow Eye Dog listens and then he waits. While he waits he is thinking. While he thinks me and Jennifer hold our breaths. We are afraid our breathing will blow away the thoughts he is making. When he is done with his thinking Yellow Eye Dog gets up and smashes past us and leaves his house, and me and Jennifer breathe out a heavy breath. We breathe in one more breath of the world next to a dog smell and then we leave the house too.

Yellow Eye Dog waits by the gate. I reach up high and undo the latch. He runs in the middle of the street. He starts off slow and gets fast and faster. We follow him. I do not look at the houses on one side, or the houses on the other side, just at Yellow Eye Dog and his tail waving to me, saying, Follow me. This way. Maybe it looks like chasing but it is not. It is following. That is different because I will let him take me somewhere and never catch him once we get there. I will always let him go the direction that he wants. Sometimes when there is a direction that I want to go, someone will tell me, No, you cannot go that way. But with Yellow Eye Dog, I let him go his direction.

We run to where a street has lots of cars following each other. They make a loud sound like water off of rocks. Then he stops and moves his head around to see what is there. Here the buildings are closer to the sky and there are more people walking fast and looking down. Yellow Eye Dog looks and then goes in a direction and I follow. There is a building and the letters are DEPOT and they glow blue. Yellow Eye Dog and me we do not run anymore. Even though running means to get there fastest. We walk to get close to the building with the letters. I touch his back while we walk.

I have a good feeling about this, Jennifer says. She beats fast against my leg and holds tight to the inside of my pocket like when a baby holds tight to the inside of its mother so it doesn't bounce going down the stairs.

People are standing outside the building that says DEPOT. They stand under the DEPOT sign in blue light like it is their moon. Lots of bags and boxes are all around the people. Some of the people are talking. One of the people is an old lady. She says to an old man, "The bus is already two hours late. There's no way we'll make the shower."

"We're not going to miss the shower. It's not until tomorrow afternoon."

"Well, then I'll be so exhausted at the shower I won't be able to enjoy myself."

"Oh, shush, standing out here isn't exhausting you any."

"I'm telling you it's exhausting me."

"It's your constant complaining. It's exhausting me too."

"And how do we know we're even going to get there by tomorrow? Rob said the bus had to make three repair stops on its route up here."

"I can imagine worse things than missing your niece's shower."

"It took me three weeks to do the lace on that tablecloth. You saw how hard I worked. How can you be so callous?"

But I don't hear the man answering how he can be so callous because there is a voice. Louder than the other sounds.

The voice calls, "Rusty, Rusty."

It is a boy. His face is round and brown hair falls in his eyes which are big, brown mud puddles with rain still dripping on top and when I see them I see the fox drawing. The way I know him is from those eyes because I have seen them before in my mind.

Yellow Eye Dog runs to the boy and the boy gets on the ground to hug and kiss Yellow Eye Dog and Yellow Eye Dog waves his tail high in the air and kisses back the boy and then they both look at us.

Go, says Jennifer. That's him.

That's him, I say.

That's Allen. Go to him. Don't forget now, Lucy. You've come so far.

I've come so far.

All the way from the farm.

Well, that is true. That is where I used to be. On the farm. I was Lucy on the farm and now I am Lucy by the building that says DEPOT in glowing blue letters. The sun is drowning behind the earth. There is a little orange that hasn't gotten all the way down yet. The orange is waiting for me to see it before it finishes its sinking. Orange, that is a color of Samantha's hair. Remember that, so it will always be with you, and whenever you want to think it, it will be there. Waiting for you, like Samantha is waiting for me to find Allen and Baby.

Go, says Jennifer.

Dear Lucy,

The house is so beautiful. It's the house you deserved to grow up in. I positively cannot wait for you to see it. There are bay windows in the living room and two ovens in the kitchen! Two ovens! I can roast a chicken and bake a cake at the same time. And why shouldn't I? I've become quite the cook. The backyard is full of perfectly pruned rosebushes and we have a white-and-glass garden table and chairs. Your room has a purple canopy bed! I have a little room just for my vanity. A proper dressing room. Like a movie star. Can you imagine?

It's not quite ready yet though. Monte says soon. It's just that we have to get things just so. We've spent so long, we don't want to stop until it's just perfect. We wouldn't want to jump the gun and then regret we didn't get something just right. That way, when you come, you'll fit right in. Everything will be just so. Nothing will be missing.

But I know you're having such a time out there in the country. I saw those kittens when I drove out there. You have always loved animals. You're probably not even ready to come home yet. Watch what happens. I bet I drive all the way out there to get you and then you beg me to let you stay. Am I right? After all, what child would rather spend time with her silly old mother than have a big grown-up adventure?

Love,

Mum mum

LUCY

"Rusty, how did you get out?" Allen asks Yellow Eye Dog. "I'm about to catch the bus! I told you that before I left, boy. Didn't you understand? I don't have time to get you all the way home, boy!"

Go, says Jennifer.

I'm here.

Go, says Jennifer. Closer.

"You've got me in a pickle, Rusty. I've been waiting for this bus for hours, and now it's supposed to get here any minute and the army doesn't allow people to have pets there. I asked them when I signed up. You know I'd take you if I could, right, boy?"

Yellow Eye Dog looks at me. Inside my pocket Jennifer looks at me.

Go, she says. This is it. He is the family so we can trust him. He will help us find the baby. Someone is finally going to help us.

"You are Allen," I say. I stand and he is down by Yellow Eye Dog and I am taller like a tree if they were cooling off in my shadow.

"That's right." He brings his eyes up to me. They are puddles. I felt their wetness when Samantha told me how much he loves her. "How'd you know that?"

"I am Lucy."

"Hey, there." Allen stands up and puts out his hand. "You southbound as well?"

"No. I am Lucy on the farm."

Allen laughs and puts his hand in his hair. On his face there are little dots like sand landed there and stuck in a nice way. In a way you would never want to brush off. "Except now. Now you're Lucy at the bus stop."

"Yes, but I am also Lucy on the farm."

"Well, Lucy on the farm, I am southbound. Except I'm in somewhat of a situation seeing as somehow my dog escaped from the backyard and I don't have the time to get him back inside before I'm scheduled to leave."

"You can't leave."

"Not without doing something about this dog first, I can't."

"You can't leave."

But what are the words? I only have some of them. Inside I am searching for the rest of them, but what I am finding is none of them. When I don't have the words to say something one side of my body decides to go one way to find them and the other side decides to go the other. Then there is none of me in the middle anymore. And the middle is where your heart lives and where your words come from.

Go on, says Jennifer. You can do it.

But what are the words?

You know them.

I do?

Course you do.

Maybe some of them. Maybe I know some of them.

Okay, so use those.

Some of the words are these.

Samantha. She had a baby inside of her and the baby was part her and part you. You made it together because it was a love that came out of the blue. That makes you the father. Then the baby came to live in the world with its mother and father but the father wasn't there. Samantha didn't know where you were and you didn't know where Samantha was. That is because they were trying to keep you apart but I am trying to put you together.

Then it was morning and Samantha couldn't find her baby. Mister dragged Samantha away. He put her in the truck which was away from her baby. Even though she would never leave without the baby. And that was the day I made her a promise, and mustn't you ever, ever go back on a promise. I promised I would find Baby and bring him back to her.

So now we need to find where Baby went and bring it back to Samantha and you will live together in a special place, a family place.

Those are some of the words. Some of the words are even right. But I can't say any of them. There is a hole in my throat and they are all tripping and falling down the hole back to where they came from and getting lost again inside my guts.

"I'm going inside to see if Rob can call my mom about picking up Rusty." Allen puts his hand on Yellow Eye Dog's neck. "See you around, Lucy on the farm."

"Allen." He is moving with Yellow Eye Dog toward the inside of the depot building. Now is the time for those words.

Say something! says Jennifer.

"Say something," I say.

No, say something to keep him here!

What do I say?

Say what you were going to say.

"What you were going to say," I say.

No, Jennifer says. Say what you were just going to say. About Samantha and the baby.

I can't. The words keep tripping down my throat.

Well, you have to say something, otherwise he's going to leave! Say—say you have something for him. Jennifer is getting hotter against my leg like she is sucking up all the hotness from my insides. Say, I have something for you.

"Allen."

He turns.

"I have something for you."

The skin above his eyes folds up. He doesn't say anything.

"I have something for you," I say again.

"Oh, yeah, what's that?" His smile is like a door opening to somewhere you have always wanted to be, but didn't know how to get to.

Say that you have a letter.

But that's a lie. I don't have a letter.

Just say it.

But . . .

It's not a lie. Just say it, Jennifer says, and her heartbeats take up her whole body. It pounds the words inside my brain and I say it.

"A letter," I say.

"What's that?" His smile is still unlocked.

"A letter."

"How come?"

"I just have it for you."

"What do you mean? A letter from who?"

From Samantha, says Jennnifer.

"From Samantha."

"Wait, you know Samanatha?" His smile slams shut. His words have frozen into small, hard stones. "How's that?"

"Because of being on the farm."

"That's the farm that you were talking about?"

"The farm with Mister and Missus."

"Aren't they supposed to keep you locked up there?"

"No. They aren't supposed to keep you locked up there. But you aren't ever to leave the farm or someone wouldn't know where to find you if they were looking for you."

"Then what are you doing here?"

A letter, you came to give him a letter, says Jennifer. From her.

"I came to give you the letter. From her."

"What does she want with me?"

"She wants to love the baby together. That is why you made it."

"You're sorely mistaken."

That means he thinks you're wrong, Jennifer says. But you're not.

"I'm not wrong."

"You are wrong," Allen says. "Look, for a while I did think it was mine. I used to go around saying to everyone that I knew it was mine. For months she told me I wasn't the father and really it was someone else, some navy guy passing through, is what she said. I didn't believe her. But I believe her now. I'm officially convinced."

"No. I know what wrong means and I know I am not that." I use my head back and forth to show that he is wrong and not me. Maybe now I have the right words to tell him and make him believe. "Samantha told me. You are the father of the baby."

"Nope."

"Yes. You are. And we need to bring her back the baby. I promised her."

"What are you talking about? She doesn't want the baby."

"Yes! Yes! She needs the baby back. It was the morning and she couldn't find it and I promised I would find it."

"The baby got taken?"

"Yes."

"By who? Thieves in the night?"

"Yes."

"Look, this is what she wanted all along. Rid of us both."

"And then we will need to find her house that she will live in since she doesn't live on the farm anymore."

"And she wants a house to live in?"

"Yes. After she has the baby she can't live on the farm anymore so she needs a house to live in where she belongs after her on-the-farm life."

"So that's what's in that letter?"

"Yes. That's what's in it." I have done it. I have said it all. Saying it all spreads warm blood to every corner of me. But why doesn't Allen's smile come back?

"How 'bout you give the letter back to her so she won't have to waste her time having to write it again when she needs to ask someone else to build her a house, like the navy guy."

You can't give it back, says Jennifer. Say, I can't give it back.

"I can't give it back."

"Sure you can."

"But it's for you."

"Uh-uh. I'm going to go take care of my dog now, I've wasted enough time dealing with Samantha and her stupid problems."

Allen goes inside with Yellow Eye Dog. I stand outside. The orange has drowned all the way behind the world but the tall lights have come on so I know it is night even though it is not the same night as night on the farm. There are no tall lights that come on at the farm, only the moonlight and the eggs when they shine.

Follow him! Jennifer says. What are you waiting for?

Go inside?

Yes, yes, yes, Jennifer says. She jumps to pound her words inside me faster.

The door is made of glass and it sings a little song for me when I open it. Inside Allen is talking to a man who is holding Yellow Eye Dog by his neck. I do not like it inside the building that says DEPOT. I do not know why any of the things that are inside of it are inside of it. Lots of things are on the wall with letters and numbers and lots of chairs are facing to nowhere. But there are no tables. Some people are in the chairs, looking through the windows like they are something that has been left behind and are waiting to be found.

"I can't give it back," I say to the boy that is Allen. I cannot take back the words I have said to Allen for Samantha. They are his words now.

"Look, Samantha never wanted me to be a father to her baby. So, forget it. My mom doesn't want me to have anything to do with her anymore, the way she embarrassed our family, and neither do I, especially when she's, she's out, back living here in town. Let's just forget the whole mess."

"I can't give it back."

"Hide it under a rock and forget where you left it."

"But I will never forget. Because I made a promise and what a promise is, is something you can never forget until you've done it."

"Well, if she needs more than you can offer, she'll have to track down the daddy. Who I suppose is on the high seas somewhere. As for me, my past is behind me and my future is in front of me and I'm leaving any minute. Right, Rob?"

"Any minute," the depot man says. There are rocks rolling around the bottom of his throat. "Don't worry about Rusty, I'll get him back to your mom's place."

"Can you really?"

"Don't worry about it."

"Thanks a bunch, Rob."

"Isn't nothing, kid. Good luck out there."

I know *any minute*. *Any minute* means that Allen is leaving. *Any minute* means he is leaving the past behind him and the future is what is in front of him and that he will not read Samantha's letter because that's not in the future.

"That means you are leaving," I say. I feel my words hiding in the cracks of my insides. My mind tries to drag them out but they are putting their claws deep in my insides which are pink and soft and sticking in there which is making me bleed in the places they are holding on. "*Any minute*. That means you are leaving."

"Get rid of that thing. Forget about her. That's what she'll do to you. That's a promise."

"She'll never forget about me."

"Oh, yeah?"

"Yes."

"Then good for the two of you."

The man nods and holds Yellow Eye Dog on his neck. Allen kisses Yellow Eye Dog and goes outside. "I'll miss you, Rusty. Be a good boy, Rusty."

Read him the letter, Jennifer says.

There is no letter, I say.

We'll read him the letter.

But there is no letter.

Repeat what I say, says Jennifer. Now go, follow him.

Again I follow him. Back outside. We will try to read the letter that I do not have before any minute comes.

SAMANTHA

Stella needed to save her baby, but Stella couldn't wait. Because she was all alone in the world. I have Lucy, so I can wait. I have to wait. Waiting is okay. I waited for him to come because I thought I wanted to get rid of him, and waiting for him to come was the only way to do that. So I know I can wait for him to come back, even though it feels as if I can't.

Stella had an idea. The last idea she would ever have, and she made it happen. She made sure of it. And I've got an idea too, for while I'm waiting. I'm gonna have a garage sale. I will get rid of my junk and get some money for our new lives, when Lucy gets here.

My mom's even gonna help me, to make sure it's a good one.

My mom cuts little tags out of brown paper bags. She's better at making straight lines with the scissors. And now I'm going around my room, making up the prices of everything and telling my mom what to write on the tags. Her printing is neater than mine. She smiles at me, she seems happy to help me. When she smiles, I wonder for a second if I could tell her what the garage sale is for. But I know I can't tell her. Lucy's the only one I can trust. She's the only one I can count on. But it would be nice to tell someone that I haven't forgotten about him, that all I think about is him.

So I tell Stella about it. She understands. And she's proud of me.

LUCY

My Dear Darling Allen, Jennifer says.

It feels like years since we last spoke. And though it may seem as if I have ignored your attempts to reach me in the past, I want you to know that that wasn't the case, but instead, that my situation at the farm was much like that of a captive and that it was nearly impossible and incredibly dangerous for me to do something as seemingly simple as mail a letter, and that for the sake of my baby alone, for my own life matters very little to me, I had to restrain myself from fleeing to be reunited with you, my one true love. That's why I never wrote you and couldn't talk to you those times at church. I was afraid of being punished and that the baby would be hurt. It's all I've been thinking about this whole time, I swear, Allen, you and the baby, and me, together. It's all I've ever really wanted, really. I've really learned a lot, really, being on the farm has taught me a lot and now I see things so clearly. I know you'll believe me because you always knew it was ours. So please help Lucy find our baby, who was taken from me last night. From, Samantha.

"My Dear Darling Allen," I say.

"It feels like years since we last spoke. And though it may seem as if I have ignored your attempts to reach me in the past, I want you to know that that wasn't the case, but instead, that my situation at the farm was much like that of a captive and that it was nearly impossible and incredibly dangerous for me to do something as seemingly simple as mail a letter, and that for the sake of my baby alone, for my own life matters very little to me, I had to restrain myself from fleeing to be reunited with you, my one true love. That's why I never wrote you and couldn't talk to you those times at church. I was afraid of being punished and that the baby would be hurt. It's all I've been thinking about this whole time, I swear, Allen, you and the baby, and me, together. It's all I've ever really wanted, really. I've really learned a lot, really, being on the farm has taught me a lot and now I see things so clearly. I know you'll believe me because you always knew it was ours. So please help Lucy find our baby, who was taken from me last night. From, Samantha."

"When I saw her at church, she wouldn't even look me in the eye," Allen says. "That's not how you act around a person you're calling your one true love."

A bus which is for people going away drives up breathing so hard it sounds like it might die from not getting enough air. Its doors open and it gives a big sigh. It is a tired bus that wants to stay and rest but it knows it has to go and take Allen with it.

"I've waited for her afterwards and she hid from me. Then when she saw I was still outside, she ran back inside the church and hid in the ladies' room. She watched through a crack in the door until she saw me leave. I know. I could see her shoes."

Allen gets onto the first step but turns and says more.

"I wrote her all the time. My mother made me. She wanted us to raise the kid. But Samantha had other plans. Who knows why I wasn't good enough for her. Who knows why she'd rather give it away and be alone. Who knows how she can live with herself. But I don't care to figure it out anymore. I wrote her all the time, she didn't answer me once."

This is the answer, I try to say, but the words aren't there. This is the answer. I want to say, This is the answer you never got. Now you can get it. Just reach out your arm and take it.

But he doesn't take it. He keeps his arms to himself.

"I woulda done right by her. I coulda given them a good life. She came from a decent family. They raised her good, you know, and now she hasn't got anything. You can't even feel sorry for her because she did it to herself because she's so sure that nothing's ever good enough for her."

"Hey, Romeo, let's go," the man in the bus says. "This trip's already taken long enough."

"But this is your answer," I say.

I reach my arm as long as it can go so he can take all the things I just said, so we can find her the baby and bring her the baby and they can be together from the beginning, from the out of the blue and then every day after it. So Samantha won't be alone. But Allen moves another step up and the doors close and Allen is swallowed up inside and the bus breathes loud and heavy as it rolls away and inside my mouth and heart and mind I am holding on to all the words he didn't take.

LUCY

Now what? Jennifer says.

That means, what are we supposed to do now? But I don't know the answer so I ask the world to see if anyone else knows.

"Now what?"

Nobody hears. So I say it louder to reach further.

"Now what?"

But everyone is gone. So it is a question for no one. It is a no-one question.

Jennifer says she has to think and she goes quiet. The outside goes quiet too. I sit on a bench and try to hear my thoughts through the quiet. I didn't have enough words to make Allen help me find the baby. That is the only thought that I can hear. Before, I had a thought that maybe I did have enough words. But now I know for sure I didn't have enough words.

That is the only thought I can hear. Over and over.

Then it is later. The blue DEPOT light turns out. There is an inside light inside the building depot. Now it turns off. There is more darkness than there was before. Jennifer and me, we sit and try to have thoughts in the dark and in the quiet. The door opens and the man that was inside comes out. He is holding Yellow Eye Dog on the neck.

"Next bus doesn't leave until tomorrow morning," he says.

"Now what?" I say.

"Now nothing. Come back in the morning."

"I won't come back in the morning. Because Allen already left."

"Then leave and don't come back. But don't sit out here all night."

The man and Yellow Eye Dog walk to the street.

Ask him about the baby, says Jennifer. Maybe he's seen the baby. He sees a lot of people coming and going.

"Have you seen the baby?" I ask the man.

"What's it look like?"

"Small." I think of what else it looks like. "And pink."

"Lemme think," the man says. "Nope. Haven't seen it."

Ask if they are going back to Allen's house, Jennifer says. Say, are you going to Allen's house?

"Are you going to Allen's house?"

"I've got to bring his dog back."

Follow him, Jennifer says. Remember the old lady? Maybe she knows where the baby is.

I get up and walk behind the man. He doesn't say anything and neither do I and neither does Jennifer and neither does Yellow Eye Dog. The thick dark and the thick quiet make the world feel like something that happens on the inside of you, not the outside. We walk and then go across a street to another street and do it again and then again and every time it gets darker and darker. Then we get back to the houses and the trees and the grass and there are lights in the houses but they only make the outside look darker.

The man goes to a house that is Allen's house. He goes to the gate and shakes it and it stays closed. Yellow Eye Dog barks at the gate.

"How did you get out if the gate was locked?"

Don't say anything, Jennifer says.

I don't say anything.

"Give me a hand, will you?"

I go and put out my hand and the man shakes his head.

"I'll lift you over and you open the latch."

The man puts his arms around my legs. It is like a hug around my legs but so tight that I can't stand. It turns my legs into a feeling like when you step on a beetle and feel it smash. Then he lifts me off the ground and I smash against the gate and bend around like a thread trying to go into a needle. Jennifer beats very hot against my leg. She is a little scared but she doesn't say anything. I feel the latch and move it up and the gate goes wide-open and we fall against it into the yard. Yellow Eye Dog looks at me. I tell him, Thank you. I tell him, Even though Allen won't be the family and even though the baby is still gone, you were still helping. Then I say good-bye and Yellow Eye Dog runs in.

The man puts me down and closes the gate and walks to the street.

"First bus eight o'clock tomorrow morning," he calls.

Now I have an idea. Now is time to knock. Now is time to ask the old lady if she has seen the baby. We had a sameness about us and it means she knows where to find the baby.

My knock is loud. My knock is strong.

But nobody comes. And then nobody comes.

Appears nobody's home, says Jennifer. Let's go.

I knock louder. I knock stronger.

But nobody still comes.

I knock harder, harder, harder.

Enough, already, says Jennifer. You're just tiring yourself out for nothing. Now go to the fence, it's a good vantage point.

We go up the hill and across the ditch with mud and sticks. Here there is nothing else but the fence. We are alone with the fence. In my mind though, I can be with Mum mum. She puts her arms on my shoulders and looks hard at my face because she wants to never forget any part of it. I look at her face hard too but already will never forget any part of it. "Be good, my dear Lucy," she says to my mind. "Be a good girl for Mum mum."

Every time I close my eyes they weigh more than the time before. I want to go to sleep with Mum mum here inside my mind. She will watch my mind's face while I sleep and keep me safe.

Stop and let me think, Jennifer says.

We stop and let her think.

It is too dark and too quiet. I can't hear Jennifer through the quiet. Her words melt in the air before they get into my ears. I sit with my head on the fence. I pull my arms inside my dress to keep warm. The darkness pulls down on my eyes.

In the darkness, there is Samantha. She was there from her baby's first day, and that is a promise to be there always, but Mister said she didn't do a promise and he was helping her do it. But why was her promise to leave the farm in the truck?

There is Rodger Marvin. He said that Samantha didn't want to be in the same place with Baby. But Samantha told me she would never leave without Baby and that as long as we are together, everything is fine.

There is Allen, he told me about the letters he wrote. He told me he never got an answer, but then I had an answer, so why didn't he want it?

There are Mister and Missus. They had Stella. She used to be their daughter but she left. And that means they know about the love that is only for family. They know that love goes on forever. Then why did Missus stop being the mother?

SAMANTHA

I hang the signs and am bringing out my things to the front steps. My mother follows me while I do it. But she's not much of a help anymore because now she's trying to get me to keep my things. She seems to think I'm the same person I was before. I don't tell her why I won't need any of this stuff. I can't let her get in the way any more than she already is.

"Don't you want this?" She holds up a candle with the wax melted halfway down. "You begged me to buy you this at the country fair, don't you remember?"

"No." I can't remember things that happened to someone else.

"Oh, but honey, don't you want this?" She strokes the top of my jewelry box.

"No." All wearing jewelry does is weigh you down on your way out.

She opens the jewelry box. "But surely you want this necklace. You can't get rid of this necklace. Allen bought it for you. You love this necklace."

"I don't love things anymore." Maybe I could tell her why not. Maybe I could tell her what I do love. But when I needed her help in the first place, she didn't listen to a thing I said.

Finally she drops her campaign to make me keep my old teen-age junk and helps me carry the stuff out to the front steps. Every few minutes she picks something up and looks at it as if it's hard for her to part with it.

When everything is arranged, I sit on the steps and wait. My mom goes inside and brings out a kitchen chair. We sit together and don't say anything. Without looking at me, she reaches over and pats my arm. It's the first time someone has touched me since Mister dragged me into his truck. I stare at the place on my arm where she patted me, as if it left an imprint, as if I were made out of wet sand. Should I pat her back? If I weren't looking at her, I would probably miss her arm completely, swing into the air, into nothing.

What do you know, people actually come and buy the stuff. I try to sell the necklace for ten dollars. It is a nice necklace, even if it doesn't mean anything, even if it doesn't matter. I know it took Allen a while to save all the money. His face was so excited when he gave it to me, as if he were the one about to be given a big surprise.

"Don't be silly," says my mom. "We'll take three."

The girl who wants to buy it only has two.

"Oh, that's fine," says Mom.

I don't argue. It's better not to seem attached to it or my mom might get me to keep it after all. And I need the money.

An old man wants to buy my suitcase but I don't have enough money to make him change.

"Just one second," says my mom. She runs inside and brings out her purse.

I would thank her, but I don't know how. Gratitude hardens into a lump in my throat and stays there.

"Well," says my mom, "I guess now you'll be forced to buy yourself some new clothes! Twist your arm!"

We had a favorite place to buy clothes. My mother is so old compared to the other moms; dresses more like other people's grandmothers. But she let me dress how I wanted. She bought me nice things. She told me I looked pretty in them. She looked like she meant it. When we came home from the store, I always put on my new things to show Dad.

But no, Mother, I am not buying any new clothes. I'm not buy-ing new anything. I'm smarter than that. And the trick is keeping your strength a secret, so people don't suspect, so they don't keep a close eye on you, so you have a chance to get away. Stella never had a chance; they were watching her too closely. They suspected her from too early on, and even from the beginning, it was too late for options. There was only one option left. She had to take it.

"That sounds nice, Mom."

The best trick the devil ever played was convincing the world he didn't exist.

LUCY

I am going to look for Baby. The places I am looking for Baby are by the fence. By this part of the fence and that part of the fence. In the ditch by the fence, under the mud in the ditch. And by the road, and on the other side of the road, and on the other side of the road. And then Jennifer and me, we walk a little further and I look there, and a little further and I look there. And the road and other places, they are the places I look for Baby. The other places I look for Baby are inside here and underneath there. But Baby is not there, and not there, and not there either.

I am going to look for the baby. The way I look for the baby is I call to the baby, Baby, Baby, where are you? I call to the baby in this place and that place, and behind this tree and under this car, and inside this car and by this door and by this window. But the baby doesn't answer here, and doesn't answer there, and not there either.

I am going to look for the baby. The way I look for the baby is to use my hands to feel for the baby. The places I feel are this grass, and this ground, and this glass car window and this tree, and these leaves. But none of them feel like the baby. This doesn't feel like the baby, and neither does that or anything else.

I am going to look for the baby. The way I look for the baby is to say to Jennifer, Wake up, Jennifer, wake up, we have to look for the baby, because Jennifer knows the smart ways to look and find. But Jennifer, she stays asleep and cold and she feels like she is a hard thing, and not the softest thing I have ever felt.

SAMANTHA

I sold all the places a little girl would have thought to put her money: the jewelry box or piggy bank or plastic-beaded purse. But I get an idea, a different kind of idea, not the obvious kind of idea I would have had in the past. It's the kind of new perspective you can only get when your world is turned upside down. I dump all the salt out of the green milk-glass saltshaker, roll up all my money, and put it inside. The top barely screws back on, tearing the edges of the roll. But it feels right that way, just big enough. Tight and safe. Not wasting any space.

While she is setting the table, Mom asks me if I did something with the saltshaker. I don't want to lie. I'm tired of doing that. There are things I have to keep from her, but I know my baby deserves better than an outright liar for a mother.

"Yes," I say. "I took it."

We look at each other, both of us waiting. But Mom doesn't ask why. She doesn't ask to have it back.

"All right then, that's fine," she says.

Mom goes to kitchen and comes back with the whole box of salt. She puts it on the table. She finishes setting the table. The napkins are perfectly folded. The plates are in the center of the place mats. I stare at the box of salt. Why doesn't she ask for the saltshaker back? Why doesn't she ask me why I took it? Why is it fine? Why is everything fine? How is anything fine?

Mom puts down the last plate and smiles weakly at the table, as if it took a great exertion of energy to get it ready for our family's dinner: three plates, three sets of silverware, three water glasses, three faded cloth napkins with perfect edges, the pepper shaker, and the box of salt.

Right now I could tell her that everything's not fine. I could open my mouth and tell her about what they did to Stella. This very second I could tell her about the letter, where she's buried. There's no way they'd let the baby stay on the farm if she knew. It could all be over now. Right now.

Mom adjusts the box of salt and the pepper shaker so they are standing next to each other like a bride and groom in the middle of a wedding cake. She folds her arms over her chest and studies the table.

But if they didn't believe me, they might ship me off somewhere again. They might call Mister and Missus. Mister and Missus might get rid of Lucy. They might take him and disappear altogether. They might do things so bad I never thought they were capable of. I have to make sure I'm here, ready, when Lucy gets here. I know we can do it, just the two of us, Lucy and me. I can't risk trying to ask for their help.

So instead, I laugh along with Mom and Dad as Dad tries to keep too much salt from getting on his casserole. It's not even a pretend laugh, just a waiting laugh.

LUCY

The man wears blue and gold.

The man says, "Where do you live?"

I say, "On the farm."

The man says, "Where is your mother?"

I say, "In the city with Monte."

"You don't live with your mother?"

"Mum mum lives with Monte."

"Who takes care of you?"

I say, "Samantha."

The man says, "Who is Samantha?"

I say, "Everything."

"Whereabouts the city does your mother live?"

"With Monte."

"But you're saying you don't know where exactly that is, am I right?"

"Right." Because that is what you say when someone says, *Right?*

"So how did you come to live on the farm? Was there a school or hospital, or, say, church group that brought you to live there?"

"Mum mum took me. We drove in Monte's car."

"Do you remember anything about his car?"

"Blue, shiny, new, without a top."

"A blue convertible, registered to a Monte," he says. "It's worth a shot. It'll be just a minute. We're trying to find your mother for you." On top of the car lights flash like bright eyes blinking red and blue. We get inside. He knows how to find things. I say to him, "Can you find the baby?"

"What baby?"

"Samantha's baby."

"Let's get you home to your mother. She probably has some answers for you."

"But the baby. It was my promise and I still haven't done it."

"We're almost there. Hope it's the right place. But not to worry, even if it's not, I'll get you home eventually."

SAMANTHA

My mom presses her ear against the door and listens to my breathing. I know she's out there. Every night she's out there, waiting, until she thinks I'm asleep. So I try to make my breathing sound like I'm sleeping, long and rhythmic. In and out. Peaceful. Until I hear the sound of her ear leaving the door. Then I take out my saltshaker and pull out the money. I smooth it out, even though it fights to keep its pig's-tail curl, count it, and roll it back up. Every night I count it, and every night the total is the same, because I never spend any of it. I only count it at night because I don't want my mom asking about it. I don't want her to think it's for anything. I don't want her to think I want anything, want to go anywhere, want to buy anything, want to do anything. I just have to stay here, every day, every minute, waiting for Lucy to get here.

When you make a plan, you have to stick with it. I can't sneak away and go back to the farm to try to find Lucy, because I know if I did, the moment I left would be the exact moment Lucy would finally get here. Stella made a plan and she stuck with it and saved her baby the only way she knew how. What she did was harder than what I have to do. So the waiting feels as if it were killing me, but the waiting is the plan. All I have is the plan. I can't let it make me weak.

I have to be stronger than this feeling that never goes away, that I'm a page whose words all got erased. I have to be stronger than my parents, trying to protect me from everything my whole life and protecting me from nothing. I have to be stronger than wanting to trust them. I have to be stronger than wanting to be somebody's kid again, wanting my mom to know just when to give me a hug, wanting my dad to tell me, Everything will be all right, sweetie, and wanting to be able to believe it. I have to be stronger than how fast my heart is always beating, and how I can't ever fully fall asleep, and how my eyes don't really see right anymore and how sometimes I can't make out the words my parents are saying to me, as if they were speaking a new language they didn't think to teach me.

I have to be stronger than how hard it will be for Lucy to snatch him away because Missus is always watching him. I have to be stronger than how quiet Lucy will have to be sneaking out of the house because every floorboard creaks. I have to be stronger than how hard it will be to carry him all this way, especially along the river, where there is no path and the rocks are so slippery. I have to be stronger than picturing Lucy being punished if she is caught. I have to be stronger than Mister and Missus and the things they are capable of. I have to be stronger than what they did to Stella.

LUCY

Mum mum is spilling all over me.

Her arms spill over my shoulders and down my back and around my waist to bring me close. Her hands spill into my hair and get in between every piece. Her face spills around my face. Her eyes spill over everything of me and then she starts to cry.

When she spills I stand very still. I do not want us to melt together and make it very hard for us to get ourselves apart. Inside I feel that I do want to spill but I use my thoughts to make my outside very hard and keep the spilling part inside. But later when I am alone I let myself spill a little bit. My smile spills onto the pillow and leaves a wet place. My belly spills on the bed so I feel that I don't have as much weight anymore.

Now Jennifer is awake. We can't stay here, she says. We have to leave.

Oh, no, I say. Don't worry, we can stay. Mum mum said never to leave the farm because she was going to come back and get me and if I left the farm she wouldn't know where to get me. Then I left the farm and I found her. Now she knows I can be smart and she doesn't have to put me somewhere where people can watch after me. Now she sees that all my bad behavior is gone. I left all my bad behavior in the old places. Now this is a new place with no bad behavior for me to have.

I feel Jennifer thinking.

One night, Jennifer says. That's it. Then we have to leave.

Why do we ever have to leave Mum mum?

To find the baby! Jennifer says.

But Mum mum needs us.

Samantha needs us! says Jennifer. And why is your mother always crying? What's wrong with her?

Because she has lots of feelings, I say.

She's so dramatic.

Don't be scared. Mum mum doesn't cry all the time.

Who said anything about being scared, Jennifer says.

I said something about being scared, I say. I said, Don't be scared.

Obviously! says Jennifer.

Mum mum comes in the room. Her dress is green and gold and her mouth is red. Her colors fill the room like opening curtains and there is the sun. Her hair is round and big around her ears like holding flowers in your hand and it is your hand that is doing the blooming. She sits on the bed and uses herself to cover me. I move a little away so Jennifer doesn't get mashed. That pulls Mum mum's mouth tight but then she smiles again.

"Dear Lucy," she says. "I'm so grateful you've come back to me. I feel like a mother again. All the delightful feelings of motherhood are rushing back. How wonderful it is to have you home."

"How wonderful it is to have me home."

"How wonderful it is to hear all these things you can say."

"I learned about books with Rodger Marvin and the Lord, good behavior, and how it feels when there is no space between people."

"Wonderful." She makes a singing noise in her mouth and smiles at the top of the room. I look there too. I do not see what it is that is making her smile.

"This is what I propose we do this afternoon. Buy you a new dress at Miriam's and have a long lunch at the fanciest place we can find." She claps her hands and then spills all around me. "I know. We'll go to Champagne! Isn't that the cutest name? It's the new restaurant that just opened. I've been dying to go but I was waiting for an occasion. What do you say?"

I do not say that I do not need any fancy dresses because I do not go to any more parties because I already went to the last party I will ever go to. She is smiling when she says she wants to buy a new dress and if I tell her I will not need to ever wear a fancy dress she will stop smiling. It is harder when Mum mum stops smiling. If she stops smiling then sometimes she might cry and then Jennifer gets scared which is a way I hate for Jennifer to be.

"Well, what do you say?"

So I say, "I say yes."

Mum mum laughs and claps. Jennifer shakes her head inside my pocket.

The store has a sign with letters like ribbon when it gets loose off the spool. Mum mum touches the dresses and whispers things to them and holds them in the air like ghosts and pretends she is dancing in them. She smiles like sunshine through the crack of the curtains, sunshine that is too bright to stay in the outside, it wants to be on the outside and on the inside too.

She says, "What about this one, look at this one."

I look. They have colors. They have bows. They have flowers. That is what the dresses have. I put my hand in my pocket and Jennifer bites my fingers in a little way that doesn't hurt. I want her to say something. I want her to like one of the dresses so that I can say that I like it too and then Mum mum will be happy and then we can go home. But Jennifer doesn't say anything. She beats and breathes and bites my fingers but doesn't say anything about the dresses.

Help me, I tell Jennifer. But Jennifer is too scared that Mum mum might cry.

Mum mum says she has found the dress for me. It has lots of pink on top of more pink. Like pink roses on top of pink icing on a pink cake. She brings me into a room where I put it on. The room is small with a big mirror and cloth on the walls like it is a dress too. Mum mum comes in and shuts the door. She moves down the zipper on the back of the dress that Missus gave to me.

"When was the last time this dress was washed?"

"Samantha washed it in the sink."

"It's hard to imagine you were allowed to wear such a filthy dress. It smells like it spent the night in a pigpen."

Mum mum told me never to make a face at the slop and I never did.

"I hope you were cleaned more often than your clothing!" Mum mum says, and laughs a laugh that floats.

Mum mum takes the dress off my shoulders and takes out my arms and when my arms are out that is when I reach to get Jennifer. I hold her in the air in the room so she doesn't fall to the ground when my dress falls to the ground. Jennifer closes her eyes and she is shaking like what wind does to the pond.

Mum mum screams. "Lucy, is that alive?"

"Yes." Alive because of me.

"You are keeping a live animal in your pocket?"

"Yes." Alive because of me.

"Lucy! Animals are not permitted to live in people's pockets. Give it here!" She holds out her hand but keeps her body away and closes her eyes.

I use one hand to hold Jennifer up close to my heart and one hand to hide her from Mum mum. Jennifer, she is getting hotter and hotter. I am afraid she will be too hot to hold in my hand so I blow my air from my mouth on her, very gentle, to make her not so hot. But she still shakes and squeezes her eyes so tight it hurts to look at it because I feel the tightness inside me.

"Give me that animal now!"

"Shhhh," I say. That is what Samantha says to me when I am afraid of something. She knows how to quiet things because there is something quiet inside her. "Shhhh, don't be scared."

"Give it here, Lucy." Mum mum moves to be in front of me. I move so she is not in front of me. Then she moves to be in front of me again. The way that we are moving makes us move in a circle and it looks like a game. But it's not a game. It is the opposite of a game and that is what makes me laugh.

"This isn't a joke, Lucy," says Mum mum. "I've told you countless times it's not polite to laugh at things inside your head when other people are present. It makes them feel uncomfortable. Now give it here!"

I am laughing because I have no more dress on anymore and we are playing a game that isn't a game. I have no dress and only my underwear and I am holding Jennifer against my heart so my beats will tell her not to be scared and moving in a circle with Mum mum.

Then I know that we will go in a circle forever. In this small room with only a mirror there is nowhere to go but forever in a circle. Then I will get too tired in the circle and have to lie down to sleep and I will try to hide Jennifer when I sleep but then Mum mum will still take Jennifer and make her live in a cage with the rest of the chickens. But she isn't the rest of the chickens. Because she is mine. Her being her is what makes her mine and that means she is the one that is different and she cannot live in a cage. So that is why I open the door and run out into the store with all dresses that float like people who lost their bodies. The woman in the store screams something and I run past her outside onto the street and I am laughing and laughing even though now I am scared.

There is no more dress on me but that is all right. It is the summer. That is the hottest time of the year so I won't get cold enough to freeze and I will only be hot enough to feel the dancing of the sun on my back and Jennifer in my hand which are the only things I need to feel.

Then I hear that Jennifer is laughing too and she is shaking again but that is because she is laughing and then my heart weighs the same as my whole body.

Jennifer! Jennifer! I say. And she laughs and laughs and her laughing weighs the same as her whole body.

Mum mum comes out so fast she is trying to look like the wind. She is holding my dress from Missus. She throws it at me and part of it sticks and part of it slips off of me. Mum mum grabs my arm to get me close to her. Then she raises her hand in the air and whaps me on the face. The whap burns the shape of her hand.

Her voice is not loud but it is a voice that wants to get inside of me and hurt my guts. "This is not a game." Every word goes by itself, not tied on to the words next to it like normal. "This. Is. Not. A. Game."

This.

Is.

Not.

A.

Game.

Says Mum mum.

I always knew that it wasn't a game. You were trying to steal Jennifer and put her in a cage. I would never say that is a game because Jennifer is my real life and games are not about real life.

I put on my dress but can't do up the back. I put Jennifer in my pocket and she is laughing so it makes it feel like hurting to have to stop my laughing but I know Mum mum is mad because now Mum mum is crying.

"Was that my fault? That was my fault, wasn't it? You think that was my fault what happened there. I can never go back there, never. That was my favorite store! My favorite store! Miriam is a friend! I know you can't believe it but I finally had a friend! You don't think I deserve any friends. Because I have a daughter like you, you think I don't deserve any friends. Well, I had one! I finally had one! And now I can never go back there!"

"That is a place where there are a lot of dresses. If you have a lot of dresses then you don't need to go back there."

"Everywhere I go, I become an exile. I thought that was over. I am so sick and tired of moving around. I thought I had found a place where I could stay."

"Then you would miss the other places."

"I can't go back to the other places, Lucy. All the places, all those people. I can never go back to any of them. Don't you understand what that does to a person?"

"Say you are sorry and they will let you come back. If you say you are sorry then people will let you do the thing that you want to do."

"They feel sorry for me but they hate me too. And they're grateful to me for making them feel better about themselves. Then they feel guilty and that's why they hate me."

My Mum mum, she is crying. Because there are people that feel sorry for her but they hate her too. They are grateful to her for making them feel better about themselves. They feel guilty about that part and that's why they hate her. When all that happens it makes you cry. When you are Mum mum there are a lot of people who make you cry. Because she is the only one who is always crying this much.

I don't want to be on the street with Mum mum who is crying. She was trying to steal Jennifer. She was saying, Give it here. Now I don't think she can take Jennifer because she can't see right through her crying but I think that maybe she still wants to. Which makes everything feel hot and like different parts of my body want to go in different directions. And the sun is too hot and Jennifer can't breathe in a way that gives her enough air. There is still some of the hurt left on my face. The hurting part is missing its skin and the air blows breaths full of stings over it.

I start to walk to a place that isn't near Mum mum crying. Mum mum says something loud behind me that isn't real words and grabs my arm. I am very still. Nothing can happen to my insides because my outside is hard from being so still.

"Don't you remember?" Mum mum isn't crying anymore. Her crying got sucked back up inside of her eyes to wait for the next time. "The car is the other way." It sounds the worst. Even worse than the worse things she said before.

We go back to her home. That is in the city with Monte. It has lots of fancy things. All the regular things she has are fancy things. She goes to her room and shuts the door but not loud so that means maybe she is not mad anymore because people use doors shutting loud to tell you they are mad.

In my room, Jennifer is shaking.

Jennifer, Mum mum isn't mad anymore.

She shakes but no words fall out.

I hold her in both hands because maybe she is cold and hands are always warm when you hold someone you love.

Still shaking.

So I blow my inside air on her because that is how to warm fingers when they stop being able to feel and Jennifer needs to feel everything.

Still shaking.

So I take off my clothes and put Jennifer in the middle of the bed and curl over her with all my hot but not all my weight. So she is the little nut and I am her big shell.

Jennifer, what will stop your shaking? I say. Tell me and I will do it.

We have to get out of here, Jennifer says, after a long time of quiet. Right now, or else we never will.

But what she said, that is the only thing I cannot do.

SAMANTHA

When my mom goes to market, she puts away the food in the cupboards. She used to ask me to help bring in the groceries from the car. Now she does it all herself. I wait until she leaves the kitchen and then I take the food that won't go bad. I'll stick the cans of soup and baked beans in a fire pit, open them up, and Lucy and I will eat them right out of the can. And I'll be able to feed him myself for months, at least I can offer him that, until we're on our feet and can afford the good kinds of baby food.

Since everything is fine with her, my mom doesn't ask about any of the missing food. The cans are heavy and we might have to go a long way with them, but I know they won't go bad. Who knows how long the food in those cans has lasted up until now. If I can wait a little longer, they can too.

I sold my suitcase so I keep the food in a pillowcase in the closet. We'll need matches, and a can opener too, but I don't want to push my luck. We can put the box of salt on the table but we only have one can opener. I'll wait until the last minute and grab it on our way out.

I can wait. That's my part of the plan. I've even figured out how to make the waiting less painful, since most of the time, that's all there is for me to do. Gathering the food and packing the pillowcase and counting the money doesn't take much time out of all the hours that make up a day. So in between tasks, I make my mind go quieter and quieter and quieter, until nothing is left but the sound of a whirling fan inside it, and then I slowly fill my mind with helium and let it float right above me, close enough to keep an eye on myself, but far enough away that the waiting can't eat me alive before they get here.

LUCY

In the morning Mum mum comes in and opens the curtain. That is like taking off the clothes that the windows are wearing and what is underneath is the light. The light is the window's nakedness. What does the light do? Well, it goes underneath your eyes and makes them open.

"Do you smell that?" says Mum mum. Her voice is high like birds who are happy in the trees. "I've been making French toast. I practiced all morning and now I've finally got it right. Let's have some breakfast and forget about yesterday."

I put my hand down to find Jennifer.

I'm here, she says. You don't have to poke me.

"Can you smell it? It's making the house smell like there's a real wife that lives here!" Mum mum laughs. Why is her mouth so big when she laughs? It is so big I could put my whole hand in it and there would still be more room for her to smile. "Well, not technically a wife yet, but soon. You know Monte's asked for my hand. Hah! It makes me sound so young. Silly, I know! But that's the way I feel, so, really, who's to argue with the way it sounds?"

When there is no eggs or no gonging there is nothing that reaches to get you on your feet in the morning. That is what happens when you are Lucy on the farm. But I am not Lucy on the farm anymore.

"Up, up, up!" Mum mum pulls me like I am something sticky that is stuck. I sit on the bed. I am wearing a dress for sleeping that has lots of ribbons that Mum mum gave me. It is hard for me to like it because there are too many things on it, like ribbons and bows and lace, and when I want to look at a part I like, my eyes get snatched away by another part before I can really see. "Let's have a fancy breakfast. We're going to celebrate all day and your little chicken is going to celebrate with us! I've given it some thought and decided she can stay. As long as you don't show Monte."

"Jennifer."

Don't tell her my name, Jennifer says.

"That is such a sweet name. Did you name her Jennifer?"

"She named her herself."

"What a smart little chicken for a smart little girl. Now come, come!"

Mum mum jumps up fast. It makes me feel slow and I get back under the blanket. Even though it is hot it makes me feel like I can hide from anybody and they wouldn't know where to look.

"Oh, no, you don't. You've come so far. It's been so long since we've had something to celebrate together."

Mum mum grabs my foot and pulls me out like I was a gopher going down a hole. That makes me laugh. Then Mum mum laughs. Then we are both laughing at the same time which is better than one person laughing alone and then the other person laughing alone. Samantha, she is someone who liked to laugh with me. When she was laughing and I was laughing then I knew there was someone who knew there was something nice inside me, even if my words were missing.

Jennifer is angry. I can hear it even though she doesn't say it. Everything she is doing with her body she is doing fast. Breathing and her heart beating. The things that she isn't saying she is saying them fast.

"Will you pretty please come to breakfast now?" Mum mum

says. "So you can enjoy it while it's hot and see how good it can really be? Get it while it's hot—that's what they say."

"Yes," I say.

Jennifer makes another sound that I know is a mad sound but I will get up anyway because it is my Mum mum that wants me to get up. Whatever place my Mum mum wants me to be that is the place I will be.

And after that, I smell what Mum mum was saying when she said, Did you smell that? And smelling that makes me hungry and so I get out of my hiding under the blankets and go into the kitchen. Mum mum puts a lot of things on a plate and makes me sit and then puts the plate on the table by where I am sitting. I eat and everything is good. It tastes like something to eat when you are wearing a party dress, except it is food for breakfast and that is not a time to wear a fancy dress except that is what Mum mum is wearing.

Mum mum looks like her smile makes the other parts of her face hurt. I want to touch those parts of her face so they don't hurt her anymore but when I look at Mum mum it makes me want to go back to sleep so instead I keep eating and eating what Mum mum has put on the plate for me. I put some in my pocket for Jennifer and she wants me to think that she doesn't want to eat it. But she does eat it. I can feel her eating it. It feels like a lot of hard and little kisses on the inside part of my pocket. It makes me laugh. Then Mum mum laughs. Maybe she and Monte do not laugh together and that is why she has been saving all this laughing for when I have come. That means she must have known that I was going to be here soon or she wouldn't have saved all her laughing.

"Quite an improvement, don't you think?"

When someone says *Don't you think?* and it sounds like a question they want you to say yes. That is agreeing. But sometimes when someone says *Don't you think?* and it sounds like a question they don't want you to say yes. That is a trick. I don't know which it is so I say nothing.

"*Improvement*, that means it's better," Mum mum says. Her smile melts a little and then gets hard again. Now it is a little lower but still a smile. "Don't you think the food is better?"

"On the farm we had eggs and grits and it was me that got the eggs because of how gentle I was with them. Missus said she never met a girl who was as gentle with the eggs." I do not tell Mum mum that one day I did not get the eggs anymore and how much I missed them then, before Jennifer came.

"But isn't this better than the food I used to make? Haven't I gotten better? French toast! *Très élégante!*"

"What is the food you used to make?"

"I guess you have a point, my darling." Mum mum is laughing. "My little, funny darling. There is no one like you in the entire world. Do you realize that? Do you realize how special you are?"

I don't know so I do not say.

"Can't I tell you how special you are? Isn't that my right as a mother?" Mum mum's voice is hanging funny, up by the ceiling. "Bragging rights? Isn't that what they're called? Or don't I get any bragging rights with you?" Her sounds start shaking the words. They might fly away or sink.

I don't know if Mum mum gets any of those. So I don't say either yes or no. I don't want to say the wrong answer and then make Mum mum get mad again and try to take Jennifer.

"Well," Mum mum says. "Anyway."

Then she takes my plate but I was still going to eat everything on it. Sometimes before I didn't know what Mum mum wanted me to eat and what she wanted me never, never to eat. Sometimes I would eat the thing I didn't know about anyway and sometimes I would not eat anything. Mum mum ties another skirt around her waist. That is called an apron. Missus likes to wear an apron and never take it off so she can keep things in the pockets and always have something to wipe her hands on.

"Now, Lucy," says Mum mum. "Listen carefully, this is important."

Mum mum sits next to me and makes an important face at me.

"Monte spoke to Mister and Missus, and they are willing to take you back, even though you ran off. And you know, the house isn't quite ready as we would have liked. But since you're here, I was thinking that maybe you could make an effort to show Monte that you could stay. We've been planning on hiring a girl to help out around here. Now, if we got a girl to help out in the beginning and show you some things, then eventually *you* would be the one helping out here. You would do the things we hired the girl to do, but you'd do them all by yourself. That would show Monte that things would be manageable with you around."

No, Jennifer says.

"You could make an effort to show Monte that you could stay, right, darling?" Mum mum says. "That you've improved?"

No, Jennifer says.

"Well, what do you think?"

No, says Jennifer.

Jennifer is sticky from the things I gave her to eat. I lick my finger and put it in my pocket to help clean her off.

"What do you think, my darling?"

Jennifer bites at my finger. I am just trying to clean you off, I say.

I can do it myself, she says.

But my mouth is bigger and has more wet than yours.

"Lucy, I'm speaking to you! Do you think you could find ways to help out around the house during the day?"

No, says Jennifer.

"Yes, Mum mum," I say.

"Because that would be just wonderful. We would share the

burden of maintaining a household. It would be different than when it was just you and me and I was alone, always having to put the pieces back together by myself. It would be a lot of responsibility for you. But I know you experienced that on the farm. They looked after you, but you did a lot for them in return, aren't I right?"

"Yes, Mum mum."

"And then you could stay!"

"Yes, Mum mum."

"That is what you want, isn't it? To stay here?"

"Yes, Mum mum." Always stay. Always be the found daughter, never the lost daughter like Stella.

"So, we'll see. We'll see if you can keep to your chores and not be difficult."

"Yes, Mum mum."

"Because sometimes you made things very difficult for me. You might not remember, but I had to give up a lot."

"Yes, Mum mum."

"In that case, why not start today?" Mum mum puts her hands together hard so it makes a noise. That is called claps. "Let's start right now!" Mum mum takes off her apron and ties it around me. She ties it so it feels like choking around my middle. None of my words or my breathing can move up from my belly or down through my mouth. She puts her hands on my middle. "Sometimes I look at you and think you have the most beautiful figure. I am almost jealous of your figure sometimes."

Mum mum, she is small. Small like a toy that you could throw as far as you wanted to if you didn't want it to be around you anymore. That is not like me. You could not throw me if you didn't want me to be around you anymore. You would have to think of another way to get me not to be around you anymore.

"So let's start. I'll clear the table and you can wash the dishes."

On the farm, Missus washed the dishes. Samantha would use

a towel to make the dishes dry. It was a hard job because a dish is something that can break easy and having water on a dish makes it so it doesn't want you to hold it.

Mum mum moves me to the sink and turns on the water. She puts my hands on the water and puts something in my hand for the washing and holds it against the dish and that is what it looks like to wash. I do the same moving that Mum mum did with her hands and that is cleaning but the dishes they keep sliding like wet feet on wet rocks. It makes me tired, trying to hold and hold the dishes that do not want to be held so I put them into the sink and walk toward outside where I see sunshine playing.

"Oh, no, you don't," says Mum mum. "Sharing the burden and all that, remember?"

"I remember."

"Then back to work!" Mum mum laughs. But back to work is not funny. It is hard. Like not soft, and difficult.

I hold some more dishes. Some more dishes do not want to be held. They want to be free and let the water run over them. So what they do is fall through my hands and break in the sink.

"Well," says Mum mum, "if a house girl started breaking dishes on her first day, we might have a problem."

I do not know if that is a problem. But I do get back to work with more dishes because of sharing the burden and being able to stay.

"Easy, easy," says Mum mum. "I don't know how many more of this set I want to part with." She takes the dishes out of my hands.

But I thought sharing the burden meant the washing dishes and then the showing to Monte and then being able to stay with Mum mum, who is my family, who was the only one there on my first day. So why does she take the dishes away? With no dishes, how will I show Monte I can stay found?

LUCY

Now a girl comes to help Mum mum's home stay nice and fancy. She also tells me what to do. Things to show Monte that I can stay here and that I am an improvement.

The girl says to me, "Look, it's not your job to keep this place clean. That's what I'm getting paid for. But your mom wants me to try and get you to help out so I'm going to ask you to do some things. But don't get too worked up about getting any of them right. You can just hang around and do whatever. I'll make sure everything's in order by the time your mom gets home. Deal?"

She grabs my hand. I do not grab back.

I can't say anything. I never heard so many words so close together before. As close as Rodger Marvin and Lizbeth and my hands used to be when the fishing-line feeling tied us together.

Jennifer, I say, help me know what to say to the girl.

No way, says Jennifer. I'm not wasting my breath helping you do chores. Not when Samantha is out there all alone.

The girl says, "I'm going to tell you some things to do and just do whatever you can. Okay?"

"Okay."

"You understand, right?"

"Right."

Some of the things she tells me what to do are make the beds, fold things, put things away, and wash things and do other things.

The way she tells is she says, "Lucy, why don't you do this thing?"

"Lucy, why don't you make the bed?"

"Lucy, why don't you fold the laundry?"

"Lucy, why don't you sweep the front steps?"

I think she means she wants me to say the reasons I don't do those things. The answers would be I don't know how. Until I learn she means I should go do it anyway. So why didn't she say, Lucy, do this thing? I am missing too many words to know why. I ask Jennifer to help me know why but Jennifer doesn't say anything. All the different why-don't-you-do-this-and-thats tie part of my brain into a knot. It hurts by my ears. That is the part of my brain that got tied up. Jennifer is the only one who can untie it because of how small and sharp her mouth is, but she pretends she doesn't know about the knot. Even though I know she feels it too.

I don't do any of the why-don't-yous right. The girl comes and does the things I did again and does them right and so Mum mum's house stays fancy. The girl never says, Lucy, you did this wrong, what's wrong with you? Can't you do a simple thing? She never does say any of that. But still I wonder why I am doing them one time and then she is doing them again, another time.

Jennifer, help me do them right, I say. Help me show Monte I can stay.

Jennifer just shakes her head.

But then I remember when Missus said to me they had never known a girl as good with the eggs. So I tell the girl, There are things I can do. I can do the weeding and I can get the eggs. I know how to be gentle soft with them. But the girl says those are not things that need to be done.

"The gardener does the weeding. And your mom buys eggs from the store," she says. "But thanks. You're sweet."

The girl's name is Mary. I know that is her name because that is what Mum mum and the boy call her. But I just think *the girl* when I think about her. She is not as pretty as Samantha and her hair is the color of corn and she is small and most of the things she says I do not know what they mean and she talks fast because she is worried her words will escape if she doesn't say them fast enough but mostly she doesn't talk to me. She talks her fast talk to the boy.

The boy is very tall so he makes himself smaller to come inside the door to the kitchen. What he likes to do is take food, then sit and eat it. I stand in the kitchen and watch him. My hand is in with Jennifer. She tries to suck herself away from it but my hand is bigger so she has to feel part of my hand even though she doesn't want to. I know she doesn't like it but there is nothing else that I like when Mum mum is gone so that is why I still do it.

The boy moves his head up and down when he sees me.

"Hi, boy," I say.

He moves his head again.

He is eating and the girl comes in and kisses the boy and the boy kisses the girl. Monte kisses Mum mum and Mum mum kisses Monte but none of the kissing people kiss me. They do not kiss me and Jennifer does not kiss me even when I touch her a lot and I think she likes it, or that was the way I remembered that she liked it. It makes me think I remembered something wrong about the way Jennifer liked to be touched. Even though I try to remember things the right way because Mum mum always wanted me to remember, remember.

"Let's have a smoke," the boy says. They stand up and go to the door that opens up to the outside. I go behind them.

"Stay inside, Lucy," the girl says. "Your mom will kill me if she comes home and you smell like cigarettes."

I watch them in the window. They blow smoke out of their mouths like fires in their stomachs. The girl puts the front of herself against the back of him so there is no space between them. The front of her and the back of him are the same skin. The boy throws some rocks on the street. They move to one side and then the other side like a tall plant when there is wind. They throw the smoke into the street and come inside. The boy sits down at the table and eats. The girl washes dishes.

They say some fast things to each other.

Some of the fast things they say to each other are "Think your parents are going out of the town this weekend? I don't know, I can't figure it out, I think maybe my dad is taking off somewhere but my mom is staying. I don't think things are going too well for them, if you know what I mean, not that I care, those two can kill each other for all I care. I just wish they'd shut the hell up at night and both leave the house at the same time. You don't think they want to work it out? No, I do, they do, but they both think the other one is seeing someone else and they're both so lonely and pitiful that neither one wants to break up with their significant other-other in order to work things out because they don't want to be the one without a significant other-other when the other finally calls it quits on them. If they don't go, want to get a motel? Jeez, Frank, with what money? I'm making pennies here and you don't seem to be in a hurry to do much of anything. My back is thrown out, you know that. Yeah, yeah, I know, but isn't there something you can do without a back to make some extra bucks? Not that I know of, my mind's not good for much, as you know, ha ha. Ha, do I ever!" the girl says, and hits him but I don't think it makes him hurt.

They laugh. I laugh. They look at me. I laugh. They look at each other. They laugh harder. I try to laugh harder but something is stuck in my throat and that is called choking. I thought laughing felt like someone giving you something special but not this laughing. This laughing only takes all my air away but doesn't give me anything.

The girl and the boy, they throw their laughing back and forth and it never gets dropped, it never gets stuck. With Jennifer my laughing always stays high in the air. But Jennifer pretends living with Mum mum made her lose all her laughing. If we go look for Baby, would Jennifer find her laughing again? But leaving Mum mum is losing more than laughing or smiling or words. It is losing your beginning. And a beginning you can never find again, once it gets lost.

LUCY

We leave today, Jennifer says. Learning to clean your mom's house is fun and all, but enough already. We have to find the baby. Every day we stay is a day that Samantha is away from her baby.

But this is our home. This is where we will live. Mum mum was going to come and get me on the farm but we found her. So then she didn't have to get me.

She wasn't ever going to get you, and we didn't find her either. A policeman brought us here.

Because we were trying to find Mum mum and he helped us find her.

That's *not* what we were doing.

But finding Mum mum is the best thing and the worst thing would be if Mum mum didn't know where I was when she went to find me.

Don't you remember what we were doing before we came here?

We were looking for Mum mum.

No, we weren't. We were looking for Samantha's baby. Don't you remember? Don't you remember your promise?

But the worst thing would be if I left and Mum mum came to look for me and I wasn't there and then she had nowhere to look so then I would be lost, like Stella.

Remember when Samantha got taken away? Remember what she asked you? Remember what you promised?

No.

Are you really that dumb? Or are you just pretending?

Then I don't say anything.

I asked you, Are you really that dumb?

Then I don't say anything again.

Because I need to know if you remember what you promised Samantha.

Yes.

You do remember?

Yes.

Do you remember who we were looking for?

Yes.

Who?

I know who.

Then say it!

I know who.

Why are you acting so stupid?

I'm not acting.

Yes, you are.

Acting stupid is the same as playing a game.

You're acting like you're stupid so you don't have to do something that you know you should do. But I know you're not stupid.

What I should do is wait for Mum mum on the farm but then we found her so that means you shouldn't wait on the farm for Mum mum anymore.

But we left the farm. Remember why we left the farm?

I don't know.

To help Samantha. Remember? Remember when Samantha left the farm and her baby was missing?

Yes, I say. I don't want to remember but my mind says I do.

Do you remember?

Yes.

And do you remember when she said, You have to find my baby and bring her to me?

Yes.

And you promised that you would!

But family they are there from the beginning of you and the only one that was there from the beginning of me, that is Mum mum.

But Samantha, her baby has been there since the beginning of him! And he's been taken and you promised you'd bring him back! Why did you promise you were going to help her if you didn't mean it?

Yes.

What does that mean?

If you don't do a promise then you are lying.

Then do your promise!

There is no dirt but there is gray, flat rock that is the sidewalk outside of where I live with Mum mum so that is what I sit on to do my crying. Crying is something that I try never to do because then I see lots of things that spin and go all together and then I can never get them not to be together and I am lost inside.

This is what the inside is.

Mum mum made a face when she smelled the farm. She scrunched her nose. I made the same face to show how we are the same, but it was a wrong kind of face. She said I should never make it. I said, But, Mum mum, it is the face that you are making. It doesn't matter what face I am making. You aren't to make faces like that or Mister and Missus will send you away and I won't know where to find you.

Samantha got dragged to the truck. She said, Lucy, I can't live without him! You have to bring him back to me. Promise you will help me. Samantha, her eyes were clear and green and showed how beautiful it was inside of her, where the baby used to live.

Jennifer said, Are you really that dumb? She said that because I said I didn't remember my promise. Except that was a lie. Because then I said I remember, I remember all the things that happened. I do remember my promise.

Every little parts of those things have melted into crying. The crying has to come out of my eyes because having all the tears on the inside was drowning me, which is being buried underwater. As the tears come out, they pull on corners of my insides. It makes me hurt in all different places, but at the same time. That is worse than hurting a lot in one place, because now there is nowhere inside of me that is safe.

Stop crying, Jennifer says. You're not the one in trouble. You have me. Samantha has nobody. She has less than nobody.

I go inside. Mum mum is in the bathroom, looking at her beauty in the mirror. I put my arms around her and hug her as much as I can and she turns around and calls me her Dear Lucy and hugs me too and every part of the world that is Dear Lucy is being hugged by every part of the world that is Mum mum and she is my only Mum mum and she is the only one that has been there since the beginning of me and that is why I am not leaving. Because nobody else was there from the beginning. Nobody else was the first thing I saw. That is the only thing that family is. Even though there is a love that isn't for your family you still can't change the beginning.

So then what was the first thing Samantha's baby saw? yells Jennifer.

I don't know, I say. I try to only hug Mum mum and not hear Jennifer.

Yes, you do! Don't lie to me.

I wasn't there.

You still know! Now tell me! What was it? Jennifer stabs her hard, sharp mouth into my leg. I drop my arms from Mum mum.

Answer me, Lucy! yells Jennifer.

I wasn't there, is true. But I don't know, is a lie. I do know it was green eyes and orange hair and smiling.

Who was smiling? yells Jennifer.

Samantha. She was the first thing that Baby saw.

Yes, says Jennifer. You got it. Let's go.

But my arms reach back for Mum mum and nothing will keep us apart, not Jennifer stabbing my leg or the blood that bleeds through my pocket.

SAMANTHA

———————

When it's still on my head, I'm looking at it and thinking, There's so much of it, it's going to take forever to get rid of it all. I need it gone now. When Lucy comes, we'll be able to get away that much easier; I don't think anyone has a clue what I look like without my hair. It's the only quality of my appearance that ever gets a mention.

I grab a handful and hold the scissors right up against my scalp. But I can't seem to start. I'm remembering things people said about it. Lucy loved to pet it and try to braid it. My teachers said it made me special. My parents marveled at it and said they didn't know where it came from. Allen loved it because his grandpa, who he never met, had red hair. The guys at the Depot called me Poppy because they thought it was the color of California poppies. I can see all these people huddled around me, watching me in the bathroom mirror, saying those pretty things.

Baby's father strolls in and joins the circle. That night under the bridge, he had told me it looked like the sunrise. Before he has the chance to repeat that sweet nothing, I hack through the first handful.

Starting was the only hard part. Then really, it's easy. My hands know what to do. They were probably secretly jealous of my hair and ready to see it go. It takes a few minutes and it's done. I finish up with my dad's razor, which takes a bit more finesse than the scissors. Now none of it's on my head. It's not mine anymore. It belongs to the bathroom floor. I look down and think, That's it? That's what all the fuss was about? All these years. What's wrong with people that they made such a fuss over a bunch of hair? It's nothing but a big mess on the floor now. But I suppose I let them make a fuss. I never stopped them. Until now.

I look pale. My eyes look darker. I look hungry. I was right. I barely look like me. Or maybe I look more like me. Maybe the hair was the disguise. All this time I had the world fooled, thinking about how beautiful I was, what with my lovely hair and all.

Except, what about him? To him, I was probably just a blur of orange. Babies can't really see, right? Is orange all he saw? How will he know it's really me? Is there some way to tie it back on? Glue it back on?

I start sweeping it up with my hands until I realize he spent most of his time inside me. He'll recognize me by my insides.

LUCY

The girl tries to teach me to show Monte that I can stay.

"Lucy," she says, "why don't you wipe down the bathtub?"

Because I don't know how to wipe down the bathtub. That is why don't I. But now I know that is not the answer to her question. At least I do know where the bathtub is, which is in the bathroom. I go in there and shut the door and get into the bathtub and lie down and it is like living inside a smooth, cool, white stone and I say, Jennifer, Jennifer.

She is not saying anything.

I take her out and look in her little eyes. She moves them around fast so I can't catch up. I put her away because if I can't see her I don't want to look at her. Jennifer never talks very much to me anymore. She likes to ask for a lot of food and I give it to her because that is the only time that she is talking to me and I want her to do it more. But then afterwards there is nothing more that she says.

Then what happens is she is getting very fat and very heavy. Her toes go through my pockets and scratch my legs. Her fur is turning into little feathers and she makes a big hump in my pocket. I do not care about her getting heavy or the scratches or holes in my pocket or how low it hangs on my legs, but now she gets hit on more things when I am trying to do some things. Sometimes she will yell if I hit her on something like a drawer that is opened when it should be closed and I say, I am sorry, Jennifer, I am sorry that I did that. But she doesn't say that it is okay or even that she is still very mad. She doesn't say anything. What she likes to say now is nothing and so all I can say to her is mostly nothing. I know I am missing lots of words, but I still have some, except never saying them makes me feel like I have even less than that.

Because now, if I want to say something to someone, who can I say it to? Jennifer, but she doesn't listen anymore. Mum mum, but she is away all day and doesn't listen when Monte is here. I know who listened to me the most before. It was Samantha. I want to say things to Samantha, but she's at her house now. I can't go there, because of never leaving Mum mum. And Samantha, she can't come here because of waiting for Baby to get found and brought to her. Because of how much she loves Baby and Baby being the favorite thing that matters most of all. Samantha can't leave because if she did, the person would bring Baby to her house and Samantha wouldn't be there.

Stella was missing just like Baby is now. But nobody ever found Stella and nobody brought her back to Missus so Stella wasn't the daughter anymore. Somebody has to bring Baby back to Samantha. Somebody has to make sure that family is forever. But I don't know who the person is. Because I am the only one who promised, but I am with Mum mum, and I cannot leave her.

So who is the person? Who is the finding person and who is the bringing person?

Then I hear the front door open. I know it is Mum mum because she is the one that opens the door that way. The way she uses her hands on the door makes the air push against the door in a way that is just hers.

I get out of the bathtub and I open the door and I run and I run into the kitchen and the girl is there doing something and Mum mum is putting down her purse on the table and I grab her and I am bigger so she goes all into my arms and isn't touching the floor which means that the only way she can get down is for me to put her down on the floor but the only place that I want her to be is me holding her. She laughs. Well, that is the best thing I have heard this day, because there is not very much that is good that I have heard today and the best means that it is better than anything.

"Well, hello, my darling," Mum mum says.

"Hello, Mum mum."

"How was she today?" Mum mum asks the girl.

"Fine, same as always," the girl says, and looks only at the something that she is doing.

"You can't know how wonderful it is for me to hear that," Mum mum says, and climbs down off me and I let her go. Mum mum touches the girl's arm.

"She's never any trouble," the girl says, and still looks at the something she is doing which means not at me or Mum mum.

"Lucy, did you hear that? *Never* any trouble?" Mum mum says, and she touches my head. I try to bring my head closer to Mum mum so more of my head can touch her hand. "You can't know how proud of her I am."

Then the girl leaves. Mum mum sits in the kitchen and I sit next to her. I put my head on her shoulder and rub it around so I can feel a lot of what her shoulder feels like. It feels like her dress, which feels like a flower petal, like it will break if I rub too much but I don't want to stop rubbing.

"Darling, the oil from your skin is going to stain the silk," Mum mum says, and moves her shoulder away from me. "Let me change and I'll be right back. What do you say?"

"I say, yes."

Mum mum laughs. "Since when have you been this clever? Who would have ever thought my little Dear Lucy would have become such a clever girl?"

Mum mum likes such a clever girl and she likes that such a

clever girl is me. That is what Mum mum always deserved to have and never got.

Mum mum comes back in her fancy-ribbon nighttime dress and we go to the sofa and she puts all of herself around me like she is my coat and it is her job to keep me warm, and holds me close-close-closer and what happens then is I shrink so I am smaller than Mum mum and she is able to touch all of me. I put my head down to her belly and smell all her smells and use my arms to make me as close as I could ever be to her. Because she is my Mum mum and I am her Lucy. What she is does is she touches my hair and she tries to touch every piece of the hair so every piece feels that it has the same amount of love from Mum mum as every other hair.

"Lucy, you know I will always take care of you. Even if we are separated again, you will be taken care of."

But now I am back from the farm. You said never to leave the farm and I never did leave the farm, except to find you, and now that I have found you I am never leaving and that means that we will never be separate again.

"I have put things in order for you. That is what I am out doing during the day; making sure you will be taken care of, my darling. Do you understand?"

"You will always take care of me."

"Yes, my dear, that is what I mean. I have seen to it that you will be taken care of as long as you live, even if we're not together."

"But we will always be together."

"Even if you don't live with us anymore, you will always be taken care of."

"But I will always live with you anymore."

"Let's not worry about it now, darling, not until more things have been decided."

Nothing stops the light from Mum mum's eyes. It is the feeling of being touched on your inside world, by something you could never touch on the outside world. It is about the feeling when you are split together and then you are taken apart. It is the feeling when you are an egg on the floor and the rest of you is taken up with a spoon and some is still stuck on the floor and other people wonder if it hurts and you know about the hurt. That is the feeling of looking at Mum mum's eyes and knowing your family is the only one there from the beginning.

Then the door opens again. The first time it was Mum mum and so the next time it is Monte. And Mum mum she is up. She is part of the egg that was taken up with the spoon after it fell on the floor. I am the part that is still on the floor. Monte is coming in and bringing in the outside air. They are together, trying to get themselves together with kissing and arms around each other. Me and Mum mum, we went together more easy than Monte and Mum mum. They have to make noises when they try to put themselves together and they have to open their mouths so much to climb inside each other.

Yes, I am bigger than Mum mum. But when she opens herself up to me then I suck myself all in and try not to breathe and try to be as very small like the inside of a nut as I can be. Then Mum mum will think that I am someone that can fit inside and she won't think I will become too big and she won't have to keep me outside. Outside is what I am now.

I will be on the inside with Mum mum, even though Monte is here now.

There is still space in between them and I squeeze into it.

"Lucy!" cries Mum mum.

"Here I am!" I say. They come apart. Now there is more space in between for me, but space is not what I wanted.

"You know better than to interrupt Monte and me like that! You and I had our time together earlier. Now it is Monte and my time for each other."

"What is it my time for?"

"I've got an idea! Why don't we show him what things Mary has been teaching you? Let's see . . . dishes, laundry, floors. Which would you like to show Monte?"

"Dishes, laundry, floors."

"Yes, which one? How about floors, that's easy. Now, Monte, watch this."

Mum mum pulls me and Monte to the kitchen. She gives me a cloth with some wet. I get down to be near the floors. "There we go now, just back and forth on the floors."

"Just back and forth on the floors."

"Yes, dear. Just like that. That's lovely."

"Just like that."

"Oh, Monte, hasn't she come so far?"

"Pretty impressive. Mary's tutelage has paid off."

"Oh, you and your big words. Let me fix us a drink and then tell me all about your day."

"Lovely job, Lucy," says Mum mum. "Now keep at it, just like that."

"Just like this."

Back and forth, back and forth, just like this. Back and forth is a lovely job. Back and forth is pretty impressive. Just like this, it is lovely and impressive. I will keep at it, back and forth and forth and back, until they let me stay.

Monte, he has to watch me to see that I can stay. But Monte and Mum mum, they take their drinks and their kissing and smiling at each other to the backyard. If Monte is not watching the back and forth, then the back and forth will not get me to stay. It is a back and forth that doesn't mean good job, or pretty impressive. It is a back and forth that means nothing.

I go to my room and shut the door. I take out Jennifer and look at her. She is sleeping. I know that I am being loud enough to wake her up but she still sleeps. My words don't have strength to wake her up anymore. I put her on my pillow and watch her while she sleeps. She looks like a heart. That is what is inside of you and makes you beat. There is Jennifer inside of everyone that makes them beat. I say, Jennifer, Jennifer, tomorrow will you talk to me, Jennifer? Jennifer, tomorrow will you talk to me, Jennifer? How will I do the chores without you? How will Monte let me stay without you? My insides are yelling because the piece missing inside of me is the exact same size as Jennifer. Tomorrow?

Tomorrow will you talk to me?

MISSUS

Over and over these days I have to tell him, Yes, he cries, but what baby doesn't cry? Tell me about a baby you know who doesn't cry? When he is quiet, I say, If you are going to judge me, then please just name me a baby who doesn't cry.

"Please, dear, calm down," he says.

I say, "When I feel your judgment coming down on me, it's hard not to react. You have always trusted me to know best, and now that he's finally here, you are judging me."

"I do trust you, but I'm worried about him too."

"Listen to you! I am not worried about him." I have to laugh, it's such a silly thought. If Mister could see the peace on our son's face as he falls asleep in my arms, he couldn't be worried. "Not one bit."

I'm the one who has suffered through everything to bring him here for you, I want to tell him. I'm the one who suffered the shame of being deficient. I'm the one who watched Stella grow into a kind of girl I could never have been. I'm the one who sacrificed to keep Stella safe during her pregnancy, only to be betrayed by her, and only now you decide you don't trust me? You trusted me enough to bring in Stella, enough to take in Samantha, and now that he's finally here, you don't trust me? Now that I finally have your son for you? The very son you were almost too weak to make for yourself?

Mister takes him out of his basket.

"Well, of course he's crying now!" I tell Mister. "You took him out of his basket."

"But, dear, is that basket made for a baby? It's rough inside. Let me get a blanket."

"It doesn't need a blanket. Put him back."

"Missus, dear, it's dirty."

"It's not! Please put him back in his basket! You don't know about these things. Give him back to me."

"The basket is scratching him. Let me buy him a nice bassinet in town. Or I can make one for him."

I take the baby from Mister, mustering all my calm. "Look. Look at him. Where is he scratched? Show me."

"There, there, take it easy." He puts his hands on my shoulders.

I pull away from Mister and I lift the baby to his face. "Show me where." This isn't about my being right or proving Mister wrong; I really do want Mister to see, to understand, to trust. To be at peace, as I am.

"Nowhere. You're right."

"You have to trust me. A mother knows."

"I do. I trust you."

"Yes, he cries, of course he cries, but what baby doesn't cry?"

"You're right, dear. Every baby cries."

Mister folds me and the baby into his arms, tight and warm against his chest. He rocks us back and forth. He has always trusted me. He is too old, he has done too much. He won't stop now.

"What baby," I whisper to his strong, loyal heart, "do you know who doesn't cry? What baby?"

But of course his heart can't answer. Because every baby cries.

And of course it is the man who asks about the baby crying. It is the man who asks if we should take the baby to the doctor. It is the man who worries something is wrong with the baby. The mother never asks such questions. Because a mother knows that if the baby has her, he has everything he needs.

SAMANTHA

I am cleaning up the bathroom when my mother appears in the doorway. She gasps.

"What have you done to your hair? How could you do such a thing to yourself?"

Because I wouldn't be able to go far with it. Mother, you have to admit that red hair is the first thing you would have put on the Missing Girl posters. But I took care of that. I have to think about these things, I'm a mother now too.

"I gave myself a haircut," I explain to her. I kneel down to sweep the hair into the dustpan.

She reaches a hand toward me, then recoils as if my barren head were an animal that might bite her.

"You didn't cut your hair. It's all gone."

"Yes. You're right."

"Why, Samantha?"

Did it hurt when you breast-fed me at first? Did it make you bleed? Were you worried if it was okay I was drinking your blood? Did you get any sleep? Did you tell yourself you didn't need any? Did you try to read my thoughts while I slept? Did you count my toes over and over and marvel that you made them and then gave them away so I could have them? Because even though they were the best thing you'd ever made, you know I needed them more? That's why.

"I needed a haircut."

"No, Samantha. This isn't a haircut. You—you shaved it off."

I know it must be hard to see someone deliberately strip themselves of something that the world considers so beautiful, but these are the kind of things you find yourself doing when someone else matters so much more to you than you mean to yourself. Or don't you remember feeling that way?

"You're not well, Samantha."

"I'm perfectly fine, thank you."

I'm better than I've ever been. The waiting was getting at me, that's true. But I've found a way to get away from the pain of it. Like now. Now I'm listening to you, and I'm sweeping, but the important parts, the real, bloody parts of me, aren't listening, and they aren't sweeping. They are floating next to me, just far enough away.

I empty the dustpan in the trash. I use my hands to get the pieces that are stuck to it.

"I'm calling the doctor," says my mom.

"Are you going to ask him to make me a wig?"

"Oh, Samantha! And the food you've been taking."

So you did notice. Why didn't you ever ask me about it? If you had asked earlier, I might have told you. You might have forced it out of me. I might have told you about the letter, I might have told you what they did to Stella, I might have told you what kind of people you let me live with, eat with, sleep under the same roof with. The kind of people you let me make promises to. I might have told you about waiting for Lucy. Maybe you would have remembered what it felt like. And maybe then you would have helped me.

But it's too late now. I won't tell you any of it now. You're causing too much of a scene, you're getting too hysterical. You have to stay calm, Mom, you can't let your emotions get the best of you in situations like these. I can't fall to pieces imagining him all alone, imagining if they even know how to feed him, wondering if Lucy will know to bring a bottle and diapers. Thinking that way will destroy me, and I can't let it. What use to my baby am I then?

"You could use a little help," my mom says.

No. Not anymore. Thank you, but it's too late for your help now.

I shake my head and keep sweeping. There really is so much hair. Each strand a time line of comments and compliments and wisecracks cut short by the scissors, laid to rest in the trash can.

"I think a little help would be for the best."

My mom leaves the bathroom. She's on the phone now.

She is saying that her daughter needs a little help. Could the doctor come down here, please? But she doesn't tell them I cut my hair. She saves that for her next call. To the wigmaker. I wonder if they have my color. My special, special color. Nobody else has it, you know, and it makes me so very, very special.

LUCY

In the morning there is a sound. A beautiful sound I have been begging to hear. And that sound, it is Jennifer. She is standing on top of me. It hurts in a way I love. Her toes are sinking into me. They make holes on my skin and each one means she loves me too, again. There and there and there. She is saying, Lucy, Lucy! Wake up, wake up!

I am awake! Here I am! If you say, Wake up, I will never sleep again! Oh, Jennifer, Jennifer! And I kiss her feathers. It feels even softer since I have forgotten what a kiss on them feels like.

Lucy, get up, get up!

I stand up and put Jennifer in my pocket which is the place she used to love to be the most, but now she says, Leave me out, there's something I have to show you.

So I keep her out in my hand. I am so glad I always had this hand here waiting. My hand feels not like just a normal part of my body anymore, because Jennifer who didn't want to be there, now wants to be there again.

Go to the kitchen, says Jennifer.

There is the kitchen. There is the light coming in. There is all the shine that all the light makes and all the clean that the girl makes. Shine is what the kitchen does best of all.

"Where is the girl?" I say.

She's outside, Jennifer says. Sit down.

I sit down.

Put me on the table, Jennifer says. She hops to a paper that is an envelope, which is a word that Samantha told me. It means there is a letter inside and also means it is a word I love.

Look, Lucy! Look! Do you know what this is?

An envelope.

Exactly. And it's from Samantha! Jennifer says. It's a letter from Samantha!

I pick up the envelope. But I do not know if they look like Samantha's letters.

"I do not know if they look like Samantha's letters."

Samantha's letters look like lace and vines that grow up on the porch in whichever way that want to. These letters look small and hard like words from the Bible.

Of course it is, says Jennifer, look at who it's from, it says right here, it says her name. The envelope says, this is a letter from Samantha.

I don't know if that is what it says. The letters are these: *TO THE RESIDENT OF.*

Of course you don't know, but I do! Open it! Jennifer says. Read it!

I open it. Inside there is a paper with lots of small, hard letters. I know Samantha's letters. They make me see Samantha's face and smell the salty oranges. These do not make me see Samantha's face or smell those smells.

Is it from her, Jennifer says. I know it is. You can't read and I can so you have to believe me that it's really from Samantha. Now let's read it together.

I do not have enough words to read it together. I do not know what to do and I sit and hold it in my hands and look at the letters that do not look like Samantha's letters. But then I have a clever thought.

"I will have the girl read it!" I stand up and go to the door.

No! Jennifer says. No, that's silly. I can read it. Put it down here on the table so I can read it.

But I thought you didn't know how to read these kind of words.

No, Samantha's words I can read.

But you couldn't read her book.

You always wanted someone to write you a letter, didn't you? And now someone has! Samantha! But the words inside the letter are private. Samantha wouldn't want the girl to know her secrets. Samantha only wants to share her secrets with you.

But Samantha knows how many words I'm missing.

Yes, but she also knows how smart you are, and that you would find a way to read her letter and keep her secrets at the same time. Now put it down so I can see.

So I unfold it for Jennifer to read.

This is what the letters are.

TO THE RESIDENT OF —————,

The purpose of this letter is to inform you of routine scheduled maintenance to your gas line during the hours and dates listed below. Disruption to your home's gas supply is to be expected during these times.

This is what Jennifer reads.

Dear Lucy,

Why haven't you done your promise to me? You promised you would help me but you have deserted me. Every day I wait for you to come with Baby. So please find Baby and bring him to me. Because he cannot live without me, and I cannot live without him.

From,
Samantha

We have to leave and find her baby, Jennifer says. And bring the baby back to her.

Does that mean we have to leave Mum mum?

Just for a little while. Then we'll come back to get our things and say good-bye.

But if we leave and Mum mum comes back and we are gone then she won't know where we are.

We'll be back here by the time Mum mum gets home, and then we'll have our chance to say good-bye, get our things, and meet Samantha at the place by the river.

But I don't want to say good-bye to Mum mum. Not for a little while. Not for any while.

Then Jennifer says, Sometimes there are people that you use words to say good-bye to because you are going to separate from them. But other times there are people that you say good-bye to with words, but inside your heart you never say good-bye to them. Mum mum is one of those people. There is a thread, and the thread is so long that it lasts forever. Your heart is tied to one end of the thread, and your mother's heart is tied to the other end. So really it's not a good-bye. No matter how far away you go, you never have to say good-bye. But we do have to go. We have to go now and find the baby.

I never have to say good-bye to Mum mum?

You never do.

If I never have to say good-bye.

So you'll do it?

Yes. I will do my promise.

All right, let's go fast so we can get back before anyone knows we're gone. We'll go to Samantha's house. We'll ask Samantha where to look. We have done everything else we can do. She is the last person we have to ask. Maybe she will remember a clue that can help us know where to look. We'll start at the beginning and ask her everything she remembers about the morning the baby got taken.

When Jennifer says those words they are the fastest words she has ever said, they are faster than when the girl talks to the boy, they are faster than a firefly you are trying to catch in a jar, it is faster than the kittens when you wanted them to stay on your lap, so you can feel their inside shapes, but as soon as you try to keep them, as soon as you lift your hand so you can put it back down to pet, then they are already gone.

We have to take the bus in town, says Jennifer. I know how to get there. Go in your mom's room and get some money from Monte's dresser.

But Mum mum told me not to touch Monte's things.

It's okay, we'll pay him back.

But Mum mum said . . .

Look, Lucy, says Jennifer. A promise means no matter what. And we need the money for the bus fare.

Okay, I say.

We go into the bedroom. It is dark and cool and smells like spilled flowers. The ground is soft as fresh-dug earth. Every step my feet sink into a place just their size, made just for them. Jennifer shows me how to take the money from Monte's dresser.

But is this stealing? I ask.

Was it stealing when you took me from the coop?

I don't know, I say.

Yes, you do. You know it wasn't, says Jennifer. That's because in certain situations, words like *stealing* don't have any meaning.

I put the money in my pocket with Jennifer and we walk outside. There is the girl and the boy and they have their smoke sticks and they are talking and touching and what they do not do is look at me when we leave. Jennifer and I walk to the bus stop. The sun is everywhere getting in all my cracks. But it is okay. It gives a good feeling. The sun gets straight to my blood and makes me walk as fast as I have to, to do my promise. Because a promise is a thing you can't ever forget, even if you pretend that you did.

SAMANTHA

—— —— ——

The doctor is a young, surprisingly large man. I thought doctors were white haired and gentle. I guess this is a different kind of doctor. I am still sweeping when he and my dad drag me to my room and pin me on my bed. My mother watches from the doorway, crying quietly.

The doctor fills the needle from a vial and puts the needle in my arm. It doesn't feel like a prick on your skin. It feels as if someone is pumping cement in your veins, against the current of your blood.

I don't look at the doctor, and I don't look at my dad. I watch my mother the whole time. Her eyes are obscured by her tears and her hands, but I know she feels me looking at her. Otherwise she would move her hands away from her eyes, to get a better look at the excitement.

I won't be here for long. I know my body will be here, lying in this bed, but I'll be no good to him when he and Lucy arrive. My parents will probably just bring him back to the farm. They don't care about what's best for him. They haven't even asked about him. They didn't ask if my body knew how to make him just right, if the back of his ears are soft as peach skin, or if his ribs are like strings of the most perfect instrument. I won't be able to stop them from taking him. I won't even be able to try to explain. I can't open my mouth.

Suddenly a beam of light cuts into the room, laying itself

across my body. More power is in that slice of light than in my father's arms, or my mother's tears, or the cement from the doctor's needle that is now hardening in my bloodstream.

Stella?

A whirlpool of dust spins in the corner.

Stella, is that you?

A fly buzzes near the window, as loud as if it were inside my skull.

Stella, can you hear me?

Stella, listen, Lucy isn't here in time. It's not her fault, but it's too late. I can't fight them anymore. They beat me. Not like you. You figured out a way to beat them.

The dust spins faster.

Stella, listen to me, you have to take him.

Stella, if he can't be with me, let him be with you. You know how to be a mother. You've been with your boy this whole time. Please let my boy be with you in the clearing, under the tree, where it's safe.

Take him, Stella.

The fly's buzzing gets louder. The whole room is buzzing now. All the air in the room is spinning with the whirlpool dust. The ray of light is getting brighter and brighter until I have to close my eyes. But I still see it. It has found its way inside me.

But can I say good-bye first?

He weighs so little, but he's so heavy, because I wasn't ever sure if I was strong enough to be his mother. But I'm sure now. And I can see him. This whole time I haven't seen him once. Not in a dream, not in my mind's eye. His eyes are so big, there is so much for them to take in. But they are also at peace, they know they are safe now. I thought I wanted to say good-bye, but now I realize how silly that is. I will see him soon, so soon. I'm right behind him, it's just going to take me a little longer to get where we're going.

LUCY

First we wait for the bus at a place Jennifer knows about. It is just another part of the sidewalk, the same as all the other parts, except Jennifer says it is actually a special part because the bus will come here.

How do you know the bus will come here? I ask.

Because I've seen it stop here before.

How did you see it stop here but I didn't see it stop here before?

I was watching for where it stopped. I knew eventually we were going to have to find a way out of here.

Jennifer was right because the bus does come, and it sighs its doors open, and we pay our fare, which was stealing but without any meaning, and sit in a seat just like all the other people on the bus, all the people that know the secrets of where to wait on the sidewalk and that it is okay to steal the fare. We watch the outsides move, past places I know and then to places I don't know and then the bus stops, and the bus doors open. We get off and we are at the Depot.

My feet can walk to Samantha's house with having to tell them where to go. I remember the this ways and that ways.

Will you look at that? This is it! Jennifer says. We're already here!

Will-you-look-at-that is the house with brown grass and the small, yellow flowers and the sick-with-the-dust trees.

What should I do? I say.

Just walk up and knock on the door.

But first I pick a yellow flower for Jennifer. She says thanks but she doesn't smell it. Maybe she will have time to smell it after we find Baby.

There are some stairs. I go up them. There is the door and I wrap up my hand tight and knock it on the door. Then for a little while there is nothing. Then there are the sounds of footsteps and the opening of the door.

The lady has some brown hair and some white hair and her skin around her eyes is crinkled. That means tired. Maybe she is so tired because she is thinking about the baby and wondering where the baby is, the way Jennifer does when she pretends to sleep but I know she is not sleeping.

"Yes, dear?" the woman says. "May I help you?"

"I need Samantha. I have to ask her a question."

"She is asleep right now. Are you a friend from school?"

You will wait until she's awake, says Jennifer. Say, I will wait until she is awake.

"I will wait until she is awake."

Say you are a friend from school, Jennifer says. Say you really want to see her.

"I am a friend from school. I really want to see her."

"You know about her condition?"

Yes, says Jennifer.

"Yes," I say.

"The doctor was here earlier this morning. She was given something for her nerves, and she's still asleep."

Say, I will wait.

"I will wait."

The woman doesn't say anything. She looks inside the house and then at me again.

"Well, I'm just not sure it's a good time." She starts to close the door. But then it opens again. "Yes, all right. Please come in.

I'm sure she'll be happy to see you, and maybe it will do her some good."

"I will come in."

"You can wait for a little while, and if she doesn't get up, then maybe you can come back tomorrow."

"No. I will wait."

"What is your name, dear?" the woman asks.

Tell her your name is Jennifer, Jennifer says.

"I am Jennifer."

"It's sweet of you to come, Jennifer. Samantha hasn't had many visitors during this difficult time. They stay away out of courtesy, I'm sure."

The woman opens the door wide. Me and Jennifer, we go inside.

Even though the outside has lots of sun the inside of the house is dark. There are windows but they are too dirty to let the light come in. The whole room is like the pictures in the farmhouse you couldn't see without wiping away the dust. But you could never wipe away all the dust in this room. The woman tells me to sit in a chair and I do. It is a chair with big flowers on it and some of the inside of the chair is getting out and what it looks like is clouds. But I do sit there and the woman sits in another chair.

"Are you a friend of Samantha's from school?" the woman says again.

"Yes."

The woman puts her hand on my hand and it feels like a brown leaf when it floats off the branch to the ground. "That's very nice to hear. I don't think she's stayed close with many girls since she was away in the country. And it is very nice of you to come see her. I think it will raise her spirits."

Jennifer says. Say, how can we see the baby?

"How can we see the baby?"

"I'm sorry?"

That means say it again.

"How can we see the baby?"

"I'm not sure what you mean."

"How can we see the baby?"

"Well, dear, I'm sure that isn't possible."

"Why not?"

"The baby is with her family."

"Samantha is her family. Allen doesn't want to be the family anymore. So that means only Samantha now."

"Oh, no, dear, I'm afraid you're mistaken. The baby is with her family in the country. The country is a nice place for children to grow up, don't you think?"

"What family?"

"A nice family."

Who are they?

"Who are they?"

"A very kind older couple who cared for Samantha during her difficult time."

The farm! Jennifer screams. Of course! The beating from her heart is spilling heat down my leg and getting in my shoes. My shoes are filling with hot Jennifer heat. Ask if that was where Samantha lived during her pregnancy?

What about the farm? I say. Why the farm? I ask Jennifer.

Just say it! says Jennifer, in a voice that makes it so I can't do anything else but say it, like she lived in my throat instead of my pocket.

"On the farm? Was that where she lived?"

But the woman just makes a noise with the sound of *mmmm*s.

The farm! says Jennifer. The farm! We have to go to the farm.

But Samantha, we have to tell Samantha where we are going. I told her I would come for her and she is here and we are here and she thinks I did not do my promise but I will do my promise, I will be doing it, now and until it is done.

No, no, listen to me, says Jennifer. Let's get out of here. The farm! The farm!

I stand up and walk to another part of the house because maybe that is the part where Samantha is. I need to tell Samantha that I was only pretending when I said I forgot.

"Dear, what are you looking for?" the woman says.

"Samantha."

No, no, Jennifer is shaking and shaking like when she was still inside her shell and trying to come out so she could meet me and be in the world.

"She was given something by the doctor to help with her nerves. But she'll be so happy you've come, she hasn't had a visitor yet. She hasn't stayed close with any of the girls she knew in school. When she goes back in the fall, it will be so nice to have a friend. But please, just wait. I can make you some lunch, some tea. We can sit in the yard. Gary is out there raking the leaves now, but he'll be done in just a minute."

"Where is Samantha?"

The woman stands and holds my arm hard. "Please, it's such a beautiful day. Let's sit outside in the yard until Samantha is finished getting her rest."

I take my arm away from her and go one way in the house even though it is dark and I do not know which kind of way it is. There are some doors and I open a door and there is no Samantha and the woman is behind me and grabs my arm again.

"No!" I say. "Where is she?"

"Gary!" the woman calls.

There is fear dripping from her voice. I have heard that fear before. It is the fear of me and my no words and my bad behavior. Except now I don't wonder about my badness and my not-having-ness. I don't wonder. Because now I know. I know I have enough.

"Gary, please come quick!"

Jennifer is hopping and hopping and saying things and all

those things stay in my pocket and I don't let them come out because I am looking for Samantha. Looking is not something that needs Jennifer's words. My heart knows where to look all by itself.

Then there is an old man. He says lots of things. Some of what he says are What is going on here? Is everything okay? Who is this girl? Is Samantha all right?

Now Jennifer is screaming. I try to put my hand over her mouth. Now my hand and her mouth are fighting, but her screaming is winning.

Too many people are saying too many things. Except me. I am quiet so nothing can get in the way of my looking. No sound, no screams, no hands waving, no arms grabbing, just my eyes looking for Samantha's eyes, my heart looking for Samantha's heart.

"Please escort this girl out of our house. She's a friend of Samantha's but she's become very upset and she needs to leave," the woman says, and then she goes into one of the doors. I know that is Samantha's door. I can smell her smell and it is of oranges and salt and also another smell which is metal that has been melting in the sun.

"Samantha!" I yell, but the door is shut and I am getting pulled backwards and the pulling is strong, stronger than me, and I try to move myself so fast that nobody could keep holding on to me, fast as the fish when you put your feet in the river, fast as the kittens off your lap, but the man is faster. So I am not strong enough and I am not fast enough so I try to be loud enough. But there are too many tears to keep my yelling going.

So I get an idea.

I try to pray to the Lord, who I have never ever talked to by myself, only with Rodger Marvin. I don't know if the Lord knows who I am, but I pray. When you pray you tell the Lord what He needs to do for you because you are weak and bad and can't do things yourself and then you how much you will love Him if He does it. I pray that Samantha wakes up and comes out of the room and says,

Lucy, my darling, I have missed you so, Lucy, let's go away to-gether and find our baby, I remember a clue about where he might be, and we'll then find the place that we were always supposed to be, the place that I told you about and you said you would come, so let's go, let's go. And then I would go with her!

Samantha, I will come, I will come, I will come, I will come. I know a promise is no matter what. I always knew, believe me, Samantha, I always knew.

I pray those things. I pray so hard I think I hear the door open-ing. But really it is only the sound of how bad I want it to open. The Lord doesn't remember me from the basement with Rodger Marvin because the door stays closed and Samantha stays inside. Or maybe the Lord does remember me, but He won't help me because He knows I don't really need Him like other people do. He knows I can do it myself. And so I tell Samantha I will find the baby by myself, I will find him for her. Some noises I almost cannot hear come through. But those aren't people noises, it is the noise of a hurt animal far away on the farm. It can't be Samantha.

Let's get out of here, Jennifer is yelling, and I am not hearing.

"Stay here, Samantha! Stay here so I can find you! I will be right back! I will be right back!"

I know what to do! Jennifer yells, and I am not listening.

The man opens the front door. He uses his stronger and faster arms to push me out. He says, "Don't you ever come back here. If you only knew what my poor family has been through."

Then the door shuts and there are metal noises of him making it so I can never come back inside, the noises Mum Mum made when she ran outside to meet Monte and I watched out the win-dow. But not this time. This time I am using myself to bang the door, bang the door, so Samantha will hear the sound of my body and know I have come to finish my promise.

Stop, stop, you're going to hurt yourself, screams Jennifer.

"Samantha! Can't you hear me?"

She can't hear you.

She can always hear me.

She can't hear you now, she's all drugged up. Let's go.

There is nowhere to go but here! The promise!

The farm!

But . . .

Lucy, don't you get it?

No.

It's the farm. It's been the farm all along.

MISSUS

I remember the way I felt when I first met Mister. The corset of my red velvet dress was unable to subdue the butterflies in my stomach. He took me to the Home Improvement Exposition. He knew so much about everything they were showing. His face lit up as the machines started up, as if they shared a common switch. When you love a man, you wonder what his son will look like. I have wondered for so long. Sometimes I still wonder, about that little boy, looking like my Mister, with Mister's name no less.

I named him after Daddy.

I suppose it is only logical to imagine that he would look like Stella too. But after what she put us through, I stopped picturing wide, dark eyes and high cheekbones and saw him only in Mister's likeness.

Stella was a beautiful girl. All the boys were always looking at her, following her around the room with their eyes. She loved the attention. I never preened in the mirror the way she did.

She looked especially beautiful the night of her first school dance, in a white, eyelet dress bought especially for the occasion, from town. Her special shoes. Silver sandals, not like shoes I ever had. I let her use my lipstick, the same lipstick I wore on my first date with Mister. I bought it for the occasion. I'd never used cosmetics before, but with Mister, it's sacrilege to say, I wanted to be more beautiful than I really was. I still have it, if you can imagine, after all these years. Cajoling Carol. The color is just perfect, it brightens up any face. There doesn't seem to be a suitable replacement.

Before he left to take Stella, he told me that despite everything we had discussed in the weeks leading up to this night, despite everything we understood about faith, about promises, and His path, he wouldn't. When I asked why not, he answered that physically he couldn't.

"Just see how you feel when you're alone with her," I said. "She's a beautiful girl. You're a man. You forget because I've deprived you for so long. That's my fault, dear, but it's nothing that's wrong with you. It's just that you forget. The feelings will come naturally, like they did with me, in the beginning."

"It doesn't matter how I feel when I'm alone with her because I'm telling you now that I can't do it."

"You don't have to decide now."

"She's our daughter."

"Well, not exactly." He hated when I reminded him of that, but in this instance it was necessary.

"We raised her. She's my daughter. She will always be my daughter. And I won't."

"But, darling, you must see the way she looks at you. It's not the way a girl looks at her father. I know how much she wishes you looked at her the same way. Don't you remember when He made us both that promise? In the beginning, when we were praying to Him? He is asking you to help Him help us—"

"Don't ask me again." He grabbed the keys to the truck.

I didn't say anything more.

The screen door slammed. The door to the truck slammed. But my heart remained still. I did not have his words to assure me, but I had faith.

Stella flounced downstairs, her new scent floating in front of her, introducing her to the night.

"Where's Daddy?" she demanded.

"He's waiting for you in the truck."

When he came home, he told me he was tired and asked if I wouldn't mind picking up Stella after her dance was over. Of course I didn't. He was the leader of our family and I supported him in whatever way he needed. In our bedroom we prayed. We remembered the promise the Lord made us all those years ago. But also we remembered that the Lord helps those who help themselves, and we thanked the Lord for giving us the strength to follow His plan. Our faith and hope were strong that night. Mister fell asleep clutching my hand. I whispered, "Amen," for the both of us. I crept out of our room and waited in the kitchen, watching the clock, my stomach in knots, until it was time to leave.

The second I saw her I knew.

She waited outside the school gym, under a fluorescent, orange lamp, clutching her beaded purse in her hands. My heart was in my throat. She looked too beautiful—white, eyelet dress, silver sandals, flushed cheeks, and still a trace of that coral lipstick—it had to be true. We were so lucky she was so beautiful. He couldn't have resisted her. I could barely swallow. She climbed in the truck slowly, almost limp. She leaned her head against the window.

"How was your first school dance?" My voice quivered.

She murmured something, speaking to the window instead of to me.

"I'm sorry, I didn't hear you," I said.

"Where's Daddy?"

"He fell asleep. Is it all right that it's me instead?"

"Why didn't he come?"

"He fell asleep. So, please tell me—how was the dance?" I waited to start the truck, my hand on the key already in the ignition. I hoped she didn't notice it was shaking.

"What did he say?"

"What did he say about what?" I was gripping the key so hard my knuckles ached.

"About why he wasn't going to get me."

"He didn't say anything. He went to sleep. Now, dear—please, tell your mother about your first big dance."

She didn't say anything. I felt my blood rush faster, my face heated up, I was about to ask her again, I was afraid that my voice would come out shrill, alarming, demanding, I opened my mouth. But she finally spoke.

"It was okay," she whispered, the last word dissolving into the space between us.

"Just okay? Why, dear? Why just okay?" My heart was holding its breath. My palms were sweating. I wiped them on my dress.

"I mean, it was good." She pulled her legs on the seat and hugged her arms around them. She rested her cheek on her knee.

My heart breathed a sigh of relief.

"Good," I repeated, my lips fluttering into a smile. "Good."

I loved the word. *Good.* I cupped the word against my chest to soothe my racing heart. "I'm so glad to hear it." I patted her head.

She sat up and turned to look at me. She opened her mouth. Her eyes darted back and forth, scanning mine. I smiled at her. Beautiful little thing. He couldn't have resisted. I started the car, she shut her mouth. We rode in silence while my heart surfed a wave of joy.

A mother knows.

And he has always trusted me.

LUCY

And so we go that way and we go fast. Jennifer is breathing so hard because of the ways we are going and how fast. She does not talk except to say, Go here. Go there. So I do not talk about how there is a feeling in my throat that makes me feel like I have no weight. I do not say that and she does not say anything back, but no words are enough to let Jennifer know about my feeling, it is the feeling of doing your promise, and for Jennifer to let me know that she hears me.

We pass the steeple. We cross the bridge. We run down the hill to the river and we follow the river. Every step my feet touch the exact right spot on the exact right rock with no slipping. I know I am going fast. Splinters dig into my chest when I breathe. I know it is far. I know it takes a lot of time, because what happened before is so far away. But I know I could go faster, farther, and longer, if that was how much the promise needed me to do.

Then we climb up from the river. I am seeing some fences with the horses inside, and then I am seeing the rows and rows of the plants where we did the weeding, hard and gentle, soft and strong, and there are the barns where sometimes animals sleep in them except for sometimes when they like to sleep outside with the stars, and then there is the flat, hard dirt that goes in a line up to the farmhouse, the dirt that gets more smooth and hard every time you run up to the house. We are getting closer and closer to the house and then there is the coop.

Jennifer makes a noise inside of me like when I bang her against something.

Jennifer, are you hurting?

No, I'm fine. It's just that seeing the coop brings back a lot of memories. Inside was the last time I saw my mother.

Do you want to see her now?

First we have to find the baby and then maybe we can go inside the coop, just for a minute, just so I can say good-bye.

But I thought you never had to say good-bye to your mother.

You never have to. But sometimes you want to anyways so you can remember when you were very small and you felt like you and your mother were the same person. Even though now you know you aren't, sometimes you want to feel that way again.

I loved to go inside the coop, I say.

I know you did. I was there, remember?

Yes, I know, but I didn't know you were you yet.

Well, I was still me, even if you didn't know I was me yet.

I didn't know you were you until you were born and came out and told me who you were.

Yes, but I knew you even before that.

How did you know before you were born?

Because I know everything.

Then we are almost there. *Almost there* means if my arms were as long as the branch of a tree that tapped on my window at night, saying hello even though I was sleeping, I could put them out in front of me and be touching the house and the house would be touching me back. That is how close we are. I stop my walking and look at it and I feel the feeling of looking at a face you have been trying to see in your head but you couldn't see it in your head even though you tried so hard. Then when you finally see it you feel a feeling and part of the feeling is being happy that you are finally seeing it. The other part of it is wondering why you couldn't get your own head to see it. But now you know. Now you know you would remember it, if you were away from it again. You really do know that you would never forget, you really do know you would never have to say good-bye, because it would always be so close inside your head.

Well, Jennifer says, go on.

"Just one more second," I say, and I hear those sounds in the air, my words are the only sound in the air other than the sounds of the animals telling each other secrets. *Just a second* means that you are going to do something in just one second, which is as small a piece of time as you could ever live, and then that time comes, the just-a-second second comes and I am watching the house and feeling the feeling of remembering the face.

It is waiting for a person to say a thing to you because you don't have the words to say whatever it is you want to say. It is hoping the other person will say it for you. But they never do, and the waiting stays inside of you.

Except this time. There is a flapping inside of me and I think that maybe, but maybe, I do have the words to say what I want to say. So I say to the farm, "It is me. Lucy. Lucy on the farm. I came back to do my promise."

We've got to hurry, Jennifer says. We've got to get the baby and get back to Samantha's. I'm getting tired.

Do you need to rest?

Don't worry about me, just hurry.

I just hurry. Nothing else. Up the steps. Across the porch. I open the door. There is an empty sound of wind blowing in the house that wasn't blowing in the outside. I want to make a sound to make the quiet go away so I open my mouth.

No, stay quiet, says Jennifer. And I do and so does she.

I walk in the house. I try my best not to touch the ground. Touching the ground is where a lot of noise happens. There is nobody in the kitchen where we ate like a family but we weren't. There is nobody in the room with the chairs and sofas and pictures

332 | Julie Sarkissian

with the dust I cleaned off to see the underneath and where we did our sewing when I was Lucy on the farm. There is nobody in Samantha's downstairs room where she slept when she was too heavy for the stairs but, yes, a little bit of her smell is still smelling there and I stop my walking so my nose can touch that part of her. Inside my head the smelling dances around. It wants someone to dance with and that someone is all the Samantha things I remember. The sweater that I wore, even though it was hers she let it be mine. She let its warmness be mine. The letters she read to me, even though they were written for her, she let them be mine. She let their insides be mine.

Lucy! Hurry, remember? says Jennifer. Up the stairs.

I remember the hurrying and leave the dancing in Samantha's room. We go to where the stairs begin. I walk up the stairs, quiet as I need to be. I know how to be that quiet because that is how quiet I used to be when I was Lucy on the farm and I was as gentle with the eggs when I stepped out in the night and scared away the foxes that were a little like me. We are almost to where the stairs stop, which is the top. I am being my best quiet, and we are at the top of the stairs.

I open the door to Mister and Missus's room and when the door is opened it is a room filled with a lot of light.

And there he is, the promise I made. Also there is a rocking chair, which goes back and forth and lets you feel like you can go places without touching the floor. Missus is on the chair. And on Missus is a white blanket and then on the white blanket is the baby, which is the promise, which is a person who has just been born who is small and soft and doesn't know how to hurt anybody yet, and doesn't know how to use words to say how things hurt them, or when they want to eat, or say that they don't understand about something. And this baby has pink skin and orange hair like the sun when it starts to spill on the sky when the day is almost over and that is also the color of the hair that Samantha has. Because that is what your baby is, and that is what your mother is, that is the person who was the first person you ever knew and who ever knew you.

Missus is asleep and the baby is asleep. I stand over Missus and look at her face which is the face of someone who is dreaming about finding something she lost. I stand over Baby and look at his face, which is the face of someone who is dreaming of something beautiful that he doesn't understand what it is yet.

I use my hands to pick up Baby. Missus she wraps her arms around herself and makes a noise but not an awake noise, the noise of something inside a dream. And now I hold Baby. His head is in my hand up by my face. His eyes by my eyes, but, no, we do not see the same thing. We see each other.

He is heavier than he looks and softer. It is a feeling of thinking a thing will be one way, and then it is not that way. It is a way you never could know until it happens. In your mind, it is a way it will never be in the world. And it is okay. Because in the world, it is better, because it is heavier and softer. And the heavier is the heaviness that lets you know you are strong. And the softer, it is the softness that lets you know that there will always be things to feel, if you can remember to touch.

Then Missus makes a sound like *mmmmm*.

Let's go, says Jennifer. We can't risk sticking around.

Then Missus says, "Thank you," like she is awake but her eyes are still closed, and she still has the dreaming face on.

Jennifer goes cold. We don't move, don't blink, don't think, don't beat.

"Thanks for putting her down for her nap, darling. Being a mother is so tiring."

Jennifer doesn't say anything, but I know. What do I know? *Go.*

And I say, it's because I made a promise, Missus, but I say it in my mind not in the air and then I turn around and I walk out the door and down the stairs, down with Baby and Jennifer, holding them both tight and safe with no bouncing until there are only two more stairs.

But then there is a noise, a downstairs-door-opening noise. The noise of the outside sounds and smells and dust all blowing inside. Outside leaves and dirt and weather are inside now and it turns Jennifer cold, cold like the moon in the middle of the night if you could touch it.

Mister, says Jennifer.

I press the baby in my neck.

Quick, hurry, but quiet, says Jennifer, fast and scared.

I quick, hurry but quiet.

Into Samantha's room, says Jennifer. Stand behind the door. And don't breathe.

Don't breathe, Lucy. Don't breathe, Jennifer. But I know I cannot say, Don't breathe, Baby. He is too little to know about stopping your breathing when you need to be the quietest you can be, how to hold your breath just the right amount of time, and then take a long, quiet breath, and then hold for some more.

Outside the door Mister's footsteps make our hearts beat harder. Every time his foot hits the ground it makes a boom that booms inside our chests. Booming and beating but no breathing. His booms go from the kitchen past the door where we are and then the baby cries into my neck. The booms stop. The booms stop right outside Samantha's door.

I hold him tight, no breathing, no crying, just for this moment, just for this moment. And we all stop breathing. Baby, I am sorry, I say with my mind and I am pressing him into my neck and I hope it's not too long and I hope it's not too long and now I know it is almost too long, it has been almost too long but still, he cannot cry yet, he cannot cry yet and Mister cannot hear it and find us, because I know what a promise is. But now it has been too long and I have to let him go. Let him breathe.

But Mister is still here, not moving, listening and waiting, but then Mister's booms they start again, they go up the stairs, up the stairs, I hear them go up all the steps, and Baby gulps in his air and I gulp in my air and Jennifer does too and we slip away and our hearts beat wild like all the horses in the world running together.

Baby, Baby, I am sorry, I am sorry and he smashes up his face and closes his eyes but he understands I would never do it if I didn't have to. We are outside now. In the last little bit of the daytime with the smells of the farm that made Mum mum make the face I would never make and I ask the baby, I say, Baby, what do you want your name to be?

But he doesn't say anything.

So I say, Baby, what is your name?

And he opens his eyes and they are green like the grass but also like you could see through the other side of them and into something wonderful, a wonderful place you would never leave, the place you were before you were born.

I can't tell you, he says. I can only tell my mother.

The baby doesn't say anything else. His hand is like a person's hand but more small and more round and it smells like a smell I have never smelled before and he reaches it to my mouth and I smell the smell even more. And now I know his smell and that is how I know he is something I will never forget. Even if I lost all the words I ever had and ever will have I would never forget his smell.

Lucy, Jennifer says, take me to the coop.

Her voice is melting into all her feathers and getting stuck there, so it is hard to hear. I try to pull out her words from the feathers but I can't, but I still hear her enough to know where she wants me to go and so I walk to the coop and I go inside. Inside the eggs shine with all their white. The chickens are at the top. They are mostly not doing any moving, with their eyes closed and their feathers big and covering everything with quiet.

Which one is your mother? I say to Jennifer. But she doesn't answer. I hold the baby with one of my arms and one side of my body and I use the other hand to take out Jennifer so I can show her.

Jennifer, I say, which one is your mother?

But what she says is nothing.

Jennifer, I say. Please talk to me.

But what she says is nothing and what she does is blink black and shiny blinks.

Which one?

I hold her up to all the chickens so she can see which is her mother but she is not looking at those chickens. She is looking at the ground and then at the sky and then all around and then she is making a noise which I have not heard before and it is a noise that a chicken makes when it wants to make a noise. It is the same noise that I have heard all the chickens make but never Jennifer. After she makes the noise a big chicken lifts its head up and looks at us. And then Jennifer looks at it.

Is that one your mother? I say to Jennifer.

Baby puts some of my hair in his hand and tries to pull it for himself and I laugh because that is something that I have done before but not something that someone has done to me since a very long time ago. He does not care if he hurts me because he is a baby and they are too young to want to hurt anyone. Then I put Jennifer by the chicken that is lifting her head to look at us.

Good-bye, Jennifer, I say. But Jennifer is quiet.

Will you say good-bye to me? I say. But she is quiet.

Please will you say good-bye to me? I say.

The first thing Jennifer ever said was Hello, Lucy. That was when she was covered in slime and had a piece of her shell still on her head. And I was there waiting for her. Waiting for her first day. Waiting for her beginning. I waited for her to say hello. I will wait for her to say good-bye.

I think I hear it. I think I hear it. But it's not her. She never will have any more words. But she can still say it, because I will be her words, like she was my words. I will say it for her. I put my hand on her mouth.

Good-bye, Jennifer, I say.

Good-bye, Lucy, I say.

Baby and me, we walk back towards the way we got here and I think I remember it. Because there are some things I know, like the way that I know Samantha's letters and they make me see Samantha's face. And some things that I see, I can feel their shape in my heart, but I do not know what the word is for the feeling their shape makes me feel, but I know it is a word that I will find soon. And when I do I will use that word to let other people know and they will use a word they had found to let me know about the shape of things inside of them.

We are walking by the trees and by the river and the flowers where I sat with Samantha. I feel how hot the rocks got in the sun today and I tell baby about his mother, who is Samantha. I am telling him, Your mother is very pretty. Her eyes are green, which is like the color of grass. That is a word you need to remember. Remember green, the color of grass that is still growing, right before your eyes even if you can't see it moving. It seems like it is still but it is not. And her hair is orange which is the same as yours, so if you forget you can just look at your hair and it is the same color as that. And that is orange, and that is a word you need to remember.

I tell him, there are a lot of words you need to remember. There are a lot of things that you will see and things that you think are living inside of you and you will wonder if there are words for them and you can find those words and use them so other people will understand what are the shapes of you underneath your skin.

I tell him, there are a lot of secrets that you will find out. You can tell your secrets to anybody, but the best person to tell a secret to is yourself. One of the secrets is the secret of growing. You are part of the secret of growing. You can't see the secret of growing while it is happening. That is part of the secret. You can only see it while it is over, but even then, it is still happening, it is always happening, it never stops happening, and that is why the secret of growing is the very best secret there is.

ACKNOWLEDGMENTS

———

I am honored and humbled by the support I have received on this project.

My deepest thank-you to James Fitzpatrick, for believing in me and my work, for supporting me, for always listening, and for sharing in the highs and the lows.

Thank you to my mom and dad, Sarah and Geoff Sarkissian, for encouraging my pursuit of the arts and for inspiring in me a love of literature from a young age.

Thank you to my brother David, for your brilliant intellect and for being such an enthusiastic supporter.

Thank you to my inspiring grandmothers, Dita Martha Sarkissian and Dita Mary Helen Post.

I am so grateful to my dear friend and fellow writer Haley Tanner for being the first person to ever read a word of this book and for all the love and support throughout the years.

Loving thanks to friend and reader Joanna Simmons for continous enthusiasm and encouragement. An enormous thank-you to Sarah Knight, my editor, for believing in my manuscript, for your preternatural ability to understand my characters and draw out their truth, and for all the TLC you put into this book.

I am deeply indebted to my agent, Judy Heiblum, who saw the potential in the rough first drafts of this book. Thank you for your wonderful suggestions and thoughtful, sincere advice.

Thank you to everyone at Simon & Schuster for making this book a reality. A special thank-you to my friends who read early drafts of this book: Sam Rosen, Lucy Lobban-Bean, Devon Taylor, Chris Korman, and Kati Skelton.

Thank you to my dear friends Katie Kitselman, Jessie Nagin, Yasmine Ryckebush, Phil Merkow, Eric Laronda, Steve Kitselman, and Kristin Brancaleone for keeping my spirit buoyant.

Thank you to Allen, Sally, Kate, and Lilly Fitzpatrick, and to Kenny and Laurie Nagin for the continuous support through the years.

Thank you to Tom Bailey for encouraging me to apply to Princeton's writing program. Thank you to Gabe Hudson, for inspiring me to pursue writing after college. Thank you to Chang-rae Lee, Joyce Carol Oates, Edmund White, and the rest of the Princeton Creative Writing Program. Thank you to Ann Hood and the rest of the New School MFA program.

A warm thank-you to Edward Youkilis for employing me while I wrote this book, and to all my talented, amazing friends at Edward's Restaurant in Tribeca.

READING GROUP GUIDE

This reading group guide for *Dear Lucy* includes an
introduction, discussion questions, and ideas for enhancing
your book club, and a Q&A with author Julie Sarkissian.
The suggested questions are intended to help your reading
group find new and interesting angles and topics for your
discussion. We hope that these ideas will enrich your
conversation and increase your enjoyment of the book.

Introduction

Dear Lucy tells the story of an uncommon woman with
a unique voice and boundless compassion. Lucy has been
abandoned by her mother and taken in by an older couple,
known as Mister and Missus, to work on their farm. It is here
that she meets Samantha, a pregnant teenager with whom she
finds an unlikely connection. When Samantha's baby disappears
shortly after he is born, Lucy pledges to help Samantha find
him. This is the first time in her life that Lucy has been trusted
with an important task. Armed with Samantha's letters and
diary, which Lucy cannot read, and in the company of a talking
chicken named Jennifer, Lucy sets out to reunite Samantha
with her child. What follows is a poignant story of faith and
friendship, heartbreak, longing and loyalty.

1. Discuss the structure of *Dear Lucy*. What is the effect of having multiple narrators? Did you trust all of them equally? If not, whom did you doubt, and why?

2. At the beginning of the novel, Lucy says, "I don't have the words yet. I am still looking for them." (p. 4). What does she mean by that, and how does it affect her interactions with others? Do you agree with her that "Not every time is a time when you need words to tell things?" (p. 11). If so, give some examples of where this statement is true in *Dear Lucy*.

3. Discuss the epistolary elements of *Dear Lucy*. Why do you think that Sarkissian includes both the letter from Samantha as it actually is and as Jennifer reads it on p. 312? What is the effect of doing so?

4. Missus's first words in *Dear Lucy* are "Life constantly reminds us of all of the things that could have been different if betrayal weren't in human nature." (p. 9). How does this statement set up her character? Do you agree with her? What sort of betrayals occur in *Dear Lucy*?

5. What is your initial impression of Missus and Mister? Did your feelings about them change by the end of *Dear Lucy*? If so, why? Did the revelations about their relationship with Stella surprise you?

6. Samantha and Lucy seem to be kindred spirits. Why do you think there's such a kinship between the two girls? In what ways are they alike?

7. Stella symbolizes something different to each of Missus, Samantha, and Lucy. What does she symbolize to each? And what do each of the character's reactions to Stella reveal about them?

8. Who is Jennifer? How does she guide Lucy, and why do you think Lucy needs her? Jennifer is afraid to speak when Lucy is reunited with Mum mum and again when she returns to the hen house with Lucy. At the hen house, Lucy says, "She never will have any more words…I will be her words, like she was my words." (p. 337). What does Lucy mean?

9. When Lucy meets Rodger Marvin she thinks he "will be the first person to ever read my words, to help me get them ready for everybody else." (p. 90). Does he help her? Do you think that Rodger Marvin is as pious a man as he initially seems?

10. Samantha says, "the trick is keeping your strength a secret, so people don't suspect, so they don't keep a close eye on you, so you have a chance to get away." (p. 261). How is Samantha trying to keep her strength a secret? Are there other characters in *Dear Lucy* who are doing the same? Why? And, are they successful?

11. Lucy tells Jennifer that Mum mum is always crying "Because she has lots of feelings." (p. 270). Do you think that is the reason for her tears? Describe Mum mum's reaction to Lucy's return. How do you feel about Mum mum's treatment of Lucy?

12. Of a child's relationship with her mother Lucy says, "There is a thread, and the thread is so long that it lasts forever. Your heart is tied to one end of the thread, and your mother's heart is tied to the other end." (p. 313). Are the mothers in *Dear Lucy* connected with their children? In what ways?

13. Describe Samantha's behaviour towards Allen. Why do you think that she treats him as she does? Do you agree with her assessment that "I didn't have any love, or any goodness or anything to give"? (p. 99). After hearing Allen tell Lucy about how Samantha treated him, did you feel differently about either Samantha or Allen?

14. The phrase "the secret of growing" recurs throughout the book. What does Lucy mean when she talks about it?

15. Several of the characters make promises to each other that they try to break. What are those promises? With regard to each of these cases, do you agree with Lucy that "If you don't do a promise then you are lying." (p. 293). Explain your answer.

ENHANCE YOUR BOOK CLUB

1. *Dear Lucy* has drawn comparisons to *The Curious Incident of the Dog in the Night-time*. Read both books, then compare and contrast them in your book club. In what ways are Lucy and Christopher John Francis Boone alike? How do they differ?

2. Read Julie Sarkissian's short story, *"The New Saint Claire Restaurant"* here: **http://www.tinhouse.com/blog/14398/the-new-saint-claire-restaurant-by-julie-sarkissian.html** and discuss it with your book club. How are the themes that she tackles in both works similar?

3. When Lucy makes her home with Samantha, Mister, and Missus, she says, "We aren't a family, but nobody says that part. A family, they are there from the beginning of each other. But we all got here at different times and now we are leaving at different times." (p. 119). Talk with your book club about what you think binds individuals together as a family.

A Conversation with *Julie Sarkissian*

Although you've written short stories, Dear Lucy *is your first novel. Did the experience of writing a novel differ from writing short stories? How? Can you describe your writing process?*

To me the experience of a short story is like a solo performance by a singer with an incredible, not necessarily beautiful but totally distinctive, voice, which needs to hit one or two notes really well and very clearly. A novel is more like conducting an orchestra, and playing all the instruments as well. There are so many working pieces, and so many moving targets, and not every instrument is as strong as the next. You can't afford to miss a note in a short story, and in a novel you're sure to miss a few.

I am inspired by voice, so I usually begin writing a piece with stream of consciousness narration, and when I feel like I have enough material I work backwards to figure out who the narrator must be, based on the clues the voice has given me. Plot doesn't come as easily to me and ties my brain up in knots and it is often difficult for me to commit hard and fast plot elements and stay constant with the "facts" of my fictional world. Working with an editor is a great resource for untying those knots.

Logistically speaking, I have worked in restaurants since I was 18, so I have been waitressing and writing for over ten years now. So I write during the day, and waitress at night and I like the balance it provides.

As a first-time author, do you have any advice for aspiring novelists?

One phrase about writing I think is brilliant and can really relate to is by EL Doctorow: "Writing is like driving a car at night, you can only see as far as your headlights, but you can make the whole trip that way."

There is so much about an unfinished book that is impossible for the writer to know until it is written. It is easy and natural to feel overwhelmed at how to move a story through space and time, but the process is made up of a million tiny steps. If you have the courage to write a sentence, over and over and over again, you can write a book.

Haley Tanner says that, "you'll want to linger of the poetry of each and every sentence" of Dear Lucy. *How did you create Lucy's unique and poetic voice?*

Thanks Haley! Lucy created her voice herself, I was just lucky enough to be the vessel through which she entered the human world. I think Lucy, and her voice, are part of the collective unconscious.

Originally Dear Lucy *was titled* This is How To Find Me. *What made you change the title? Did it reflect a change in the way you were telling the story?*

My agent, editor and I decided together to change the title after we learned that Junot Diaz had a novel forthcoming titled *This Is How You Lose Her*. We were worried the close similarity in titles might do my book a disservice. Additionally, it seemed that most people couldn't remember *This Is How To Find Me* correctly. It was a practical decision to change the title; not artistically motivated.

All of the characters in Dear Lucy *are flawed in some way and some of their actions seem unforgivable. How did you feel writing those characters? Could you identify with their choices?*

While I felt different things for different characters, I did have some sympathy for everybody, especially as I recognized how desperately they were trying to believe their own stories. And I can certainly identify with that. We all hold specious conceits about ourselves that we are desperate to believe, but never truly can, so we become determined to have others believe it about us. I think Missus in particular demonstrates this.

A lot of the unforgivable actions in the book presented themselves to me as the solution to little mysteries. For example, Stella was always a character in the novel, she was always the adopted daughter of Mister and Missus, and she was always "missing." I always knew something terrible happened to her but for a long while I didn't know what it was and I didn't feel like I had to know. But subconsciously the question of what happened to her was developing in tandem to my writing and creating Missus and Mister. So when it came time to address what happened to Stella, I had subconsciously already decided what happened. Once I knew it, I couldn't not know it, it seemed to be true, whether or not I chose to address it overtly in the book.

Dear Lucy centres around the power of words. The characters can't often say what they mean, either because they have "no words" or they're unwilling to face certain truths. How did you get those voices to come together?

With so many characters selling their stories and telling half-truths, it was a challenge to reveal enough to the reader to allow him or her to put the pieces together, while still allowing the characters to be manipulative and partly obscured. Some amount of trial and error went into what was revealed and when and by who. And often what one character couldn't say, another character could, either deliberately or inadvertently.

Gabe Hudson calls Dear Lucy *a "gothic noir." Were there any gothic writers who inspired you while you were writing?*

Absolutely! Southern Gothic writers are some of my very favorite. Faulkner has long been an inspiration to me and was for this book. Other include Flannery O' Connor, Nathaniel West, Carson McCullers, Eudora Welty. *The Book of Ruth* by Jane Hamilton is a more recent novel that is certainly meets the darkness criteria for Gothic writing that I was really inspired and moved by.

Dear Lucy *is told from multiple points of view. Why did you choose to structure the story in that way? Was it difficult to switch between the voices of the characters as you were writing?*

After writing about eighty pages in Lucy's voice I realized I wanted a foil point of view, both to Lucy's innocent truthfulness and her cognitive limitations. Missus' POV was born out of that desire. Missus was already a character, and her voice became a good parallel to Lucy's; Missus is completely shrewd and perceptive, but she is incapable of real honesty.

I liked the layered effect of the voices, like looking through multiple panes of old, weathered glass. It's harder to see what's behind the glass, but all the cracks and grime enrich the experience of trying to make out what it is you're seeing.

Having multiple narrators was certainly a challenge, not so much in switching between the character's points of view, but in distinguishing the sound and quality of the voices from one another. Lucy's voice is so distinctive and it would creep into other POV's, especially when it came to metaphors and similes.

What kind of research did you do while you were writing Dear Lucy?

Dear Lucy is timeless and placeless so really no research felt necessary. There isn't much physical description of the farm, so there wasn't a high risk of being factually incorrect when it came to farming. Likewise, any Biblical references are so vague I didn't feel I ran the risk of being inaccurate.

As Dear Lucy *ends, it is unclear what will happen to any of the characters. Why did you choose to end on such an uncertain note?*

I decided to end the book at the most victorious moment in Lucy's life. It is a choice when to end a book, and certainly I can imagine what could come in the moments and days after Lucy leaves the farm with the baby. But when Lucy is explaining her secrets to the baby, it is one of the longest, most intricate dialogues Lucy has in the book without displaying any self-consciousness about missing words. So not only has Lucy followed through on her promise to Samantha, she has fulfilled her promise to herself to find words for the shape of things inside her, and tell them to someone. Lucy is grateful for her words and for the intimacy they provide. She is proud of her words for perhaps the first time.

What would you like readers to take away from Dear Lucy?

Lucy's sense of wonder at the things other people take for granted.

What are you working on now?

I am working on a novel about a pirate carnival, which is a floating fair of music, food, and entertainment collected from around the world. It is run by a mysterious community of gypsies, and travels up the eastern seaboard, spreading its celebration of life, passion, and indulgence. When the pirate carnival docks in a sleepy New England town, the lives of three young women will never be the same. Clarissa, a beautiful, painfully polite, modest young woman unlocks the dangerous power of her beauty. Sweet, chubby, Betsey, who has left college to care for her ailing mother, abandons her duties to become the loyal muse of a charismatic pirate baker. And Sue, the narrator of the book, falls in love with a pirate who speaks the language of her heart but won't give her straight answer about anything. Up against her own desires, the beliefs of her family, and the twisted magic of the ship, Sue fights to uncover the troubled history of her beloved and save those she loves from disappearing into a world where ego, indulgence and beauty, seem to trump all else.